Also by Cathryn Grant

NOVELS
The Demise of the Soccer Moms ♦ *Buried by Debt*
The Suburban Abyss ♦ *The Hallelujah Horror Show*
Getting Ahead ♦ *Faceless* ♦ *An Affair With God*

THE ALEXANDRA MALLORY PSYCHOLOGICAL SUSPENSE SERIES
The Woman In the Mirror ♦ *The Woman In the Water*
The Woman In the Painting ♦ *The Woman In the Window*
The Woman In the Bar ♦ *The Woman In the Bedroom*
The Woman In the Dark ♦ *The Woman In the Cellar*

THE HAUNTED SHIP TRILOGY
Alone On the Beach
Slipping Away From the Beach
Haunting the Beach

NOVELLAS
Madison Keith Ghost Story Series
Chances Are

SHORT FICTION
Reduction in Force ♦ *Maternal Instinct*
Flash Fiction For the Cocktail Hour
The 12 Days of Xmas

Cathryn Grant

THE WOMAN IN THE PHOTOGRAPH

An Alexandra Mallory Novel

D2C Perspectives

This book is a work of fiction. References to real people, events, establishments, organizations, or locales are intended only to provide a sense of authenticity, and are used fictitiously. All other characters, and incidents and dialogue, are drawn from the author's imagination and are not to be construed as real.

Copyright © 2018 by Cathryn Grant

All rights reserved. No part of this book may be used or reproduced in any manner whatsoever without written permission except in the case of brief quotations embodied in critical articles and reviews. For information, contact D2Cperspectives@gmail.com

Visit Cathryn online at CathrynGrant.com

Cover design by Lydia Mullins Copyright © 2018

ISBN: 978-1-943142-45-3

1

New York City

During one of my last conversations with Gavin, he suggested that I hadn't yet found work I was passionate about. Gavin assured me that when I discovered what that work was, it would take me to a level of satisfaction that was *almost spiritual,* a plane of altered consciousness.

When he said those things, I knew he was wrong, but I couldn't argue with him.

As much as he seemed to understand me, as much as he seemed to recognize something about me that he wasn't saying, it was impossible to tell him I'd found that work several years ago. I couldn't tell him that I spent a certain amount of my time planning and committing murder. He wouldn't understand that. No one would understand. My work isolates me from the human race. I enjoy people from a distance. I'm entertained by their emotional trajectories through life, I can carry on interesting conversations, but there are taboo subjects. Even I know that.

It's not the physical act of taking a life that gives me satisfaction.

I do not enjoy seeing a person without life animating their body. I do not enjoy seeing a corpse. I do not enjoy seeing a human being suffer. My feelings are the same regarding animals — I loathe suffering and torment. I don't understand emotional suffering quite as easily, but I hate physical suffering. I know how that feels and I don't want to be the cause of that in another person.

This is why I prefer to use a mind-numbing substance to ease my victims into unconsciousness, then across the final threshold — taking their lives while they aren't aware except in the very deepest crevices of their minds.

Killing people isn't some sick pleasure for me like it is for those psychopaths everyone is so fascinated with.

I'm driven by the desire to make the world more equal. I recognize that's a mountain I'll never conquer, but I have to try. Women have been treated like substandard humans since time began. Sure, there were anomalies. In ancient Egypt, women had some property rights. They could refuse a marriage offer. And oddly enough, they had equality in facing the same criminal penalties as men. There are lots of mythological traditions that put goddesses on equal footing with male gods.

But overall, men are deemed the creators of the very universe. Religious texts are dominated by male deities. For most of history, men ran the governments and the religious institutions. Until recently, they've written the vast majority of books and plays and works of history and philosophy. They've made the laws, composed the music, painted the images, invented new technologies, and pretty much directed the entire show. Women were there to serve and clean, to give birth and prepare food, to admire and submit, to cheer and to fuck.

Despite all the legal and societal changes in the past thousand years, the past hundred years, the past ten years, shifts within human hearts clearly take eons.

Misogyny is perpetuated when people procreate and then form children's conscious thoughts into mirror images of their own mindset. And it never stops. Removing some of those people from the gene pool will surely advance the human race at a faster pace, no matter how minuscule each step might be.

To be honest, I also get extreme satisfaction from cleaning up, from wiping away all traces of myself — every fiber and hair and sloughed off piece of skin. I've always loved the soothing appearance of a spotless surface, dust wiped out of a room, grit sucked from carpet fibers and mopped off of tile floors. There's an added layer of pleasure from knowing that I'm not leaving an imprint of myself. People could search a room or a house and never know I was there.

The rewards in my work come from the pleasure of accomplishing what I set out to do. I'm rewarded by the satisfaction of helping individual women and helping, however slightly, to move society forward.

Whether my work puts me into the altered state of consciousness Gavin spoke of, needs further consideration.

My reward also comes from executing my plans without being caught.

Of course, there's always a chance I'll miss something tiny — an eyelash, or the faint smudge of my fingerprint on a surface that isn't obvious. No one's perfect.

This is why it's important to keep as much of my identity as possible off the internet — that giant sucking machine that's cataloging everyone's lives, preserving every thoughtless word, and every casual photograph. For eternity.

2

I love shopping. When I was told that the first task in my new job involved shopping, using another person's credit card, I knew I'd made the right choice for the next rung in my unorthodox career ladder.

Before I even showed up at the offices to meet my new co-workers and see the layout, I received a text from Trystan Vogel telling me I needed to purchase a DSLR and a video camera.

According to a follow-up message, Trystan wasn't into online shopping. Making an important purchase is a physical experience, he said.

I saw his point.

I love the ease of surfing the web, comparing and clicking and shipping while I nurse a martini or smoke a cigarette, or both. But there's nothing like the tactile pleasure of picking up items, turning them over in your hands, feeling fabric and wood, metal and even finely crafted plastic. I like trying on clothes, and I like the perfect lighting of a department store fitting room. I like the click of hangers as I move them along a metal pole. I could take a nap in the neatly folded sweaters and baby-skin-soft T-shirts stacked on tables, a display of gentle and exciting colors that can melt your heart. None of that is captured online.

Trystan wanted to be sure I received full-service assistance in choosing the perfect equipment, so he provided the address and contact information for a nearby camera shop. He instructed me to follow their recommendation and to sign up for classes on how to use the camera.

The primary responsibility in my new job would be photographing and filming clients. Trystan's first, admittedly unconventional, step in transforming his client's behavior and mindset, was to take photographs capturing every area of their lives.

In the past, he'd hired professional photographers to take care of this. But often, they didn't capture the subtleties he was after. He wanted a photographer who thoroughly understood his objectives and the nuances of what he provided to his clients.

When they signed up, clients were required to hand over certain elements of their privacy via a very carefully-written document which allowed me into their homes, their offices, and their nightlife. According to Trystan's directives, I would take candid shots and video clips.

These images helped his clients see how they appeared to the world, how they interacted with society, how they spoke and laughed and carried themselves. The photographs and video were meant to reveal poor posture and facial ticks, expressions and tone of voice that were off-putting or made the client appear weak.

The image and the energy they were projecting was presented to them without flattery, in order to help them see where they needed to adjust their behavior. The avoidance of flattery was what the hired photographers couldn't get their heads around.

All their skills had been acquired with the sole purpose of taking flattering photographs — lighting, tricks for getting subjects to relax, and of course, touch-ups after the fact.

Trystan believed I would be good at this cold-eyed approach. He was right. I couldn't wait to get started.

3

Per Trystan's instructions, I showed up at the camera shop in Tribeca. The building was narrow and deep. The entrance was a Dutch door, although judging by the corrosion around the lock that allowed the top to open separately from the bottom, it hadn't been opened since the turn of the millennium. I guess the friendly days of neighborhood shops with wide open doors were disappearing, one Dutch door at a time. This shop appeared to be holding on because it had been in business for decades, patronized by long-time customers. It also held on because a lot of professional photographers used it, and it was one of only a handful of photography businesses that still developed film.

The shop area was filled with nicely displayed cameras. In back was a formal portrait studio and office space. Upstairs was the developing lab. The third story with its curtained bay window looked as if it might be the owner's apartment.

And of course it was the owner, not a clerk or even the manager, that Trystan had directed me to. Trystan and Leon were old friends. It made me realize that Trystan's low-key boasting about his vast network of social and business connections might be more accurate than I'd assumed.

I took a deep breath of cool air, a relief from the sweltering September weather that had already reached seventy-eight degrees at ten in the morning.

Leon Sharp stood behind the counter, his eyes fixed on the door. He was a tall, slender man with longish hair and a mustache. "Alexandra. How are you? Trystan told me you would arrive on time, and here you are." He extended his hand but didn't make a move from behind the counter, forcing me to cross the shop, weaving around a pedestal with a very slick-looking Minolta sitting on top.

I shook his hand. Then, as if that were the secret code unlocking his service, he stepped out from behind the counter.

He proceeded to walk me past every prominently displayed DSLR camera in the shop. As he described the virtues of each one, his voice was overcome with a passion that most men might use in describing a lover. He threw in occasional disparaging comments about phone cameras and the proliferation of poorly executed photographs — images that gained *notoriety* simply because they were posted on the internet and managed to attract an enormous number of undiscerning eyeballs. "It's a shame, really, where the world is headed. Where art is headed. Quality is secondary." He sounded like an old man, but he looked like he was about thirty-five, possibly younger. "I blame a lot of it on digital," he said. "That's what really started the decline, in all the arts, if you think about it. No one takes time any more to frame a well-thought-out shot. Little attention is paid to lighting. You can take a hundred shots and wait for the light to catch up with you. Photographs are turned into vapor that can be deleted by the truckloads with the tap of a button."

"Doesn't that mean only the good shots are saved?"

"Good is relative," he said.

I smiled.

"But you know quality, or at least Trystan does, and I assume by default, you do as well." He pulled his lips back into a tight smile. "Which is why you're here. I understand you've never used a DSLR?"

"I haven't."

"So you'll be taking our introductory class?"

"Yes."

"With the purchase of your camera, it's only three-hundred-seventy-five dollars."

"Such a bargain."

He gave me another tight smile.

"And Trystan told you I'm buying two cameras?"

His nose seemed to twitch with disgust. I didn't actually see it move, but I felt the desire shimmying through the skin of his face.

"Yes. The video camera as well."

"Not exactly classic photography is it."

He almost laughed with relief that I understood how crass videography was. "If you're a filmmaker, that's one thing. But we don't stock that kind of professional equipment. And amateur videos…" He shrugged.

"Film is an entirely different field," I said.

"Yes." He nodded, wobbling his head vigorously to be sure I was fully aware of his agreement. "I don't like carrying video cameras for hobbyists, for over-eager parents."

"Of course not," I said. "This is a shop for artisans."

"Yes!" He softened his smile. He ran his fingers over the edge of his mustache as if to brush the hairs off his lips. "But we do have to cater to a wider audience."

"I'm sure. Is there an additional discount for the class, since I'm buying two cameras?"

"Well." He smiled. "You're not exactly buying them, are you? And you're not paying for the class either, so I don't think that should concern you."

"Just curious."

He took me around the shop a second time, explaining again the features of each camera.

It wasn't clear why I needed to listen to a list of the features and optimal uses for every single camera, twice, but maybe he didn't get a lot of foot traffic. Maybe he hadn't had a chance to talk about cameras for weeks, and all the information had built up inside of him until he couldn't contain it. I'd seen a prominent URL on the window and imagined that like most specialty stores, he did a large part of his business online.

It's sad, in a way. Losing the tactile pleasure of shopping. No matter how good virtual reality becomes, will it ever allow us to touch the objects? Maybe it will. Maybe it will tweak our brains so we'll think we're touching something — simulated soft and hard surfaces.

In the end, Leon recommended the Nikon D3200 as the perfect candidate for my photography adventure. He actually called it that — an *adventure*. His chuckle and emphasis on the word suggested he was also looking down his nose at Trystan, just a tiny bit. He recommended a light-weight, easy-to-use Panasonic for video.

After the cameras had been brought from the back of the store and placed into a thick plastic shopping bag with sturdy handles, he gave me his card. "It was a pleasure doing business with you."

"With Trystan, you mean."

He nodded. "Yes. But you also. I can see you're a

woman who appreciates quality."

I wasn't sure how he was able to see that since I'd mildly mocked him once or twice, but maybe he was living in a world of virtual reality already, picturing me as the customer he desired. He'd only slipped out of his virtual world for a moment when his anger at the idea of every person on the planet holding a mobile phone, snapping away at their food and their pets, flooding Instagram and Facebook with crooked over- and under-exposed landscape shots and pictures of drunken parties.

Unlike Leon, I was happy to be living in the era of digital photography. Photography is more interesting than it's been in the past. Pictures are more brutally honest since they don't have to be taken with care for the cost of developing. The photographer can remain unobserved with a phone as a camera or a lens that brings someone across the room into the chair beside you. At the same time, photographs can be edited into something false. Maybe that's what Leon didn't like — the blending of truth and lies that are impossible to separate.

4

My new apartment was small. For non-millionaires, there was no escaping that in Manhattan. Small and semi-affordable didn't mean a slick, new high rise. It meant tired linoleum and kitchen cabinets without doors. It meant a slightly sagging parquet floor that made me feel as if I was about to fall through the glass when I stood at the front window, watching passersby on the street below.

The apartment had a small living room with enough space for a dining table and four chairs, a galley kitchen, one bathroom, and a bedroom almost as large as the living room. The best feature of the apartment was the set of French doors that separated the living room from the bedroom.

My apartment was on the third floor, no elevator. I liked it for the view of the sidewalk and interesting passersby as well as a few decent-sized trees spreading their leafy branches to within a few feet of my window. I figured the daily stair-climbing would be a good addition to running.

I would have liked more space and more glitz, modern appliances and flooring, but I didn't want to lose sight of my long-term goal. When it comes to my future home, I've been pretty good at deferring pleasure. Spend the minimum now for the home I dreamed of sooner rather than later. I chose the apartment because it was close to work, close to the subway, located in a relatively safe area, and had a certain world-weary charm. Especially those French doors.

The first thing I did was wash and polish every single pane of those doors.

Lying in bed with the doors closed, I could see every inch of the apartment. With those doors, I felt like I lived in another era when things were less utilitarian and less sensible. Unless you have a luxury home, most modern apartments focus on functionality over flair. Building exteriors are all straight lines and unadorned windows — high rises, for the most part. The early twentieth-century building where I lived was brick with a classic fire escape and decorative yellow tile that ran across the exterior on each floor, up and around the narrow windows — flair that served no practical purpose.

Best of all, my apartment building had a roof garden. I couldn't wait to sit up there, smoking a cigarette and watching the city hum with life. If I stayed out there late enough on a hot summer night, I would feel the city ease its way into sleep for a few hours before traffic and pedestrians stirred themselves again, long before sunrise.

There were four apartments on each floor. Rather than running along a hallway, the doors all opened onto a landing. I imagined there would be a lot more crossing of paths compared to what I'd experienced in the long, narrow, often dimly lit hallways of my previous apartments.

The landing floor was an expanse of black and white twelve-inch square tiles, mostly un-scuffed, even after decades and hundreds of feet passing over them. The tiles were clean, and the sharp contrast of black and white made the area seem bright, even with the muted light coming from a few sconces. There were no windows. A thin black line of grime had collected along the floor beneath the railing surrounding the stairwell. It looked as though my cleaning would need to extend beyond my apartment door.

Inside my apartment, I opened one of the packing boxes and pulled out a pair of jeans and a tank top. I dressed and brushed my hair into two stubby pigtails since it was too short for a single ponytail. I walked two blocks to a Dwayne Reed store, New York's all-purpose pharmacy, cosmetics, household supply store. I bought a bucket, sponges, scrub brushes, a mop, and a variety of cleaning fluids. The apartment had been cleaned before I moved in, but there's the removal of dust and grit and stains, and then there's *clean*. I wanted to scrub away as much accumulated grime as I could, seventy or eighty years of it.

Once it sparkled, I would take the train to the Long Island Ikea to buy a few pieces of furniture. The journey promised to be a full-day trip between subway and train. Until the furniture was delivered, I'd be sleeping on a folded quilt with a second quilt covering me.

By seven that evening, I'd cleaned every corner and surface of my apartment. It still looked a little tired, but there was no build-up of dirt along the baseboards and in the corners of the ceiling. The cabinets were free of grit and crumbs missed by the cleaners, and the bathroom porcelain and fixtures glistened. Even the chipped tile looked fresher. Furniture and a few framed posters would emphasize its charm and cover its tiredness, just like a bit of nicely applied makeup and well-fitted clothes do for a woman's appearance.

I refilled my bucket with warm water and took my scrub brush and cleanser and a fresh box of toothpicks out to the landing. Toothpicks are a near-perfect tool for digging into the crevice between baseboards and flooring. Dirt and damp and dust and dead skin, and whatever else swirls unseen through the air, finds its way into these small openings. Welded with the moisture from fog and rain and humidity that creeps inside, it turns to a glue-like substance. A sponge can't reach it, and even the bristles of a scrub brush don't have the strength to dig into the tiny slit and scoop out the years of accumulated filth.

A sturdy toothpick with a sharp tip fits easily into the smallest spaces, not unlike the way it fits between the gum and tooth in the human mouth. It can pluck out the most stubborn pieces of oily dirt.

I started near my door and worked my way steadily along the wall between my door and the railing. I had just turned the corner, digging and wiping off the sticky stuff onto a paper towel, when I heard the door behind me open.

I shoved the clean end of the toothpick into the crevice and dragged it along.

"What are you doing?"

"Cleaning."

"Did Sam hire you?"

I looked up and saw a woman about my age and height. She had short dark hair, ironed straight and sticking up at the front, combed back at the sides. She wore a tie-dyed dress that hung to just above her ankles. Instead of normal dress straps, the fabric was tied at her shoulders, making it look as if she wore a curtain she'd yanked down on the spur of the moment before venturing outside. Her toenails were naked, and her feet looked clean and soft and tender, unused to going barefoot, placed snugly inside dark brown Birkenstock sandals.

I had an urge to grab my new camera and photograph her, standing there with the shadows cast by the placement of the sconces, her eyes full of irritation, her milky skin pale against the bright colors of her dress.

I sat back on my heels. "Sam?"

"The manager."

I hadn't met him yet, hadn't known his name. All I knew was that he occupied apartment number two on the first floor and that I was only allowed to contact him with non-emergency issues between the hours of five and six in the evening Mondays through Thursdays.

"No."

"Then why are you cleaning?"

"It's dirty."

She stared at me, uncomprehending. "It gets mopped every two weeks."

"There's a lot of gunk collected in here."

"Who cares?" She flipped the leather jacket she was carrying over one shoulder. "Do you live on this floor?"

"I just moved in." I held up my left hand so I wouldn't be reaching out with the hand that was dealing with extracting gunk. "Alexandra."

She recoiled, and her lips spasmed into a smile as she tried to cover up her revulsion at the thought of touching my hand, even the clean one. "It's really not necessary to clean the common area," she said.

"I don't mind."

She stared at me. "How long have you been in New York?"

"A few days."

"You might want to re-think that. Someone like you will get eaten alive in this place."

I laughed.

"I'm not kidding. You're too naïve."

I gave her the most naïve smile I could find inside of me.

She moved to the end of the landing and began the descent without saying good-bye, or telling me her name. For half a second, there was an opportunity to dash into my apartment, grab the video camera, and capture her progress down the stairs, turning at a right angle every eight steps. But then she was gone.

It was possible she would come to regret misreading me.

5

When I walked into the lobby of my new office building on Monday morning, I was still feeling like a transient. My apartment was clean. It had towels and sheets and an adequate supply of cookware and dishes, but the furniture wouldn't arrive for three more days. I'd found a guy via Craig's List who would put it together for me, and I'd decided it was worth the cost to have it done quickly while I was at work.

My shoulders ached from sleeping on the floor, and my tailbone was stiff from sitting on the hard surface, my back against the wall, my tablet on my thighs while I got myself hooked up to the internet and watched a few shows to pass the time.

As I crossed the lobby, I was aware of all the aching parts of my body, not to mention a film of sweat from the steamy, motionless morning air.

I was starting to realize that living in New York City was going to toughen me up. It was nothing like San Francisco, and although the subway seemed nice from an anonymity and convenience and cost perspective, I saw how dependent I was on getting where I was going without a lot of thought about logistics. Uber had its downside, but so did subway travel. Still, it seemed important to become familiar with the subway, to travel like most of my fellow New Yorkers, if I could be so bold as to call myself that after just a few days. Besides, from what I'd seen of the traffic, the subway was faster than any sort of free-standing vehicle.

So far, it seemed like the simplest task in this city required monumental effort. I supposed that within a few weeks, it would all become familiar, hardly worth a thought, extra travel time baked into my schedule, but for now I felt like I spent half my day studying subway routes, checking the street map on my phone, and trying to figure out where to find food or vodka or a new pair of sandals that would support all this walking. Once I located those things, I had to walk six or eight blocks or go underground to wait for a train, and lug my purchases back home in the same way.

Trystan's offices were on the eighteenth floor of thirty-seven. The company, if you could call it that, truly had no name. All that was listed on the building directory was *Trystan Vogel* and the suite number. I pressed the elevator button and waited.

He'd asked me to be there by ten, which seemed rather late, but maybe he wanted time to get the rest of our small group together or maybe he liked to sleep in on Mondays or maybe ten other things. He hadn't explained the late start time and hadn't given me any hint of what my regular schedule might look like. I had a feeling it was going to be rather fluid.

The elevator doors opened, and I stepped inside along with five other people. We rode in silence. I was the only one to get out on the eighteenth floor. I walked down a narrow hallway to suite eighteen-twenty-two. I pressed down on the handle and went inside.

I was standing in the tiniest lobby imaginable, no larger than my walk-in closet at Sean's house in Sydney. There was a single armchair and a potted plant that was classy enough to hide the fact it was artificial until I touched one of its leaves. On the wall adjacent to the chair was a large photograph of the Brooklyn Bridge. I felt slightly more at home, knowing I could identify a significant landmark.

Trystan appeared at the entrance to a short hallway. "Welcome to New York." He wore a white shirt and dark brown slacks without a single misplaced crease. He gave me a warm smile to accompany his welcome.

"Thanks."

"Are you settled?"

"Almost."

We traded pleasantries as he led me down the hallway, showing me the four offices, all relatively similar in dimension, nothing flamboyant for him as the head of this unconventional operation. His office had two windows, and a few extra feet of floor space. There was also a locked document storage room and a small conference room, barely large enough for six people. A TV screen was attached to one wall.

New York real estate is expensive, he informed me, as if I didn't know. He preferred not to over-invest in floor space that existed simply for show. Space could be found in other ways — in one's view of the world. In an office that wasn't filled with unnecessary furniture and decor.

I smiled and considered the trippy view of the world I was going to experience working for Trystan, the self-proclaimed Provocateur.

My office had a single narrow window that looked down onto an alley. I had to press myself against the glass to see the pavement. There was a pale green ergonomic chair and a thin laptop and a wireless mouse. The walls were empty, ready for whatever I wanted to look at while I worked. There was a single visitor's chair and several large hooks behind the door for my winter gear. A narrow set of three shelves stood in the corner on the same wall as the window. On the top shelf was a bud vase holding a white rose.

From the street, the tall building looked glamorous alongside its equally tall neighbors. But inside the office suite, the glamor faded somewhat. I hoped my job didn't require an excessive amount of time at a desk, which made me realize again that I had a very sketchy idea of what my job involved.

Trystan and I rode down to the lobby, talking about Australia as we descended. He purchased a tray of coffees, and we returned to the conference room where my new co-workers were waiting. He introduced me to Stephanie and Diana. We took our seats in the comfortable cream-colored chairs. They surrounded a white ash table with a dark stripe down the center. There were narrow crevices in the wood as if it had been sliced from the center of a tree.

While Trystan talked about the research and the project management work my co-workers did, the compiling and analysis of data for our clients, I studied the two women seated across from me.

For the foreseeable future, they would be within arm's reach five days a week, throughout most of my daylight hours. They studied me as intensely as I looked at them, although they were slightly more obvious about it. I kept my gaze trained mostly on Trystan and nodded and murmured more frequently than they did, still able to make an assessment.

My gut response was that I would love Diana and

encounter a power struggle with Stephanie.

Diana was black, an immediate observation that caught in my throat like a fishbone. I never note the race of white people. They're just there, the landscape of my existence. I suppose we're wired to categorize — race, gender, height, weight, age. And which categorization comes first? It's impossible to say. Had she categorized me as easily as I did her? I pushed the thought away.

She was my age, with a look of intense scrutiny and intelligence in her eyes as they flicked over my face and as much of my body as was visible above the table. She had long hair done in thick braids across her scalp, narrowing into thinner, braided spears that hung to the center of her back. Her makeup was perfectly done — a lot of it, dramatizing her eyes in a way that made me feel they took in everything I was seeing and more.

She had on a black sleeveless blouse, and her forearms were decorated with silver bracelets. Her fingernails were perfectly manicured, short, with cherry-red polish. She wore as many rings as she did bracelets and I loved every single one of them.

Stephanie was older than me, but I couldn't pinpoint her age. She didn't look like she was lacking intelligence, but there was something about her tightly clenched lips that said she had a higher estimation of her intelligence and skills than was warranted. She had dark brown hair, sleek and straight, cut just below her earlobes. Her skin was creamy with rosy cheeks and free of makeup except for taupe gloss and a hint of brown mascara. She had dark brown eyes and wore large gold hoops in her ears.

Her shirt was dark gray, also sleeveless — these women

were obviously used to sweltering New York late summer weather. Both of them wore sandals and blue jeans. I was glad that Trystan, despite the dark slacks and white shirts he preferred, didn't have a business suit dress code.

Stephanie's top was cut low, showing a bit of cleavage. Front and center on her breastbone was a three-inch gold cross. While Trystan spoke, she stroked it absently, as if she were petting it.

I can't say why, but I had the feeling it wasn't a decorative piece she'd chosen that morning. I had the impression, from the way she fondled it, that it was something she wore every day.

6

During Trystan's and my four-block walk to a bistro for lunch, he talked about the neighborhood while I thought about that gold cross.

It was too big.

Yes, her earrings were also over-sized, but that was a fashion statement. Madonna and a few other rock stars aside, a cross is not a fashion statement. But it's definitely a statement.

Tiny gold crosses, especially those with fake gems, or diamond or ruby chips in the crosshairs, announce a quiet belief. They say that the wearer is tied to something that's been with her most of her life. Those slender crosses proclaim that she has a certain way of viewing the world and won't take kindly to cruel gossip or crude jokes, but that she won't be in your face with her beliefs. She's subtle. She wears it for spiritual comfort.

And why is it always *she*? Why don't men wear crosses around their necks, except for your desert-preacher types or hippie-believer-types who favor leather necklaces with crosses made of nails?

In general, men don't wear a lot of neck jewelry. I suppose they've been socialized to strangle themselves with neckties. When they break free of that convention, why would they wrap chains around their necks? Bracelets are somewhat common on men, rings more so, and of course, there's a proliferation of lone earrings. Necklaces are rare.

I don't know if women need that visible assurance more, or if they need to tell people where they stand without a lot of conversation. Maybe it is a fashion statement after all. If I got to know Stephanie better, I might ask her.

But getting to know her better looked to be a minefield, because of those quarter-inch-thick gold bars, crossed in just the right way.

We stopped at the corner of East 53rd and Park to wait for the traffic light. I took a deep breath and looked at the people walking toward us on all sides, coming down streets that were formed into a near-perfect grid. The layout of New York City was so different from the wandering streets of the suburbs where I'd lived. San Francisco and Sydney had some of that grid-like structure, but not like New York. You had the impression some dude slapped a sheet of ruled paper over the island, and the roads were constructed according to his template. Suburban streets can take their time getting somewhere, designed for tranquil movement, even if that's not how they're utilized. They dead end and turn for no practical reason and loop back into each other making you feel lost even when the GPS is telling you where to turn. A grid, especially one as precise as New York's, says efficiency. Business.

The light changed and we crossed, pressed by people in suits and others in shorts and T-shirts and flip-flops, some in traditional Indian and middle eastern robes, others in outfits that looked like they were headed to nightclubs, and plenty wearing jeans and Doc Marten boots and tank tops, tattoos covering their bare arms and shoulders.

As the faces and clothing blurred around me, my mind

returned to that enormous gold cross.

I wondered what Trystan thought of it. I wondered if he'd even noticed it. Men have a way of not appearing to see some things, things that jump out to women like glittering knife blades. For the most part, men don't take much notice of shoe styles or manicured nails or new haircuts or expensive jewelry. They definitely don't notice purses, unless the bags are large and a man can laugh at the size before casually asking the owner to take charge of sunglasses and a pack of cigarettes and any other clutter spilling out of his pockets.

There was still a slim chance that Stephanie's necklace was a fashion statement. It was New York, after all. It might be an ironic piece of jewelry. It might have been created by a famous designer, although it lacked flair, so that possibility was remote.

The rest of her outfit and hairstyle and makeup argued against it being any of those things. There was something telling me that she was out to proselytize everyone in her path. She was starting off by silently declaring her view of life in a shiny wordless statement, and slowly the admonitions of sin and repentance and punishment would emerge.

Having those thoughts was biased and judgmental of me, but they weren't thoughts of wanting to stay away from her, of ostracizing her, or not treating her with respect. It was reality. Knowing how she was likely to behave, and knowing how I would be compelled to disagree with easily half the things she was bound to say.

I hadn't even spoken to her beyond our group small talk. It was bigoted of me to make assumptions about her beliefs and potential behavior. But experience makes you that way. If it's happened too many times, you walk into a relationship expecting the same. You can try to fight it, but it's part of the hard-wired learning process of the human brain. Difficult to fight, impossible to completely overcome. It's why the old get jaded, I suppose.

It wasn't that I begrudged her a faith of any kind. What I didn't like was the advertisement. The announcement that she had strong beliefs. In my experience, a woman with a cross that large doesn't give a rat's ass about your beliefs. I suspected that cross meant her views were a frequent topic of conversation and woven into nearly everything she said.

We'd reached the Bistro, and all my thoughts had done was wander in circles. It was too bad the straight lines of the streets hadn't directed my mind in a more orderly fashion. You'd think the lines and corners would do that, but perhaps the weaving in and out among throngs of disparate people flooding the wide sidewalks fought against the structure of the layout.

Trystan opened the door, and we stepped inside.

The tables were close together. The noise of people talking was warm but not cacophonous. We were seated at a table near the back wall. A watercolor painting of a European outdoor cafe hung on the wall over our table — Paris or Italy, possibly Greece.

The table was pristine, with a crisp white cloth and pale blue napkins and a tiny dark blue glass jar filled with sand and a succulent.

We both ordered a glass of white wine, shrimp bisque, and a small salad with goat cheese, plum tomatoes, and candied walnuts.

Trystan took a roll out of the wire basket. He bit into it

without adding butter. I cut mine in half and smeared a thin layer of soft butter over the open surface. I took a bite, and we chewed in silence.

I managed to finish first. I put down my roll. "Tell me more about my co-workers."

"What do you want to know?"

"Anything that will help me start off on the right foot."

He seemed to like my desire to be a team player, my desire to get along and adapt to my new environment. I smiled, glad that I was giving the right impression.

"I'm still not sure what you want to know," he said.

"How long have they worked for you?"

"Diana for two years, Stephanie for five months."

After that, he mostly talked about their roles and more about my role. He didn't mention any of the useful things such as views on smoking, the existence of partners or spouses, the propensity to talk too much, or religion.

After only five months, it was possible Stephanie hadn't yet revealed the agenda behind the cross. Maybe he had no idea what that piece of gold was declaring, no idea that she very well might be coming for him, for Diana, and now, for me.

7

Tess and I had an appointment to Skype. Other than exchanging a few text messages with bits of mundane information about what we were up to at any given moment, we hadn't spoken since I'd arrived in New York.

When she suggested the call, it proved we would both make an equal effort to stay in touch. The nine thousand miles between us could shrink at any time. And we had a connection that was hard to put into words — more intricate than employee and boss, more solid than mentee and mentor, or roommates, or workout partners.

Before our call, I got out the supplies for a martini. I left them on the counter and started up to the roof garden, climbing the three remaining flights as quickly as I could to give myself a pathetic few minutes of cardio for the day. My heart was thudding pleasantly and my skin steaming unpleasantly when I reached the garden. The sun was going down in a haze of orange, like spilled juice across the horizon. I loved the feeling of so many buildings around me, rising into the sky, filled with people, standing close as if to shore each other up.

The world felt secure when I looked out at all those towering structures and imagined the people whose lives were playing out inside. There was only an extremely rare threat of an earthquake in New York to make me think about everything crumbling into a pile of rubble.

At the same time, there was the constant reminder of September eleventh floating unseen around the city. The anniversary was the following day, and that date and those remembered images and horrors hung in the air. Still, it had been one of those occurrences that shocks and horrifies once but is a singular event. Nothing like that could happen again. The unimaginable happens only once. Of course, there are a host of future unimaginable things, but that event had its moment in time. It then became a permanent part of the city, a wedge in the psyches of everyone who lived and worked there. Their hearts were torn apart but eventually managed to grow thick scar tissue and new strength. The whisper of those magnificent towers turning to dust held the place together in its wake, and the city retained its dignity and sense of superiority.

I smoked my cigarette and basked in the warm, moist air. It was soothing, standing there without the biting cold wind I experienced most evenings in San Francisco.

When I was finished, I went downstairs. I cut a few slices of cheese and placed them on crackers. I ate them while I mixed the martini, thinking about how I needed to get my act together with dinner. Rarely having to cook anything during all those months at Sean's, I'd lost my will to put effort into planning meals. Even though I don't like to cook, I had to eat more than cheese and crackers, toast and avocado, or a slice of pizza. Soon, before the weekend, I would make a serious trip to the grocery store.

With the martini in one hand and my finger tapping the screen of my iPad, I waited for the minutes to tick past.

I pulled out the swizzle stick and sucked off my first olive. I chewed it slowly. The Skype app began ringing, and a moment later, Tess was in my sweltering apartment, looking cool and relaxed in the lush greenery of her backyard. Of course, it was early spring there. She would have her own chance to swelter in a few months.

I did not miss the situation with Sean and the near confinement to his house, and especially not the social media activity — a job that was both ridiculously easy and impossible. I missed the climate, and there was a void without Tess, of course. I thought about Gavin often enough, and we'd also exchanged a few text messages. I guessed those teasing, flirting notes would fade to a trickle, or end suddenly when he met someone else.

Tess raised her wine glass toward the screen. "Cheers, Damien says *hi*."

I raised my martini. "Cheers to you and Damien."

We both sipped our drinks.

She told me about the status of the TruthTeller app, which sounded pretty much the same as the status at our final group meeting. It sounded the same as the status when I'd resigned three weeks earlier. It sounded the same as the status she'd sent when my plane landed at JFK. She didn't seem to mind the leisurely pace, the meandering toward announcing the product.

"Tell me about your new job." She took another sip of wine.

Damien laughed. He wasn't captured in the range of the camera on her laptop, but I pictured him bobbing around, tilting his head, and chatting to anyone who would listen.

I described the building where Trystan had offices. I told her about my camera purchases. I told her I was still intrigued and eager to get started. I told her about my apartment and the strange woman next door. Tess corrected my assumption and suggested I was the strange one, for my detailed cleaning of a public area. She couldn't see my point that the landing was basically my front patio.

She asked about my new co-workers.

"I've only just met them. We didn't really talk."

"Too bad. I'm curious."

"I think I'll get along with Diana. We're the same age, and…"

"So?"

"It's not just our ages. She…I can feel it. The look in her eyes, right?"

"No wonder Trystan wanted to hire you from the start. He thinks the same way — snap judgment. Thinking you can read a person the moment you meet."

"Because you can."

"It's not always accurate, you know."

"In my experience, it is."

"I had a great feeling about Sean when I met him," she said.

I hadn't had a positive reaction to Sean, but she seemed to have forgotten that. "He's not so terrible."

"Well, he's not what I thought. I read him as easy-going. Instead, he's neurotic."

I laughed.

"And the one who isn't your age?"

"I said it's not only our age…I just mentioned it as a detail."

"And the other is young? Old?"

"About forty, maybe a little younger."

"Okay. And why won't you get along? Sounds rather

closed-minded of you."

"She's religious."

"How do you know, and so what?"

"She wears a giant gold cross. And I had enough preaching when I was a kid. I prefer not to spend time around people who want me to repent."

She laughed. "No one wants you to repent. Unless they knock on your door and ask to be invited in for a chat."

"You'd be surprised."

"It's an office. I'm sure she's not going to try to convert you."

"That cross is huge. It's really in your face."

"Then don't look at it."

"Hard not to." I pulled an olive off the stick and ate it. I took another sip.

Tess told me a woman's body had been found floating in a pond, dead from a stab wound. "At that park where we went running, remember?"

"Yes." I ate the last olive and swallowed the remainder of my drink. I waited for her to tell me the woman's name, waited for her to say they'd talked to Sean and Gavin, and Tess. And they wanted to get in touch with me.

"They haven't identified her yet. But isn't it awful? Right where we were running?"

"It is."

"I thought that area was so safe," she said.

I wanted to correct her...reassure her it *was* safe, that the killing might have been personal. But I couldn't.

8

It was nearly eight o'clock when I finished with Tess and my martini. The air outside was still sultry, flowing through my open window, enticing me to consider having another drink and drifting into a semi-unconscious state, sitting beside the window and allowing myself to be mesmerized by the never-ending river of foot traffic.

Pushing the desire for a martini out of my head, I ate two slices of cheese and half an apple. I took a bottle of water out of the fridge. I slung my new camera bag over my shoulder and went downstairs.

I hadn't started the instruction classes. I hadn't even read the manual. But Leon had pointed out the automatic setting, and the button to snap a photo was prominent. I could take a thousand blurry pictures of people with their heads cut off and make them evaporate into the ether.

A few blocks from my apartment was a tiny alleyway, dead end, so not really an alley. The buildings on both sides and the brick wall at the rear were covered with ivy. The space was about the same as the footprint of the buildings on either side. For whatever reason, the space had been left vacant and then transformed into an open patio with a fountain and small tables and chairs where people brought takeout food. There were several benches where I'd seen old men reading The New York Times when I passed by during daylight hours.

There was a lot of activity for a Monday night, although nothing like on the weekends when people squeezed together on the benches and used the edge of the fountain for overflow seating and children chased each other back and forth.

I found an unoccupied bench, sat down, and unzipped the bag. I pulled out the camera, removed the lens cap, and settled the camera on my lap. I connected the flash attachment to the top of the casing. The recommended lens, or rather, the lens imposed on me by Leon, would take decent distant shots, allowing me to be far enough away that most people wouldn't be aware I was photographing them.

I turned on the power, aimed the camera at the fountain, and snapped three pictures. I put the camera in my lap. The buttons for advancing the images were obvious. I pressed them and looked at the photographs. They were worse than what I might have taken with my cell phone. The flash captured the water and turned it to a white smear, leaving darkness all around.

My first class was the following week. I definitely needed it.

I aimed the camera at two men playing cards. Those images were better. There must have been something about the water and flash combo that distorted the lighting. Maybe the water had its own light.

I photographed the cards on the table, the back of one man's head, the bent head of the man across from him. I shifted slightly and took a photograph of a couple arguing, trying to hide their anger, which gave their faces stiff, contorted expressions. Their jaws were tight, their lips barely moved. They leaned away from each other.

They wore wedding rings, although whether they were married to each other was impossible to tell.

The man had his arms crossed. He flexed his biceps as if it were some sort of intimidation tactic to let the woman know he was the more powerful of the two of them, the one who would ultimately win. It wasn't that I had the impression he was flexing his muscles because he intended violence, but that some kind of psychological violence was making his body respond, possibly outside of his awareness. He was going to win that fight, and she was going to see that he had the upper hand.

At least that's what I imagined. And I doubted I was that far from the truth.

I put the camera on my lap and looked around for another interesting subject. The disagreement seemed to be at a standoff. Unless they started moving, raised their voices, it couldn't hold my interest for long, and there was nothing else to photograph. Their expressions hadn't shifted, and their bodies remained rigid.

In the far corner was a table and chairs occupied by three women. They were chatting and pouring wine out of an insulated canister. They weren't being discreet about drinking wine, but I was pretty sure it wasn't allowed in a public place without a liquor license. Still, they were quiet, and I supposed it was unlikely a cop would walk into the area unless someone called.

I took a close-up of each woman. They were in their late twenties, all of them with long, flat-ironed, light brown hair. They all wore shirts with collars, linen slacks, and black high heels so that you'd think they all looked the same. But they were very different.

Their faces, even when they were just talking, without any dramatic expressions, were remarkably different. It's quite stunning, when you stop to pay attention, how there's an infinite variety of faces. People keep reproducing, the population keeps growing, and every single instance of a human being looks unique. Over seven billion of us.

If you went back through all of history, I wonder whether that would hold true, or would you eventually run into duplicates? Since DNA seems to be unique with each reproduction, probably not. It really boggles the mind.

The woman who seemed to be controlling the wine had a narrow nose, thin eyebrows, and thin lips. The rest of her body wasn't significantly thinner than her friends' bodies, but her face was narrow and delicate and looked as if it might crack easily. The woman to her left wore an incredible amount of makeup — her face smoothed into a sheet of skin without any variation over her cheekbones or jaw, as if she'd been fired from clay. Her lips were a red so dark they were almost black. I zoomed in and took two shots of her face. She wore false eyelashes, and her eyebrows looked painted on. Her eye shadow and liner were smokey black. She had very large eyes, and they probably didn't need all that makeup, but she looked dramatic, and I couldn't blame her for going for maximum effect.

I turned the camera to the third woman. She had a large nose, almost to the point of being a distraction, but her smile, and she smiled a lot, was fantastic, making her look like the happiest person alive.

Suddenly, she was no longer smiling. She stood and walked quickly across the cobblestone, stopping a few feet from me. "Are you taking pictures of us?"

I cradled the camera in my arms — a mother protecting her child from attack. "I'm experimenting with my new camera. Just trying it out."

"Stop it. Delete them. Right now." She folded her arms and moved closer. She jutted one hip to the side and began tapping her toe.

I laughed. "I'm just practicing. I won't do anything with them."

"Delete them."

"They belong to me."

"It's illegal to photograph someone without their permission."

I removed the flash attachment, put on the lens cap, and fitted the camera into the bag. I zipped it closed and stood. "It's not illegal to take photographs. It's illegal to *use* the photographs without your permission."

"I have no way of knowing whether you'll do that."

"I won't."

She glared at me. "I want you to delete those pictures." She moved closer. I wondered what she would do. Surely not grab my bag, although I could see that she very much wanted to do that. "You're a bitch," she said.

I smiled.

"That's a total invasion of our privacy."

"I don't use social media, so they'll never be posted anywhere."

"Everyone uses social media."

"No, they don't. And I probably will delete these. I'll probably delete them tonight. I told you, I'm just getting a feel for my new camera."

"Well, get a feel somewhere else."

"You're very beautiful. You should be flattered."

A slight blush crept across her face — hating me and feeling flattered in a single sweep of emotion. "I'm not."

I smiled. "Enjoy your wine." I turned and walked around the bench, then quickly wove past several tables until I reached the sidewalk. I wanted to look back, but I didn't.

People are paranoid about having their photo taken by a stranger, but they'll post all kinds of photographs and comments and their whereabouts all over the internet without a moment's hesitation. It's almost as if they think it's their private web, shared only by friends, and not accessible in some form or another to every person on the planet with dark intentions.

9

The next two days, my new job consisted of eight hours sitting in the conference room with Trystan while he gave me a detailed briefing about each person on the current client list. There were fifteen. You wouldn't think it would take two solid days to read profiles and questionnaires and talk about people's lives, but it did. You would think two solid days of that might be boring, but it wasn't.

He broke up the stream of information with nice lunches — the first day at a steakhouse that was holding on strong to its 1980s decor, and the following day at a Thai place that was dark with a copper ceiling and glimmering floor made of something I couldn't identify.

Despite all this alone time with him, I didn't feel like I knew him any better than I had when I'd accepted the job offer. Or, more accurately, when I'd decided I wanted to work for him before there was an offer on the table, and all that existed was something indefinable between us.

And that indefinable something was still there, hanging in the air around us. The best way to describe it is a sense of understanding the nature of the other person on an unspoken level. Chemistry, but not the kind that leads to sex. Kindred spirits might be the best word.

Maybe part of what we understood was an unwillingness on both our parts to reveal much of what was going on inside. Like me, he talked about himself, but when he was finished, you knew there was more unsaid than said. I'm not sure whether people are aware of that with me. I expect some are, and others are clueless. I wondered whether Trystan recognized that fact. Some people talk, and you know it's all out there. Of course, there are always going to be some hidden crevices, but they don't filter much. Trystan did. I do.

The amount of information people gave him about their lives was astonishing.

They took standard personality tests and filled out extremely detailed questionnaires. Trystan had me read every single answer. The questionnaires consisted of one-hundred-forty questions about their childhood, their beliefs, their career path, dreams, goals, desires they were ashamed of, sources of pride, and more.

The questions had been devised by Diana. She'd started working with Trystan right after he got the idea for provoking people to achieve their wildest dreams. She had a master's degree in psychology. Under his direction, she'd done more studying of commonly used personality and career aptitude tests to compile her own set of questions that really dug below the surface. That had been Trystan's primary instruction to her — dig as deep as you can. He didn't want questions that revealed an agenda or that people might easily manipulate to give a pre-determined impression of their lives.

He'd collected financial profiles, sexual histories, and what some would consider secrets, on people at very high levels in their fields, a few in the public eye. It surprised me they would trust anyone to see inside their lives like that. And yet, they did. I guess if you believed his promise of a *transformed* life that *skyrocketed* you beyond the *next level*, and you wanted badly enough to get yourself to that next place in your upward trajectory, you would do anything.

I half expected I might read that one of them had committed murder on her way to the top. Or that another was guilty of embezzlement, they were so forthright with the shadows in their lives.

At the end of the workday, I was glad to walk outside of the building, escaping those walls and small spaces. No matter how cleanly and simply and elegantly decorated, they were small.

The air felt good on my skin, thick and warm as it was. I decided to walk the eight longish blocks home rather than crowding below ground and hanging onto a metal pole while the subway raced and stopped and sweaty people surged on and off, all pushing for their favorite spot.

Walking felt good after sitting all day, and the mental effort of mapping my way pushed all those stories and dreams and desires of Trystan's clients out of my head. The blur of people walking past, the hum of voices and footsteps — high heels clicking, athletic shoes tapping, men's shoes clomping, and flip-flops slapping bare heels. It was almost musical, a melody against the sounds of traffic.

I wasn't sure if I truly felt an energy of the city or if I was glamorizing everything because it was new to me. New places and experiences are always exciting and remarkable. It's not until it becomes familiar that the shine wears off and noise becomes noise. Too many people on what felt like a small island could become oppressive. But maybe the glamor and excitement of New York would always outweigh the crowds and noise.

When I reached the entrance to my building, I was sweating. The back of my neck was damp even though my hair only brushed across half of it now.

Despite my desire to get my heart pumping by taking the stairs, I trudged at an ever-slowing pace up to the third floor. I needed to conserve some of my energy for a proper grocery shopping. On the weekend, I would map out a place to run. And find a gym.

As my foot touched the landing, my neighbor's door opened, and the woman who'd been shocked by my cleaning emerged from her apartment. This time she wore a blue sleeveless top that barely reached the edge of her low-slung short skirt. Her feet looked as sweaty and grimy as mine, barely clinging to her ultra-thin leather flip-flops.

"Oh. Hi." She smiled. Her expression was warm and welcoming. She seemed almost happy to see me as if she'd forgotten how she'd nearly flown down the stairs to escape me the last time.

"Hi."

"It's hot," she said.

I nodded.

"I don't think I introduced myself. Last time."

"I don't think you did."

"Victoria."

I leaned against the railing and adjusted the strap of my bag. "Good to meet you."

"Alexandra, right?"

I nodded.

"Are you from the midwest?"

I ran my fingers through my hair, lifting it off my scalp, longing to hurry past her into my apartment where I could drop my bag and pry off my sandals and drink a glass of water. "Why do you think that?"

"Your accent. You don't really have one. And that you want everything clean." She laughed.

"Only people from the midwest like their environment clean?"

"No, but New York isn't very clean."

"Most places I've seen are fairly nice."

"But not the streets. And landings. And stuff like that. There's a lot of people and a lot of history. Maybe clean isn't the right word, but you know what I mean. Layers of history. But you are…from the midwest, I can tell. You're very open."

I had to suppress my laugh. "Maybe you can help me. What's the best and closest place for groceries?"

"Big shopping? Like whole chickens and twenty kinds of yogurt? That kind of store? Or just enough to get your fruits and veggies and a chicken breast?"

"How about both, then I can decide where to go, after I cool down."

"You do look sweaty."

"I walked home."

"From where?"

"East 53rd."

She nodded. "Well, there's a market that has a lot of things I need on West 57th. There's a bodega on West 50th, and a Whole Foods on East 57th, about fifteen minutes on the E train."

"Thanks." I crossed the landing and put the key in my lock.

"Where do you work?" she said.

I didn't turn. I wanted to peel off my jeans and sandals. I wanted a glass of water. I sort of wanted a smoke. "I work for an executive coach." Trystan wouldn't like that description at all, but how would he ever know?

"Sounds interesting."

"Could be. I just started." I opened the door.

"Can I see your place?"

I turned slightly. "I'm still getting settled, and right now, I need to chill. Why don't you come over for a martini on Friday."

She nodded. "I'm super curious."

I knew that sensation — gnawing curiosity, an inability to put your mind elsewhere, but I didn't usually announce it to people. I smiled. "Good talking to you."

"I love martinis. And we can compare jobs. What time?"

I suggested six-thirty, she moved it to seven. She told me her boyfriend lived with her, but she would leave him at home. "We work together. From home."

She seemed eager for me to ask what she did, but she underestimated my desire for a chair and a glass of water and bare feet. "See ya." I closed the door while she was still talking, as she wondered out loud whether she should bring the boyfriend *after all*, but then commenting I hadn't really *invited* him, and suggesting that *girl time* would be fun.

She'd seemed very convinced of my naiveté. I was happy to let her assume that.

10

I wasn't a bigot about Stephanie and her cross.

And it's not religion that I have a problem with. It's religion imposed on the entire world, the expectation that every single person is required to conform to a single set of beliefs. The idea of sinners and an angry man sitting on a throne, even if it's argued that's an archaic view. It's still presented that way.

The Throne.

The bearded man.

Yes, I know it's a spirit. A spirit called *he*.

I didn't like that cross out there in my face, marching around the office, proclaiming all the baggage hanging off those two slender arms, stretched wide, a man's hands nailed to them in the Catholic version, bare and reminiscent in Protestant crosses like Stephanie's.

I didn't like that sooner or later, I would be required to listen to Stephanie's questions about my life. They would be casual questions, posturing as friendliness, but in reality, superficial words with a monster lurking beneath. A monster that wanted to tell you how your life needed to be lived differently. Questions that turned into criticisms and accusations and finally, condemnations. As if the inside of another person's heart is any business of any other person, unless they choose to reveal it.

The chutzpah takes your breath away.

There's a reason I knew Stephanie was biding her time, waiting to accuse me of sin — the sin of thinking I know what's true and false. The sin of thinking I don't need to repent. The sin of thinking there might not be any being on a throne or a spirit in the sky. I knew because in high school, the kids in our church were given training classes in how to convert the sinners that sat beside us at school and cheered during our football games and even lived inside our own homes, every single day.

A person wearing a cross that large wants to be absolutely sure you know where she stands. It's the opening shot in her assault on your heathen life. It's there to make you aware at every single moment in time that god is watching, that the wearer is thinking of god, and wanting to tell you how much god loves and cares for you and has a plan for your life. I don't even have a fully worked out plan for my life. It's doubtful any other being does.

11

Portland

On the first Wednesday of September, at five o'clock, two hours before the evening church services, the high school kids sat in a small auditorium. We were each given an enormous binder filled with tabs and pages of lessons. The binder was filled with four-color photographs of people knocking on doors, talking to the unsaved, bowing their heads in prayer as they led the candidate to repentance. There were lists of Bible verses, forms with questions. There were scenarios that helped you know how to respond in different situations, as if every possible human encounter could be written up and illustrated with well-groomed, constantly smiling teenagers.

It would take an entire three months for us to be thoroughly trained.

We would memorize the questions and answers. We would perform role-playing exercises to help us get over our assumed fears of starting intimate conversations with people who were not interested in discussing the destination of their soul, or anything about their death. Not surprisingly, I was the only one in the class of over fifty High School Juniors who had no fear about starting an uncomfortable conversation. I relished the idea. But the conversation I imagined would not be the one they wanted me to have.

Each week Mr. B would speak to us for half an hour. Mr. B didn't typically lead the youth group activities. He was one of a select few who had been chosen to fly at church expense to a conference in Florida where he was specially trained to train others on the program.

After his lecture, his staff of volunteers, trained by him, would review our homework assignments before we were broken into small groups for role-playing. The purpose of the training material was to lead people from two opening questions all the way through a tightly controlled discussion, with proof from the Bible, and by appealing to their supposed logic, so that at the end, they saw clearly there was no other option but to repent. They would be persuaded intellectually, and their hearts would follow the lead of their heads.

They would recognize without any lingering doubt that god existed, that the only possible happiness was adhering to his guidelines, that he had a plan for their lives, that he had rules, that his rules had been broken, that he wanted to interact personally with every person on the planet, that all the things laid out in the Bible, as interpreted by Tabernacle of Truth and like-minded churches across the country and around the world, were unquestionably true. There was no room for refusing to repent, for refusing to join the church, and for refusing to also become one who went out and brought the saving news to others.

The similarity to a pyramid scheme was obvious to me, but I was told in no uncertain terms that entertaining a thought like that was the lowest form of skepticism and ungodliness. And besides, people at the apex of a pyramid scheme profited financially from those below. In this case, there was no profit. There was no self-serving motive for a reward of any kind. The parallel was still obvious, to me.

I was put in a group with Mr. B himself so he could keep an eye on me.

"I can tell you're a bright girl," he said. "But you need to turn that intelligence toward God. You need to yield your mind to Him and use it for good. Not for sowing doubt and trying to mislead others into unbelief and the destruction of their souls."

I smiled.

"Do you know that you're a very intelligent young woman?" he said.

"Probably," I said.

"There's no probably about it. You are."

I nodded.

"I'd like to set a challenge for you. To use that well-formed brain that's hiding behind that beautiful hair." He gave me a soothing smile and moved slightly. He raised his hand as if he intended to touch my hair. Instead, he let his hand waver in mid-air between us.

I waited.

"Are you ready for a challenge?"

"I don't know what it is."

He scowled at me. "The answer should be straightforward — a simple *yes*."

"Not if I don't know what the challenge is."

"When an adult asks you a question, you should say *yes*."

I gave him a tiny smile.

"Does your father allow you to show such disrespect?"

"I don't think I'm being disrespectful. I just need to know what the challenge is before I say *yes* or *no*."

He looked angry, but he caved. "I'd like you to memorize the first series of questions and answers in your workbook. You can come up on the stage with me next week, and we'll demonstrate an interaction with an unbeliever."

"Are you sure that's a good idea?"

He ran his hand over the bristles of his short hair. He left his hand there, letting the hair tickle his palm. First, he stared at me, then seemed to gaze through me. Finally, he lowered his hand and let it hang by his side, fingers twitching, looking for a place to land. "Memorize the first two questions and the various responses. If you're not prepared, it will be humiliating for you, standing on the stage in front of your peers, looking like a fool." He walked away, weaving among the scattered chairs where they'd been pulled out of their rows. He found his way to the front of the room and picked up his own three-inch binder, flipping through the pages madly, not landing in any spot for the several minutes I stood watching him.

During the second half of the session, Mrs. B took the stage. She told the story of a waitress who had recently served her at a Denny's restaurant. Mrs. B was *given the opportunity* to use the questions in the course with her waitress. As a result of following the outline, Mrs. B *led the young woman to faith*. Now, the waitress was engaged to be married to a godly man who had a calling to serve as a police officer. Mrs. B smiled and clasped her hands together. She tipped her face toward the ceiling in a way that made me expect a beam of light to fall upon her.

I wasn't sure whether her story meant we were in the match-making business, connecting lines from individual people to god who then formed couples, or if it meant that yielding to god brought you the man or woman of your dreams. Either way, Mrs. B was clearly more excited about the engagement than the conversion.

12

New York City

As I slung my leather bag over my shoulder, ready to leave my office, Diana stepped into the doorway. "Want to grab something?"

"Martinis"

"I don't drink." She smiled. "Maybe an ice cream? Coffee?"

I preferred an icy cold martini.

I couldn't imagine a woman my age living in New York who didn't enjoy at least one drink. What did she do for nightlife? I suppose she could order soda, but it's not the same. Alcohol isn't inherently bad, as long as you don't let it run your life. The pleasure of relaxing with a drink isn't any different from the pleasure of seeking dopamine in extreme exercise or yoga or rock climbing or a nightly bowl of potato chips and dip. We all want to feel good, it's human nature. And a drink or two, occasionally a few more, unwinds the brain in a very pleasant way. Until it tears them apart, a few drinks can bring people closer together.

Moving my mind back to the immediate question, ice cream sounded like it would be appealing once I left the building. But with conditioned air rippling across my skin, coffee seemed more satisfying. "Let's decide when we're outside."

"I know what you mean." She moved to make room for me.

We walked to the elevator and waited for it to arrive.

"I was surprised you don't drink," I said. "Are you religious?"

"God no!" She laughed. "I mean, I'm not, but why did I say *god*?" She rolled her eyes. "I guess we're all a little religious somewhere deep inside, or we wouldn't always have that word slipping off our tongues."

"Maybe."

The elevator doors opened, and we stepped inside. When we reached the ground floor, she walked ahead of me and pushed open the lobby door. Even standing a few feet behind her, I felt the blast of hot, damp air.

"Definitely ice cream," I said.

"Agreed."

We walked on hot pavement that burned its way into the soles of my sandals and turned the bottoms of my feet to the consistency of steamed dumplings. I commented on the sensation, and Diana laughed.

She began lifting her feet higher as she walked, suddenly aware of the heat and moisture, and attempting to cool them by keeping them off the pavement as long as possible with each step forward.

"How are you adjusting so far?" She paused with one foot in the air, then took another step.

I mimicked her movements and felt that although my feet were now slightly less damp and pulpy, it would take us forever to walk five blocks to the ice cream shop she said was the *best ever*. I returned to my regular pace. She did the same.

"To work or New York?"

"Both."

"I'm getting a sense of what Trystan is trying to do for his clients. *Our* clients. It's interesting. I'm surprised people give him so much personal information."

"At the end of the day, people want to tell their stories," she said.

"But their sex lives? The things they're ashamed of?"

"Maybe they feel relief, talking without being judged. Knowing it has a purpose to improve their lives."

"But he has a hold on them now."

"It's all confidential."

"Sometimes that doesn't mean much."

"True. But in this case, it does."

"You know the saying — the only way two people can keep a secret is if one of them is dead."

She laughed. "I never thought of that in this context." She paused outside the ice cream place. "Should we eat it here, or walk to the park? There's a small one about three blocks over."

"If the ice cream lasts that long."

"We'll probably be done by the time we get there, but walking feels good. Even when it's this hot."

"Do you always have ice cream after work?"

"Not always, but a few times a week, in the summer."

"You look too thin to be eating ice cream every other day."

"I walk almost everywhere."

We moved toward the counter. A girl with a ring through the left side of her nostril and long blonde hair woven into a braid asked what we wanted.

Diana ordered strawberry vanilla swirl in a waffle cone.

I got coffee with chocolate chips in a sugar cone, so I got my coffee after all. I'm not sure if coffee ice cream has caffeine, probably not, but the taste of coffee alone is enough to make my body think I'm getting a bit of a wake-up boost.

We licked and walked. The sharp cold of the ice cream running through my body made my feet feel less damp and bloated. Diana agreed it was the same for her.

"Are you liking New York?"

"I am. How long have you lived here?"

"Since college. I went to NYU and couldn't leave. It was in my blood from the start, I think. NYU was the only college I ever wanted to attend. My dad was so frustrated with me." She laughed and bit off a piece of ice cream, almost chewing it. My teeth ached, watching her.

"He wanted me to cover my bases, keep my options open. We fought about it for almost an entire year, but I only applied to NYU. Luckily I got in. He would have burst a blood vessel if I hadn't."

"Where did you grow up?"

"Michigan."

She didn't volunteer any more. Michigan is a big place, but I guess it wasn't in her blood.

"Anyway. Fifteen years in New York. It feels like I've lived here all my life."

We talked more about New York, and I told her a bit about Portland. By then, we'd reached the park. We sat on a bench under a tree with narrow leaves, that fluttered constantly, making me think of minnows.

"Do you feel restricted, working for such a small company?" I said.

"No. I love what I do. I'm more interested in the work.

And there aren't as many political games with fewer people, right?"

"Maybe."

"That's not your experience?"

"Not always."

"Well I think we're all pretty focused on what we're doing, on helping our clients, so maybe that has something to do with it. Plus, Trystan is easy, so he sets a laid-back tone. He treats us well, pays us well."

"What's with Stephanie and that cross?"

"What do you mean?"

"It's kind of in your face."

"Is it?" She bit her cone and chewed slowly.

"It's so big. Does she try to convert everyone?"

"No. She talks about God a lot, but it's not a problem."

For all her lack of drama, Diana could have been talking about whether Stephanie talked too much about shoe shopping or baseball. Maybe I *was* bigoted. Maybe I had a chip on my shoulder. Maybe other people didn't look at that oversized, extremely bright gold cross and assume it was coming for them.

Was it possible to see an object like that and not feel the owner had her sights on you, that she wanted to make you think like her? That she was unable to live in the world without assuring that everyone had the same view of good and evil and the afterlife?

It's not a topic most people like to discuss. And the ones that do, can't seem to talk about anything else. But maybe it was all those years of being forced to sit through mid-week classes and youth group lectures and evangelism training and prayer meetings. That doesn't even include

Sunday morning services and nighttime family Bible readings at home, the silent Bible readings, the family prayer sessions, and the prayers at dinner and before bed.

My life was dripping with religious coercion. I thought I'd escaped.

13

Victoria knocked on my door at six-forty-four in the evening. Since she'd adjusted the time to seven o'clock after I'd suggested six-thirty, it was an odd time to show up. It seemed as if she'd deliberately chosen a time a fraction closer to my suggestion than her own. It was strange to request a later time and show up closer to the earlier time. It felt like some sort of game or a grab for control. Maybe I was over-thinking, but I began to wonder if everything about her was deliberate — brushing me off as if I was somewhat unstable, and the next time we met, trying to suck me into her vortex.

A bottle of vodka and a bottle of vermouth stood on my kitchen counter beside my new martini glasses. The glasses were one of the few things I'd splurged on. I'd gone for expensive glassware over something functional, craving sleek elegance rather than thick glass with bulky stems. The jar of extra-large olives stood slightly behind the vermouth, and four delicate glass swizzle sticks with tiny glass olives on the ends lay in their box.

While Victoria stood in my living room, comparing my view of the street to her view of an alley, I mixed the drinks. She settled on the navy blue love seat, and I sat in a pale gray leather chair across from her. It was strange, observing my furniture from a guest's perspective. This was the first time I'd bought furniture in my life. If I allowed my mind to dwell on it, there was an oppressive feel to my new possessions. I want nice things, things of my own, but having those things in an apartment that was so *not* my permanent home, made me feel heavy. More objects were attaching themselves to me, adding complexity to my future changes in location.

We raised our glasses and Victoria proposed a toast to Wall Street. I took a long sip to clear my mind, drinking without echoing her words. I put down my glass. "That's the first time I've ever toasted Wall Street. Why are you such a fan?"

"I'm a day trader."

"Do you like it?"

"You don't seem shocked. Most people are."

I smiled. I tucked my newly short hair behind my left ear. It fell forward, covering my ear and brushing my cheek and jaw.

She gazed at me over her glass. "You're not shocked?"

"No."

"A lot of people consider it legalized gambling, skimming along the edge of legal."

"The whole stock market is a lot like gambling." I took another sip of my drink.

She moved the swizzle stick around her glass. "I agree, which is why I don't get the objection to day trading."

"People think it's cheating the system, I suppose. And most people *don't* think the stock market is like gambling."

"They think they're so sophisticated," Victoria said. "Day trading is just leveraging the homework others do. There's nothing unethical about that. It's also about riding the waves of human inconsistency that affect the market."

"You don't have to convince me that it's okay."

She talked for a while about their computer set-up —

two large screens for both of them. Computers that were the fastest you could buy, always the latest software, dedicated internet access. Still sounding as if she wanted to persuade me, she went on about how great it was to work with her boyfriend. It was good to have someone there to help keep the adrenaline under control, someone to bounce ideas off of, to make sure you didn't go too crazy, to validate your instincts.

She didn't define *too crazy*.

She turned sideways on the love seat. She kicked off her sandals and stretched her legs out, propping her heels on the arm and pointing her toes.

I wasn't thrilled about her bare feet on my new couch. She looked like she felt awfully at home in my place. It wasn't just the couch, it was the way she'd looked out the window when she first arrived, commenting on the street view as if she'd studied it, and envied it, in the past. "Please take your feet off my couch."

She elbowed herself up and turned, swinging her legs back to a normal sitting position.

"Did you know the person who lived here before me?"

"Oh, yes."

"Why do you say it like that?"

"Because I knew him well. Quite well." She smiled.

"Was he the predecessor to your current boyfriend?"

She laughed. "Not really. No…it's complicated." She sipped her drink.

I waited. I ate an olive. I gave her a gentle smile, meant to encourage more sharing.

She laughed. "Do you have a boyfriend? All four of us could hang out."

"I thought you liked girl time?"

She giggled. It was a disconcerting sound — nervous, as if she'd been caught at something. "Of course. But guys are fun."

"They are."

"I can't believe you don't have a boyfriend. You're...I'm not hitting on you...just commenting...you're pretty hot. I think most men would agree."

I took another sip of my drink. "Do you want anything to eat?" I stood and went to the kitchen area.

"No thanks. I should head out in a minute. One drink is enough. Especially a martini."

"Just some cheese and crackers. I'm starving." I put a wedge of soft cheese and a spreader on a plate. I arranged a layered semi-circle of wheat crackers around it.

I carried the plate to the living area and put it on the pine table between the love seat and leather chair. Victoria reached for it, picking up several crackers. She began eating them. A fine mist of crumbs fell from her fingers. She didn't seem to notice. She ate the crackers one after the other, crunching and chewing her way through, crumbs now flecked across her lips and in the corners of her mouth.

I spread cheese onto one of the crackers and ate it. I ate an olive, and as the silence took on a heavy quality, I wished I'd thought about music. I needed to buy a speaker to connect to my phone.

Victoria ate a few more crackers, her desire to talk seeming to deflate now that I didn't have a guy to add to the mix. "Really? No boyfriend?"

"Really."

"How come?"

"I don't know anyone here. I've only been in New York for a little over a week."

"Where were you before?"

"I lived in Australia for three months."

"Oh, that's cool."

She asked me what the Australians were like, whether I'd seen the Great Barrier Reef, and why I was so lucky to get to live there. She would love to live in another country, especially Australia.

"Why don't you?"

She sipped her drink and grabbed a few more crackers with her left hand. "Too busy. I'm a working girl."

I ate another smear of cheese on a cracker. I finished my drink and ate the last olive. I scooted forward on my chair. She'd been there nearly an hour. She'd said it was time for her to leave, and now, I agreed. I wanted something more than cheese. I wanted a cigarette, and I needed to get started on my homework. I only had the weekend to read two psychology books. The requirement was Trystan's, but the book recommendations had come from Diana. She said the books would give me insight into peak performance and how people achieve it, and what mindsets and habits block it.

For all the sipping Victoria had been doing, her glass was only half empty. The olives were gone, and there were two crackers left on the plate, but plenty of cheese. Her head was tipped back. She gazed at the ceiling, appearing to study every nuance in the plaster. "What are you doing for the rest of the weekend?"

"Work. A class."

She lifted her head and leaned forward slightly. "What class?"

"Photography."

"Sounds interesting."

"I haven't told you anything about it."

"Photography is interesting all by itself."

"True."

"What sort of class?"

"Instructions for my new camera, mostly."

"Where is this class?"

"At the store where I bought the camera."

She nodded. She took a few more sips of her drink. "Do you want to be a photographer?"

"It's part of my new job. Photographing our clients."

"That's weird."

I shrugged. I stood and picked up the plate of cheese. "Mind if I have those last two crackers?"

I moved the plate within her reach. "Help yourself."

She grabbed the crackers as if she expected me to yank the plate away. She put both crackers in her mouth and spoke as she chewed. "I'm starving. I should get home and see what we're doing for dinner. Want to go out with us?"

"Maybe another time. I have a lot to do."

"Where did you buy the camera?"

"Vision Photography. Why? Are you looking for a camera?"

"Do they sell surveillance cameras?"

I laughed. "Not that I noticed. But you could call and ask. Are you worried about break-ins?"

"Nope." She stood. "Thanks for the drink."

"Spying on your boyfriend?"

She laughed. "Of course not."

When she was gone, I used the hand vac to clean up the

couch, hoping to sweep up her sloughed-off skin along with the crumbs. I hoped her sweat hadn't penetrated the fabric. Still, although the couch was nice, it was an inexpensive love seat from Ikea. Temporary furniture for a temporary phase in my life. It didn't need to last for decades.

14

The class for new owners of the Nikon D3200 was scheduled for Saturday afternoon. Recalling the well-functioning air conditioning at Vision Photography, I appreciated the timing. I also appreciated that I could spend Saturday morning going for an extremely long, brisk walk that took me to the Brooklyn Bridge, through Little Italy, and back to my apartment. There was plenty of time left for a relaxing breakfast of scones and bacon, with a well-made cappuccino, at a cafe a few blocks from my apartment.

I wore a sleeveless dark blue dress and sandals, comfortable for the subway and walking to class. There was nothing to be done that would keep my shorter hair off the back of my neck. For the first time, I sort of regretted my drastic haircut. As a compromise, I let it dry naturally which gave it a tangled appearance, and figured if I got sweaty while I was walking, it would blend in with the messy style.

After a subway ride and a leisurely walk, feeling like a New Yorker, at least in my mind, I opened the door to the camera shop. Cool air and silence greeted me. I stepped inside and let the door fall closed. I breathed in the air which smelled oddly fresh for air that was running through a machine. I called out for Leon, but there was no answer.

When I bought the camera, Leon had pointed out the room where classes were held. I assumed he was in there now, with any other new camera owners, but it was surprising that he'd leave all that expensive equipment unattended. Maybe the display models had RFID tags, or the place was under the watchful eye of hidden cameras. I looked up, moving my gaze around the room, checking at each corner and paying special attention to the hanging plants. There was no sign of any small electronic eyes. Either he was extremely clever, or thieves were safe from detection.

The silence was intense. Leon hadn't mentioned how many others were in the class. Maybe it was just me, which I supposed would be fine. I could push him to cover topics faster. All of his attention would be on my questions, and I wouldn't have to listen to simplistic questions and answers that could be had through common sense.

I moved through the display area, amazed at the variety of brands and models. At the end of the day, they all performed the same function. Was there really that much difference between the shutter on a Nikon or a Minolta? Did the lens quality vary significantly from Canon to Ricoh? It was doubtful.

In the back of the display area was a short hallway. A hand-written sign on the first door to my right announced in turquoise ink that it was the classroom. I opened the door and went in.

Leon wore cargo shorts and a black T-shirt and canvas loafers without socks. He sat with one hip on the table, talking to a woman whose back was to the door.

I knew that short dark hair, ironed straight and standing at attention.

Victoria.

I'd thought her tone was overly curious when she asked about the class. I'd wondered at her interest in the name of the shop, but her question about surveillance had done a clever job of diverting my thoughts to a possible drama inside the apartment next door. I'd been so caught up in the thought of someone recording the activities of their partner, I'd let the other question fade to insignificance.

She turned and smiled. "Hi, Alexandra."

"You two know each other?" Leon said.

She turned back. "I told you a friend recommended you." She put her hand on a brand-new Nikon D3200 that sat on the table in front of her. Beside it were two additional lenses. She was far past me in the equipment arena.

I moved around the table and took a seat across from her. "You bought a camera just to take the class?"

"Of course not."

"Then why?"

Leon stood and stepped back, picking up his own version of the camera. "Let's get started." He removed the lens cap. "You know that the lens cap should always be in place when the camera is not in use. Without exception." He said this as a statement of fact as if this was information that any adult should already be aware of.

I unzipped my bag and removed my camera, keeping my eyes focused on the task at hand. I felt Victoria's gaze on me, a burning sense of triumph that was palpable.

Did she think I cared whether she spent nearly a thousand dollars on camera equipment she hadn't needed two days ago and surely didn't need today? Did she think it mattered that she'd crashed my class, that I didn't have Leon to myself, that she was stalking me? *Was* she stalking me?

It felt uncomfortable that she'd gone to so much trouble. It made me feel my anonymity had been compromised, that I was no longer alone in this amazing city, free to move about as I pleased. I didn't want her showing up at my office or at restaurants where I was eating, popping up outside the dressing room in a department store or in the chair beside me at the nail salon.

What did she want?

She removed her lens cap and turned her attention to Leon, smiling with smug confidence.

Leon put the lens cap back on his camera. "Actually, before I get started on the mechanics of the camera, let me talk about the art of photography for a few minutes. I hope you'll indulge me."

He strolled toward the far corner of the room and put his hand on the wall for a moment, pressing the palm against the cool plaster. "Photography is my first love. I fell for her when I took my first photograph at the age of four. The shot was taken with a Polaroid, a birthday gift from my aunt. Instantly, I loved the magic of pushing a button and capturing part of the world, a moment in time and preserving it the way I remembered. There was something god-like in that ability to take a piece of life and make it my own. From there, I began to learn how I could not only capture my world but shape it to my will. With lighting and angle, by waiting for the perfect moment, I could create my own reality."

My thoughts drifted around the poetry of what he was saying. Victoria slipped out of my mind, and I was only vaguely aware of her sitting across from me, her stare fixed on my face. When I did glance her way, I wanted to use that old cliché that's often spoken to someone who won't stop staring — *Why don't you take a picture?*

Leon clearly loved photography with all his heart and

hearing him talk, I wanted to see the images he'd captured throughout his life. I wanted to see those polaroid snapshots.

When he was finished, he went over the automatic settings for the camera and the details for working the flash attachment. He led us outside of the comfortable manufactured air to Broadway and asked us to take a photograph using each of the automatic settings.

As I sized up objects for my camera, Victoria followed me, her Doc Marten boots thudding on the pavement. She wore a short skirt and a loose, flowing top. Aside from the boots, she looked much cooler than I felt in the damp heat. The sun had moved to a position that cast shadows on the sidewalk in front of Vision Photography, but it was still hot and muggy.

She seemed to be looking to me to determine what she should photograph. When I snapped a shot of a cigarette butt in the gutter, she leaned in and did the same with her close-up setting. As I pointed the camera toward the roofline of the building across the street, she mirrored my movements. She didn't seem to have a single original idea. The expensive camera and lenses were wasted on her.

When the class was over, I packed up quickly and headed toward the door. She asked whether she could walk home with me. I told her I had an errand. When she followed with a suggestion she could keep me company, I said, *no thank you* and scooted out the door. I turned down the first subway entrance I came to and took the train six blocks before getting out.

I had no idea what she wanted from me, and I spent the rest of my circuitous route home wondering whether I should ask her what she was after, or wait to see how the situation unfolded. Or unraveled, which might be a more realistic expectation.

15

The smartphone Trystan provided for me had been programmed with contact information for my new co-workers, so when a message arrived on Sunday afternoon, the sender was identified as Stephanie Cook. She asked whether I'd like to meet for breakfast the following morning. *Seven-thirty, at the latest!* She suggested a coffee shop three blocks from our office, unless I had food restrictions.

I stared at the screen until it grew dim, then went dark, like it was closing its eyes for a nap. There was only one possible response to the invite. This was my new team, these were the people I was working with, people I would be somewhat dependent upon for my success or failure, and the people who would impact my fate for the foreseeable future. I couldn't refuse her invitation without proposing an alternate date. So there was no reason to say no.

It occurred to me that Trystan might have told Diana and Stephanie to tag-team me with invites in an effort to make me feel part of the team. Instead, I felt manipulated. With all of this psychological theory floating through our compact offices, my co-workers trying to see into the heads and interpret the behavior of others, I felt my own brain was at risk of too many inquiries. I placed my hands on top of my head, pressing down gently. It was apparent I would have to more carefully consider the things I said.

I arrived at the designated coffee shop at seven-twenty-nine. Stephanie was already seated at a table near the windows. She peered out, watching the street. She glanced at her phone when she caught sight of me.

I sat across from her. The server was beside me before I put my bag on the bench. The coffee shop knew their crowd was on its way to work and not patient with delays or wasted time. The server filled my coffee cup and asked whether we knew what we wanted. Stephanie ordered for us — two breakfast specials with eggs cooked to our liking, hash brown potatoes, two bacon strips, and toast of our choice.

When our eggs and toast were specified, and the server was gone, Stephanie said, "I'm happy you could make it."

I smiled and thanked her for the invitation. The gold cross was there, as it had been every day. She wore a white shirt, the collar turned up a bit for flare, and the top two buttons undone to vividly display the gold icon against the V of pale skin.

I picked up my coffee and took an exploratory sip. "Do you eat breakfast out a lot?"

"Once a week. It's my Monday treat."

"That's unique. Most people indulge themselves on Fridays. Or on the weekend."

She smiled. "I'm not an indulgent person. It's a treat to make Mondays exciting instead of something to dread."

I wasn't going to debate a *treat* versus an *indulgence*. I took another sip of coffee. "Like I said, it's a unique approach. Why do you dread Mondays?"

"Oh, it has nothing to do with my job, with working for Trystan. I love working for him. This is the best job I've ever had. But Mondays are a shift from owning your time, from doing whatever you please. It begins a period of waking with an alarm clock, less freedom, the tension of too many human beings and too much traffic. So, of course, no one gets excited about the day. That's all."

"Makes sense," I said.

Our food came, and when the server left, Stephanie folded her hands, resting them against the edge of the table. "Let's thank God for our food."

"I don't pray."

"You're not grateful for your food?"

"I'm glad I have it."

"If you'd rather not thank God for the gift of food, will you be silent for a moment while I give thanks. Is that okay?"

"Sure." Her reaction was more low-key than I'd expected. Maybe I'd judged her too harshly, and possibly unfairly. I broke off a piece of bacon and popped it into my mouth.

She eyed me but said nothing. She adjusted the position of her hands on the table, closed her eyes, and bent her head forward. She began speaking — "Dear Lord, Thank you so much for this delicious food, that it's healthy and will nourish our bodies. Thank you for the pleasant aroma and the wonderful tastes I'm about to experience. May it strengthen my blood and bones and body. May it do the same for Alexandra. Please allow her to find gratitude for all the blessings in her life. And thank you…"

I touched my fingertip to my eggs to test whether they were cooling. My fork clattered against the edge of the plate.

Stephanie wrapped up her prayer with a bit of praise and an *Amen*. She unclasped her hands and picked up the cutlery. She drew her knife through the center of the eggs. Yolk and runny white from her sunny-side-up eggs ran across the white plate, moving at a speed similar to the slow spread of blood toward the slices of bacon and the edges of the toast. "This is the best breakfast in New York."

I took a bite of scrambled eggs. I sipped coffee and buttered my toast. I had no doubt she loved the food. It was good, better than average, much better, which is hard to define with basics like eggs and bacon, but I had no point of comparison in New York.

"Don't you agree?"

"It's very good," I said.

"You like to keep to yourself, don't you." She bit a strip of bacon, holding it between her teeth while she gazed at me.

"Yes."

"That can close you off to the world."

"How I am works for me, but thanks."

"Don't be offended. I didn't mean to hurt your feelings."

"You didn't."

She chewed her bacon and gave me a smile that tried to be sympathetic. She took another bite of bacon. "It's safe here, working with Trystan. We're all pretty close. So if you've been hurt in the past, you can let go of that. You can trust me. And not just me…Trystan and Diana, too."

"Good to know." My skin crawled with her effort to insert herself into my life, to make me into a project, to assume things that obviously came from either her psychology reading or her own past, rather than having anything to do with me.

"How are you liking working for Trystan?"

"It's interesting."

"That's all?"

"That's all I need. I'm looking forward to meeting clients, to taking photographs."

"You're lucky that role was given to you. It's important. And it has to be done right."

"I think I'm up for it."

"Just don't get too big for your britches."

I laughed.

"It's not a joke."

Dishes clattered around us. Voices buzzed and hummed, with an occasional raised exclamation, often a curse word. Curse words seemed to be more prevalent here. Or maybe I'd become used to the melodic sounds of Australian voices, where even the word *fuck* sounds upper class and easy-going and elegant.

"Do you have any questions about what I do? Or about your role?"

"I have a good idea of what's expected. Trystan was very thorough."

"What about my role? Any questions about what I do?"

"Is there something important I need to know about?"

"Not right now, but insight into all areas will help you do your job more effectively."

"Good to know."

"You're not being very friendly. The point here is to get to know each other."

"Why don't you tell me everything you think I should know. That would be helpful. All the things I need to know to get along with you and Diana. And Trystan, of course."

"That's a strange request."

"I don't think it is, if the point is to get to know each other. You first."

"My pleasure. I've worked here for five months. My job is to support Trystan and Diana, mostly with data input and scheduling. Diana's very easy to work with, and I like her a lot." She laughed. Her cheeks filled with color. "It's a little uncomfortable, having someone younger be in charge of you. She's not my boss or anything like that, not even close, but at the same time…"

I finished for her. "She has more authority."

"You get it."

"I do."

"Any*hoo*, I make client appointments. I input data from the questionnaires. I make sure Trystan's schedule is manageable, which is more complicated than it sounds. Our clients are very busy people. Extremely busy. They're on the go sixteen to eighteen hours a day. Their schedules fluctuate a lot, and Trystan has to accommodate that. It's a constant juggle." She explained more — the research she did to help Diana, the preparations of PowerPoint slides for customer feedback presentations. "I suppose I'll be taking direction from you, sometimes. I don't know. So two women younger than I am. It makes me feel I missed the boat."

I placed my fork on the side of my plate. "I doubt it's that serious."

She didn't smile. She returned to telling me everything she thought I should know, all of which was rather superficial. *Trystan was nice, a great boss. Diana was sweet, easy to get along with. The job was interesting, making the days fly by. The clients could be very direct and somewhat impatient but were respectful overall, probably because Trystan set that tone. All three of them got along. She liked the atmosphere. Sometimes Trystan took them to lunch or dinner, which made everything more friendly.*

None of those clichés told me where to watch for landmines. I think the problem was that Stephanie saw the world, or at least her sliver of the world, as open and kind and trustworthy. There weren't any landmines in her view. In fact, I think she would have been shocked to hear me suggest the possibility.

In my experience, there are always landmines. You don't know what you don't know.

16

An entire week passed before I had a chance to scope out a place to go running. In the meantime, I'd smoked plenty of cigarettes and polished off half a bottle of vodka, drinking a martini every evening. For all the allure of New York nightlife, my nightlife consisted of coming home from work tired, walking to get something to eat, walking home, occasionally walking to Dwayne Reed or the market, cleaning up my dishes, relaxing with a martini, climbing the stairs to the roof garden for a cigarette or three, and collapsing into bed.

It occurred to me this was the first time in several years that I'd had a job where I actually had to work a full day. I wasn't acclimated. At Sean's, I'd hardly worked at all. At CoastalCreative, the work involved a lot of dialing into conference calls during which I sat with my phone on mute and surfed the web and listened to co-workers discuss projects. Most of the calls involved endless repetition — an echo chamber. Those hour-long calls could have been completed in fifteen or twenty minutes.

I was tired. I was studying and reading and getting prepared for my first client meeting. I'd taken some photographs and video of strangers around our office building, hoping not to be caught after that incident in the courtyard near my apartment. Trystan had been pleased, and a little surprised at how evocative they were.

Of course he was surprised. He didn't realize that I've spent my whole life on the outside, watching through a virtual lens. Watching how people behave, finding my own form of entertainment in observing their emotional dramas, and when I can, stimulating dramas of my own just to see what might happen. He'd been right to suggest I was a provocateur myself.

I couldn't wait for my next photography class when I'd start learning how to manually adjust the camera for more interesting shots. Although I wanted to learn, wanted to feel in command of my camera, I wasn't sure it would make all that much difference. My directive was to capture posture and mood and demeanor. The lighting and other artistic factors were secondary.

On Saturday morning I woke at five. I'd decided the best place for a peaceful run was Bryant Park, a beautiful nine-acre oasis in Midtown. During the day, Bryant Park hummed with tourists picnicking, New Yorkers taking lunch breaks, couples hanging out, and retired men playing checkers and chess. I thought I'd fallen into the setting for a film, watching these guys play boardgames in public. Was there any other city in the country where that kind of thing happened? I didn't recall seeing it in San Francisco or LA.

There were a fair number of mid-day runners as well, but it looked like too much of an obstacle course, dodging children and the elderly, dogs on leashes and distracted people meandering in no direction, unaware because their minds were inside their smartphones. Besides, early morning has always been my preferred time.

Eventually, I wanted to run in Central Park, but it was more overwhelming to navigate, so I'd start with Bryant. I dressed in workout clothes, grabbed my earbuds and phone and headed out.

The sun was just coming up when I reached the park. I stretched my legs, plugged in my earbuds, and started a playlist of a pianist who was new to me — Scriabin. The music wasn't quite as easy to listen to as Chopin, but it was growing on me.

I began running, feeling the burn in my lungs from all those cigarettes and nearly three weeks without even a short jog.

It amazes me how fast the body slides into decay. You have to keep on top of it constantly. I don't see that as a burden, I love running and lifting weights, and I was loving all the walking, but you can't ever sit back in your house for a month, or in a tropical garden somewhere, and think you aren't going to pay the price when you get moving again.

After two miles, my muscles were wobbly, and I was breathing harder than I liked. I spent extra time doing cooling stretches and then walked back to my apartment.

I climbed the stairs slowly, dragging my limp muscles, still breathing with more effort than normal. All I could think about was breakfast. I had planned on something large and brunch-like before heading to photography class, but now I couldn't be bothered to cook much. I wanted food right that minute.

A few steps before I reached the landing, a door opened. A guy emerged from Victoria's apartment. He closed the door, stabbed his key in the lock, and turned it. He looked up and gave me a single nod.

He was average height, even though he loomed over me a few steps above. He had short, light brown hair and dark stubble that looked like he'd been working on it for a good five days. He wore a white dress shirt hanging open over a white T-shirt, blue jeans, and Vans.

He moved toward me, and I edged myself closer to the center of the step. "Are you Victoria's boyfriend?"

"Who wants to know?"

"I live right there." I nodded toward my door and stepped up onto the landing. I leaned against the rail. "I met Victoria a few days ago. She came over for a drink."

"Yeah, okay. She mentioned you." He laughed, an abrupt sound, like a cough. "She didn't…" He gave me the once-over, his gaze lingering for a long time just below my face. He laughed again.

"I'm Alexandra."

He moved closer. "Hi-ya. I'm Rafe."

"That's an unusual name."

"So is Alexandra." He smirked

"Maybe."

"It's Scottish," he said.

"Okay."

"You and Vic are taking that camera class together?"

"We're in the same class, yes."

He winked, suggesting he knew she was behaving oddly, signing up for my class, buying a camera she didn't seem to need. "Vic said you might want to hang out sometime."

I wasn't sure I'd said that at all. I wondered if he knew his girlfriend was interested in surveillance cameras.

He took a few more steps closer. "I'd definitely be up for hanging out with you."

Was he hitting on me?

As if to prove I was being unduly naïve, he took the

final steps until he was right beside me. He stroked my arm with the knuckle of his right index finger.

"What are you doing?"

He shrugged and moved his hand away. "What about tonight?"

I walked around him to my door. "Hanging out?"

"Sure."

"Don't you need to check with her?"

"She usually does whatever I say. I mean…" He had the good grace to blush slightly. "She likes to do what I want to do, so it's not a big deal. She goes with the flow."

That hadn't been my impression, but what can you tell after one drink and a handful of crackers?

I reached into my pocket and removed the key to my front door. It was warm and sharp in my hand, sliding easily into the keyhole. I turned it to unlock the deadbolt and used my other hand to turn the old-fashioned doorknob at the same time.

"So what about it?" he said. "Want to hang out?"

"Sure. Sometime."

I didn't turn to look at him, but heard the movement of his feet and then felt the warmth of his body, standing directly behind me. "When?"

I shrugged. "Any time."

"Tonight?"

"That doesn't work."

"Tomorrow?"

I shook my head, still not turning.

"When can you?"

I looked over my shoulder. "We'll figure out something."

"When you see Vic in your class, you two can set it up. It'll be good. We can tell you all the ins and outs of Manhattan."

"Can you?"

"I've been here all my life."

"Is that right?"

"Well, in Jersey. And then the Bronx. But in Manhattan for three years now. So close enough. Even when I wasn't *technically* in Manhattan, I came into the city all the time."

"Then you must know it inside and out."

He grinned. "That's right." He moved closer again, putting his hands in his pockets and hunching his shoulders slightly, trying to look self-effacing, I think. "I love this place, and I'd love to show you around."

"I'll look forward to the education."

He laughed, and I slipped inside my apartment, closing the door quickly. There was something slippery about this guy. He was too friendly. Too eager. And giving me the once-over like that, when I knew he had a girlfriend, and he was fully aware that I knew. It's not unheard of, in fact, it happens often, but it's always unsettling.

I couldn't figure them out, and I wouldn't unless I hung out with them. Suddenly, I was interested in seeing Victoria at the photography class after all. Together, they'd become a point of curiosity, and a bit of entertainment.

17

At our second class, Leon spent the entire hour talking about lighting. I'd expected instructions on how to manually adjust the camera for different types of shots, but he wanted us to understand the importance of lighting first. He talked about how light and dark affected the mood of a photograph, how light created the artistry in photography, and how it could be manipulated and captured for dramatic effect.

It was all very interesting to think about composing an image in which sunlight struck the side of a building and fell across a pot of tulips sitting on the bottom step of a brownstone. It was intriguing to consider how the light could be used to feature the ironwork of the stair railing rather than the blossoms in the pot, and how the shadow could transform the colors of the flowers into something moody.

None of that was going to apply to anything I'd be doing for Trystan. The photographs I would be taking required the best light possible. I needed to be able to expose micro expressions, capture the look in a person's eyes, and choose the right angle to illustrate their posture.

Since Leon's thoughts were all about art and nothing about my work, I didn't ask any questions. Victoria also remained silent. Leon's voice took on a droning quality that risked putting us to sleep if it hadn't been for that lovely air conditioning. Still, I wished I'd stopped for a latte before I showed up for the class.

Glancing across the table told me that Victoria felt the same. The first time I looked, her eyes had a glassy quality. The next time, her lids were lower, obscuring most of her eyeball. After that, she began shifting her position every few minutes. She crossed her legs one way and then the other. She propped her chin on her palm, her elbow on the table. Then she leaned back and stretched out her legs.

None of this movement interrupted Leon's flow of words. He was lost in his own world. He might as well have been inside a studio, speaking into a microphone to record a podcast. He didn't seem to care whether or not we were interested or whether we were learning anything useful. He was so in love with what a person could do with a camera, it consumed him.

At five minutes past two, he summarized the things he'd said during the previous hour and assured us that next week we would learn about f-stops and shutter speed. It was almost too late for me. I would be taking my first set of photographs during the coming week. Still, I planned to keep attending his classes. You never know what you're going to learn. Even if the entire hour seems useless, there might be one important comment, made in passing as you're putting your camera into the bag.

I zipped mine closed and pushed my chair away from the table. I stood. "Thanks for the class."

"You're excellent students," he said. "Good listeners."

"You're an amazing teacher," Victoria said. "I could listen to you all afternoon."

He smiled.

Victoria and I walked out of the classroom together. We made our way through the shop and out to the street.

I slung my bag over my shoulder. "Do you want to grab coffee?"

"You're not in such a rush to run away this time?"

"Nope."

"So you *were* ditching me last time. I didn't imagine it."

"I didn't say that."

"You implied it."

"Did I?"

"I asked if…" She stopped and looked at me, trying to peer through my sunglasses. "Never mind."

"Do you want coffee or not? My treat."

"Sure."

We walked for several blocks and stopped at a shop that was packed with people but still managed to serve our iced lattes in less than ten minutes. We carried them to Bryant Park and leaned against an iron fence since all the benches and chairs were occupied on a warm Saturday afternoon. The trees offered plenty of thick shade that fell across the path and onto the grass. The center of the vast lawn was in full sun, but the heat didn't do anything to stop children from chasing balls and each other. One girl turned cartwheels, a little machine rolling across the grass, turning over and over until she looked like a human wheel come loose from a truck.

Victoria pried the lid off her cup and peered inside. "Rafe said he met you." She replaced the lid and adjusted the straw.

"Yes."

"He said you want to hang out."

"Any time," I said.

She laughed. "But not tonight. Or tomorrow, so not any time."

I watched the girl continue the cartwheels, her younger sister trying to imitate her now, falling before she got a single leg up into the air.

"You pick the time," Victoria said. "We could go out for pizza. Or Thai."

"Thai sounds good."

She nodded. "There are lots to choose from."

I sipped my coffee and watched the parents of the two girls. The man leaned into the woman, letting his head loll against her shoulder. "How long have you and Rafe been together?"

"A few years."

"Two? Three?"

"Something like that." She took a few sips of her drink. She turned her face toward the sky and closed her eyes for a moment. "The weeks fly. Trading is addictive." She laughed. "We have so much fun, we lose track of time."

I nodded.

"It's amazing how much money you can make just by watching what other people do. It's almost ridiculous how easy it is."

"How long have you been doing it?"

"I've been doing it about two years. Rafe for six years, I think."

"And that's all you do?"

"Yep."

"You make enough to live on?"

"We're very comfortable. *Very.*"

"I've heard people don't last long at day trading."

"Maybe if they're not very smart."

"And the two of you are very smart?"

"I'm not full of myself. I'm just speaking truth. We know what we're doing. Especially Rafe."

"How did you get into it?"

"I think I already told you. He was doing it, so I joined in. I'm not sure how he started, to be perfectly honest. I think just fooling around, trying to figure out what the catch was. Maybe a friend who was doing it…" She lifted the cup to her lips and rested it there for a moment before taking a sip. "Are you interested in learning how to do it?"

"No."

"You seem smart. You'd probably be good at it."

"Too risky."

"No guts, no glory." She sucked hard on her straw and rolled her eyes to look sideways at me.

"I agree, but not when it comes to money."

"It's just paper. Bits and bytes, really, not even paper."

I laughed. "I need those bits and bytes to live. I'm not going to gamble them away."

"You'd rather get up every morning and go to an office where someone tells you what to do all day? You want to do that until you're an old woman?"

She had a point, but I wouldn't want to sit in front of a screen all day either. I didn't want to buy and sell things that I had only superficial information about, making a few pennies here and there, unable to move my gaze off the screen for hours at a time. From what I knew of it, which wasn't much, you were chained to that computer during trading hours. And you could hardly breathe for the pressure of it, for knowing you had to make split-second decisions and rapid keyboard and mouse clicks all day long. I don't mind instant decisions, but I imagined it could become too much.

Victoria was very impressed with their skills, but I couldn't help wonder how well it really worked. No matter what she said, it sounded like gambling. You were betting that something you'd purchased would go up in price. At the same time, the slightest shift from something you couldn't control or even begin to predict could make it do the opposite. A politician could make a rash decision, a country on the other side of the world might pass new laws or a fanatic could blow up a public building or terrorize a festival. And I doubted her brag-worthy income. If it was that great, why were they in this apartment? Could you really make it pay day in and day out for years? For decades? Were there windfalls that made that unnecessary? It wasn't my impression.

"You're thinking about it, aren't you?" She laughed. "If you're interested, I'd be happy to show you. Any time. And when I say *any time*, I *mean any* time." She took another long, noisy sip of coffee, moved the straw away from her lips, and smiled at me as if she knew something about me that I hadn't intended to reveal.

18

Stephanie wasn't thrilled with this new person on their previously cozy team. It had been going so well with Diana and Trystan and her. Now, something had changed, suddenly and dramatically. She couldn't describe exactly what it was, but there was a different kind of energy. The air seemed to be sparking around her. She no longer felt at home. She felt downright excluded. Trystan was more interested in mentoring Alexandra than he was in helping Stephanie expand her role and grow into a more interesting and profitable position, as he'd promised. He seemed to have forgotten all about her.

She'd felt they were a family, and now there was an interloper.

Eating breakfast with Alexandra had confirmed her feelings. Alexandra was full of herself. And she had no clue what she'd stolen from Stephanie.

That photography job should have been hers. It was *meant* to be hers, and she'd worked hard to position herself for it. But no, Trystan apparently wanted someone young. Someone good-looking to flash in front of his male clients. Even the women would like Alexandra, admiring her style and her cool confidence. It was horribly unfair. It was all Stephanie could do to keep from crying when she walked past that woman's office every morning.

The idea for bringing the photography work in-house

had been Stephanie's. How dare he jet off to Australia and pick up this woman and offer her the position? He seemed blind to Stephanie's talent. He ignored half her suggestions or stole them, and now he treated her like wall decoration.

Not always. That wasn't entirely fair. He appreciated the work she did. But he was blind to her other abilities and refused to give her a chance. Just because she didn't have the charisma and hungry desire that Diana had. The same charged energy that spilled out of Alexandra, so that you felt you had to mop up the room after she left.

At first, Stephanie had considered asking Trystan if she could assist Alexandra. She would make herself humble, offering to learn from Alexandra. But she'd decided that wasn't humbling, it was humiliating. The woman knew nothing! She didn't even have a college degree. And she had no experience in photography whatsoever. What was he thinking? How did Alexandra get to sweep in here, get handed hundreds of dollars in camera equipment and set loose to do as she pleased?

Stephanie had posed the question to her Facebook group. In a Godly way, of course. She hadn't allowed the bitterness to seep to the surface. She'd been careful to be complimentary of Alexandra. But even with her care, the lashing out had been immediate and severe.

She'd posted a simple question:

Why do some people get handed opportunities without trying and people who work hard get shoved aside?

Immediately they trounced on her for her lack of gratitude. For her envy. So many sins she was accused of. They suggested she lacked humility and that she wasn't trusting God's timing in her life or His plans for her. She was accused of *choosing* to ignore the fact that Alexandra Mallory had been brought into her life for a purpose. Of course, they didn't use Alexandra's name because Stephanie hadn't posted it.

She sat in her office now, once again letting her gaze move slowly from one corner to the other, trying to map out whether Alexandra's office was larger. The general impression was that all the offices were the same size, but the suite was oddly shaped, and it wasn't possible that they were exactly the same square footage. She was convinced the other office had more space, even if only a few inches. The desk didn't seem as close to the walls, and the window appeared to be a few inches wider. That made no sense, of course. From the outside, it was clear that all the windows in the building were uniform, but every time she looked, the other office seemed to have more sunlight or something that made it seem... bigger.

She sighed and turned her attention to the screen in front of her. Four clients had asked to reschedule. One of them was supposed to meet with Trystan and Alexandra at her office in Park Slope. An entire morning was dedicated to that meet-up because the travel time to Brooklyn would prevent Trystan and Alexandra from getting back in time to see any other clients before lunch.

It was impossible to concentrate on fitting the clients' schedules into something workable. Every time she began to move a name into one of the time slots they'd requested, and every time she thought of the Park Slope appointment, which had to be the cornerstone of the rearranged schedule, she pictured Trystan and Alexandra in a cab or hired car, exchanging information about clients and whatever else, easily half an hour of private conversation and insight into their work that Stephanie would never be privy to.

The two of them would build an increasingly solid relationship. She would be further shut out every time they went to that woman in Park Slope. Or anywhere, really. Alexandra would know Trystan better than either Stephanie or Diana did. This would give her an inside track into his thoughts, his plans. It would allow Alexandra to find out more about their clients and increase her value in Trystan's eyes.

Anything could happen when two people had all that time alone.

She couldn't figure out where she'd gone wrong. Why had Trystan loved her suggestion, but it hadn't even entered his mind that she would be a good candidate for that role as his PA, or whatever he was calling it now? When he first said he was looking for someone, he called it a PA position. But he'd renamed it and redefined it while he was traveling overseas — Client Satisfaction Manager. A ridiculous title. A title that could mean anything at all. And now, it sounded like that person, the Client Satisfaction Manager — Alexandra — was the second in charge. As if she was in line to take over if he ever chose to move on to something new. As if Alexandra might be running things more and more every day, in subtle little ways.

Alexandra would know every detail about every client, and Stephanie would not.

19

The computer had gone to sleep. Stephanie had spent too much time staring over the top of it, looking out the window at the thin line of Central Park that was visible in the distance. To see more than that thin line, she had to lift herself off the chair into a partial standing position.

She pushed her chair away from the desk and went to the window. The view didn't satisfy her like it usually did, reminding her how lucky she was to live and work in this magnificent city, reminding her how lucky she was to have a job that allowed her to rent a good apartment, affordable in part because she shared the space with her sister.

She smiled.

Not really her sister. People used to say they looked like sisters, and so, out of habit, Stephanie had continued thinking of Eileen as her sister. It made her feel young, countering what she saw in the mirror each morning. Being mistaken for sisters hadn't happened in a while.

Until last year, she'd gotten along well with Eileen. They'd been close, best friends, almost. They viewed the world the same way, or they used to. They shared all their secrets. Then… She put her hands on either side of her head and slid her hair away from the sides of her face. Their intimacy had been destroyed, they were strangers now.

At least there was still another human being nearby when she woke in the morning, or in the middle of the night.

And she didn't have any of the roommate problems lots of women faced — living with a slob, or someone who did drugs, or drank, or brought home strange men, allowing them access to their beds, the single bathroom, the kitchen.

All of these things should make her fall to her knees with gratitude. Her *Living as a Godly Woman In A Large City* Facebook group reminded her of that all the time.

There was so much to be thankful for. And she'd been perfectly happy — thankful — for this job…until that woman with her streaked hair and heavily made-up face and eyes, constantly staring and calculating, flashing that secretive, haughty smile came along and spoiled everything.

Maybe it was a test…

She was supposed to practice what she knew was right and not allow herself to dwell on self-centered thoughts. Her life had been too perfect. Not perfect…too easy. Before this, she hadn't been challenged to find pockets of gratitude in every single day. Until now, it had been easy…easi*er*. She hadn't been forced to deal with someone who got under her skin and filled her head with bitter thoughts. Someone, she hated to admit it because it was such a stain on her heart, but someone she was very close to hating.

There hadn't been many people she'd hated in her life. She didn't like that out-of-control feeling that came with hatred. It consumed you. It woke you in the middle of the night, it created thick shadows at the edges of your life. It turned even the most wonderful experience into something tarnished with ugliness because that person you hated was constantly intruding into your thoughts. Now, in the space of two years, two people had stirred up violent feelings of hate.

Her colleagues were at their desks, working. They all

appeared busy. She was the only one distracted and unproductive, but she couldn't focus. She pulled her phone out of her pocket and opened Instagram. Keeping her back to the door, she scrolled through, liking photos and videos of puppies. She tapped tiny hearts on a stream of food pictures from a guy she followed who photographed restaurant experiences in New York, *sharing the flavor of the city*, his bio said.

She hadn't posted any photos of her own in a while. Every single thing had been derailed by Alexandra Mallory. She needed to get a grip, to get back to that. Soon. She slipped the phone into her pocket.

This wasn't the way a Godly woman should approach her work. Goofing off was stealing from your employer, taking time that you were paid for and squandering it. Her ungodly colleagues were diligent. The space around her was filled with the sound of tapping computer keys and the murmur of phone calls like the trickle of water in a stream.

The sound of a chair rolling away from a desk followed by the soft thud of footsteps in the hallway made her turn from the window. Alexandra was crossing the narrow space to Diana's office. She tapped on Diana's doorframe. She spoke in a low voice, more muted than the sounds of Trystan on the phone a moment earlier. "Do you have a minute?"

Stephanie couldn't hear Diana's response, but she watched as Alexandra stepped into Diana's office.

She heard the murmur of Diana's voice. Alexandra asked a question about one of the clients. They spoke softly for several minutes, and then Alexandra asked in a clear, easily overheard tone. "I need to join a gym. Do you have any recommendations?"

Again, Stephanie couldn't hear the response.

"Okay," Alexandra said. "I'll ask the girl who lives next door to me. When I find one, do you want to join with me?" There was a pause followed by Alexandra's laughter.

Stephanie turned back to the window. So. That's how it was going to be. She'd expected it, but that didn't weaken the sharp pain that shot through her chest. Not caring if you were excluded never seemed to matter, the rejection hurt, even though it shouldn't.

20

Diana hadn't invited me to sit, but I'd dragged the chair from the corner of her office so it was closer to her desk. I sat down and crossed my legs. She didn't look put out that my posture suggested I planned to sit there for several minutes.

Since our ice cream, I hadn't spoken with her alone. I wanted to hang out with her more outside of work. She was interesting and smart and gave the impression that what you see is what you get. Obviously we wouldn't be going out for martinis, although that didn't preclude trying some fabulous restaurants. But if she didn't drink, she must be into healthy things, so I asked her whether she could recommend a gym.

Two of her friends belonged to gyms, but she couldn't recall the names.

"Have you ever tried weight-lifting?"

She wrinkled her nose. "No. It looks like too much work."

"It's not hard work. Your muscles work, obviously, but it feels good."

She shrugged and moved the mouse around her desk, studying her computer screen. She clicked a few times.

"When I find one, do you want to join with me?"

She shook her head.

"I could show you what I do."

"No. I think it's one of those things that feels great when you're finished. I like doing things that feel good while

I'm doing them. And also when I'm done, which is why I don't drink." She gave me a smile that suggested she was smarter than I was, but it didn't seem offensive.

"You might be surprised."

"I like walking. I like cycling. I like hiking. I do not want to stand in a stinky gym and pick up iron bars." She shuddered. "I don't want muscles that make me look like a guy."

"It's not like that."

"I think it is like that."

"And the gyms I've belonged to don't stink."

"I have a very acute sense of smell. If people are in a room sweating, there's going to be an odor. And I would smell it."

"They have good ventilation."

"Nope. No. Don't ask me again."

I uncrossed my legs. I moved to stand up.

"Don't be offended."

"I'm not."

"Good. You looked like you were going to bolt, so I wasn't sure."

"I'm not offended." I stood.

"So you're leaving anyway."

"I have stuff to do. It looks like you do also."

"I had stuff to do before you sat down."

"Fair enough."

"So you are offended," she said.

I put my fingertips on her desk and leaned forward slightly. I smiled. "I'm not offended."

She studied me for a minute or so.

I turned and dragged the chair back to its original spot.

"We could go hiking sometime. Or cycling," she said.

"Where do you hike around here?"

She laughed. "Not in Manhattan. Upstate."

"Okay."

"When the weather cools down. We can see the fall colors."

I moved toward the door.

"I was wondering, have you ever taken the Myers Briggs or PAPI test?"

"No. I'm not fond of tests."

She laughed. "It's not that kind of test. There aren't any wrong answers."

"Still not my idea of a good time."

"I should give you one. To get a sense of what you're like. I'm surprised Trystan didn't suggest it."

"It's a good thing he didn't. I might not have taken the job."

"It's just a tool. Don't be nervous."

"I'm not. But I don't want a generic set of questions packaging up my life into something other people can analyze."

"It's kind of fun. We can all use a little more self-insight."

"Can we?" I moved to the doorway and glanced down the hall. The rest of the space was quiet. Even the tapping of keys that was constant background noise had stopped. Were Trystan and Stephanie listening to our conversation? Could they hear us? I doubted Trystan could. I wasn't sure about Stephanie.

I wasn't thrilled, thinking of Stephanie joining in, suggesting analysis was a good idea. We were here to apply psychology to clients, not to ourselves. Was this some sort of secret requirement that Trystan had waited to drop on me? Putting Diana up to it, like he'd put them up to inviting me out to get to know each other better on a personal level? Maybe they hadn't been trying to get to know me as a co-worker, maybe they'd been trying to analyze me.

I adjusted the collar of my shirt where it caught on my hair. It was a white, sleeveless business shirt, with a stiff collar and small buttons. Inside the office, it was cold, and as if my body had just remembered that fact, I shivered.

Diana laughed. "You act like I'm demanding you take a pee test."

In my mind, that would be less invasive. I hadn't smoked pot in weeks. I'm not into drugs, and even pot is occasional. Something I do to socialize, not because I love the high.

"It's a fun thing to do. Honestly. I'm not trying to analyze you or give you a hard time. It's really interesting. I think it makes you more effective at your job, and it can help all your relationships when you know yourself better."

"I know myself fairly well."

"We all have blind spots."

"Do we?"

"Yes."

"If you say so."

"Do you want me to set it up?"

"I don't think it's a good idea."

"Why not?"

"Because I don't think it is."

She nodded, her eyes unblinking as if she were waiting for a tell to spasm across my face. After a moment, she smiled and returned her attention to her computer.

I crossed the hall and settled at my desk, but I was distracted. It was my own fault for thinking of the gym when I was supposed to be working. By introducing a personal conversation, I'd flung the door wide open for her to suggest a psychological test or personality test or whatever you wanted to call it.

Unless Trystan had put her up to it.

Now I wanted to get back to lifting weights more than ever. My whole body twitched. My muscles felt both slack and wound too tightly. Doing a few rounds on the bench press would push all this stuff out of my head. That, or a martini. It was almost lunchtime, and I was sure Trystan would be up for a medium rare steak and a martini. I was equally sure he would know several good places to find those.

But after that, I needed to find a nice gym. One that didn't stink of sweat, where no one was trying to pick my brain.

21

Portland

Telling me to memorize the opening questions and answers of an evangelism assault program for a public performance was a huge mistake on Mr. B's part. If he'd run it past any of the youth group leaders who were used to interacting with me, he probably would have been advised against it. But he thought he knew what he was doing. He thought he had a divine directive that put him above everyone else.

And part of what he was doing was asserting his authority over me. There was nothing like someone asserting authority over me to make me burn with a desire to exercise my own. I didn't want anyone thinking they owned me or controlled me or had any say in what I did with my life.

That doesn't mean I don't obey most laws, that I don't see the need for laws. But when it comes to individual and insignificant choices, it's every man, or woman, for herself. I think most people feel that way. I don't like people telling me what to wear or when to smile or how to view a situation. I don't like being told smoking isn't healthy, as if I'd never received an education that included personal health.

Mr. B should not have given me a stage for expressing my views on this evangelism training program and its agenda for trying to coerce and manipulate people into believing they were destined for hell if they didn't repent.

The stage had been set, so to speak, with two armchairs angled toward each other. There was a low table between them. They'd even gone to the trouble of using a discarded door still in its frame, propped up with sawhorses so that our scene could include knocking on someone's front door and receiving an invitation to enter their home. This was part of the program. We were encouraged to learn these principles to talk to our friends, harassing our classmates and teammates. But we would also be required to make visits to people who had attended services or other events at Pure Truth Tabernacle and been careless enough to leave their name and contact information on a little card requesting prayers for particular problems in their lives.

During our role play, Mr. B would knock on the fake door, and I would invite him into my living room. We would take the chairs. I'd been told to take the one on the audience's right. After I pretended to pour coffee from the china teapot sitting on the table into the two cups beside it, he would begin by asking me the questions outlined in our study guide.

I sat in the chair. The lights were dimmed, so I saw the shadows and outlines of my classmates, but no faces were visible. There was a knock on the fake door. I stood and walked to the door and pulled it open. The frame wobbled against the sawhorses.

Mr. B greeted me, calling me Mrs. Mallory because he thought that made it seem more realistic. I thought it was creepy and weird, and I wanted to ask him why there was no boy to play Mr. Mallory, but I'd decided to let it go. I'd be giving him enough trouble soon.

We took our seats, and I mimed pouring coffee. I

handed him a cup and saucer. He took it and put it to his lips, making a disgusting sound that was supposed to mimic a sip, but I guess he wasn't expecting all that air and the echo inside of the empty china.

He chatted about the weather while I nodded and agreed it had been quite a storm last week. He placed the cup on his knee, holding the saucer with one hand, the cup with another, his fingers pinched around the lip as if he was afraid it would slide to the floor. Maybe his leg was trembling with nerves, considering all those teenagers watching and listening. Maybe he was suddenly unsure of his acting ability. Possibly, he doubted his rush to include an unknown component in his demonstration of the proper way to introduce a slow segue from outlining a person's inborn sin to their need to turn their life around.

"Tell me, Mrs. Mallory, if you were to die tonight and you arrived at the gates of heaven, and God said, *why should I let you into my heaven*, what would you say?"

It was a mouthful. They should have developed shorter questions because I'm sure he lost everyone at *if you were to die tonight*.

"It's highly unlikely I'll die tonight." I smiled directly at him, but he didn't see. He was watching the shadowy faces of the audience.

"If you *were* to die tonight..."

"Despite what you read in the news about shootings and drunk driving, less than one percent of people in America die between the ages of twelve and nineteen."

He coughed, but I talked over him. "Actually, it's point sixty-eight percent. And that's the average. Boys are two to three times more likely to die when they're teenagers. So I don't think I'm going anywhere tonight." I smiled.

He turned and glared at me. The cup rattled in the saucer. "*Mrs.* Mallory, what would you think if a woman of *your age*, a forty-two-year-old adult, were to die tonight…"

"I can't imagine that happening. I'm only sixteen."

The cup rattled again. He placed it on the table and straightened his back. He gave me a limp smile, working very hard to keep his anger inside. He released a short, anxious laugh. "I think you've forgotten how time has flown by, Mrs. Mallory."

"I haven't. And I don't expect to die."

"When you die, and God says *why should I let you into my heaven*…"

"Why would he call it *his* heaven? That sounds very possessive, rather like a despot. Does he think all of the universe belongs to him as if it's his personal property?"

Under his breath, his lips twisted to the side, Mr. B hissed at me. It was an actual hiss as if a snake were coiled in the armchair beside me. The sound was fierce and loaded with venom. But what could he really do to me? "Stop it," he said quietly. "Stick to the script."

"But…"

He turned and smiled at the audience. Sweat glittered on his forehead and above his lip, the stubble and moisture making his face appear unwashed. He spoke in a loud, strained voice. "If you were to die tonight…"

I kept my gaze on him. "I don't know what I'd say. I don't think I'd be stopped at the gate like that, angels or god looking for my wristband to make sure I'd actually bought a ticket."

"You *will* be stopped."

"I thought the Bible said…"

"I wasn't aware you read the Bible, *Mrs. Mallory*. Most people who don't attend church are woefully unfamiliar with what is revealed in the pages of that book." His voice was tight as if he thought he could change my behavior with the sheer force of his own tension flooding over me.

"I used to attend church." I smiled at him. "And I don't remember anything about having to show your credentials before they let you in the door."

Mr. B stood. He nodded his head, giving a tiny bow toward my classmates sitting in the dark. Still clinging to his role, but no longer wanting to address me at all, he spoke to the shadowy faces. "Thank you for your time. I'll be praying for your soul."

He turned and strode toward the fake door. He wrenched it open. It wobbled and tilted toward him. As if he'd been burned by the doorknob, he leaped to the side. The door crashed to the ground.

22

New York City

When my phone blinked to eleven-fifty-three, I picked it up. I grabbed my bag from the floor beneath my desk and went to Trystan's office.

As I stepped into the doorway, he looked up. "Alex. What can I do for you?"

"I wanted to get a last minute update before we meet with Jim Kohn tomorrow morning."

"An update on what?"

"I want to be absolutely sure I understand my role in the meeting. It would be great to get a bit more insight into what he expects and how the photography and video play into that."

"I believe we went over all of that."

"I'm a bit of a perfectionist." I smiled. "Since it's my first time, I want to be sure it goes exactly as you expect."

He looked unsettled by my choice of words. After a moment, he nodded. "Okay. I appreciate that." He looked at his watch. "I assume you chose this timing for your final update because you're hungry." He didn't look at me, but locked his computer screen and pushed his chair away from the desk.

"I always think better with food."

He laughed.

"My treat," I said.

"That's not necessary."

"I didn't come in looking for an invite to lunch."

"Nevertheless, I'll pay. It's a business expense."

During the elevator ride down, we talked about that safe topic favored by most of humanity — the weather. People can talk endlessly about weather. How hot it is, how unusual the heat is, even when it's not unusual. How cold it is and the atypical nature of that. How cloudy, how clear, how windy, how rainy. We discuss when it might rain and how much rain we've had or whether there's not enough and we'll be facing water rationing. We bond over too much rain and speculation, or the reality, of flooding. In New York, I expected they would talk just as fervently about snow and ice.

The funny thing is, no one ever seems bored with the topic. Maybe we're not bored because weather is so obviously beyond our control and we're in awe of its willfulness, secretly fearing what it might do to us. We're threatened by its lack of predictability, despite our computer-generated forecasts. Everything from spoiling our plans to tearing away the roofs of our houses and filling the rooms with great loads of thick, suffocating mud.

The weather might be why people tend to believe god is out to punish them. That's how it was with the ancient gods — gods of sun and rain and harvest. Instinctively we know the weather is in control, and eons ago, humanity named it and worshipped it in the hopes it wouldn't destroy their food or rip away their shelter or extinguish their very lives.

In our modern world of science and computer models and micro-forecasts, we simply discuss its behavior, as if we're still paying homage.

I suggested steak and Trystan agreed.

At the restaurant, we were seated at a table covered with a heavy pale green tablecloth and dressed with two white napkins folded to stand like tiny snow-covered mountain peaks.

"I'm in the mood for a martini," I said.

"Are you."

"Don't worry, it won't interfere with my work. In fact, it will relax me. I'm taking a few hours this afternoon to practice a bit more with the camera. Just to be sure I'm fully comfortable with it tomorrow."

He ordered two martinis.

"How are the classes going?"

"They're okay."

"Just okay?"

The server came with two martinis — gin for him, vodka for me. One olive for him, three for me.

Trystan raised his glass. "Cheers."

I said the same, then put my glass down without taking a sip. I pulled one of the olives off the stick and ate it, then I took a sip. "Tell me again what Jim is looking for, and what you want me to capture. Those are the main things I want to be clear on."

"I told you, he wants higher caliber clients."

"Yes, but what does that mean, exactly?"

"He's made some remarkable investments that have benefited a lot of extremely wealthy clients. But now, he thinks he's ready for some high-profile names."

"So not necessarily more money, *high-caliber* means names everyone knows. He wants to rub elbows with famous people."

"Yes."

"Okay, that's more clear. And why does he think that's important?"

"It doesn't matter why he wants that. Our job is to get him there."

"So I get that I'll be taking photographs and video during some of his meetings, but what will his clients think of that? If I were exposing my financial guts to someone, I wouldn't want a photographer there."

"You'll focus on Jim."

"But how can the clients be sure I'm not also photographing them? Won't they naturally get captured in some shots?"

He leaned back as the server approached with our steaks, a pile of greens filling half the plate where you'd normally expect to see a baked potato spilling sour cream and vegetables glistening with butter. We dug into our beef, introducing long pauses as we chewed each bite, savoring the flavor.

"You'll need to be discreet, and instill confidence."

"Easier said than done."

"Some people won't care. If someone objects strongly, just shut it down. There are lots of opportunities."

"So you really don't know why he wants well-known clients?"

"Don't be so curious."

"But I am. It seems like he'd be happy making fortunes for people who are starting out with less. Wouldn't that be more satisfying?"

"The well-known don't always have more money."

"Well, what does he want? How can you help him if

you don't know why?"

"That's a question he needs to answer for himself. All we're there to do is show him where he's weak, how he might be sabotaging himself in microscopic ways. Facilitate his own self-understanding."

He told me more about Jim, mostly re-hashing what I'd read in the file, what we'd discussed before. After several minutes, he put down his fork and looked at me. "Are you nervous?"

"No."

"Then what's up? We've already gone over all of this. You read his file."

"I just wanted it cemented in my head. And I wanted a better sense of him as a person. It's hard to get all of that from answers on a personality test and all of that."

"True."

"Those tests make it seem like there are only fifteen or twenty personalities in the world," I said.

"If you talk to Diana, you won't see it that way."

"She wants me to take one of the tests."

"Good idea."

"Did you suggest it to her?"

He furrowed his brow. He blinked as if he was trying to decide whether he'd heard me correctly. "No."

"Okay."

"But it wouldn't hurt. You might find it insightful."

"I doubt it."

He dragged his knife through the steak, removing a thin sliver of rare beef. He stabbed it and put it in his mouth. For a moment, he didn't chew. I felt like I had to hold my breath, waiting for him to start, imagining that piece of beef with saliva building around it, ready to choke him. Finally, he chewed quickly and swallowed.

"So it wasn't your idea?"

He gave me a look that suggested he wasn't going to repeat his answer.

"And you didn't tell Diana and Stephanie to invite me out for ice cream or breakfast?"

He laughed. "Do you have a touch of paranoia that I didn't detect when I interviewed you?"

"No."

"It sounds like you do."

"There's a fine line between paranoia and watching your back. Or noticing when other people have hidden agendas."

"There's no agenda. They're being friendly to a new co-worker. They just want to get to know you. Take it at face value."

I still didn't think someone who wore a giant gold cross wanted to get to know me better. She wanted to beat me over the head with that cross. I didn't tell Trystan that. He would absolutely think I was paranoid. But I know what I know. And paranoia truly is simply a derogatory word for someone who's careful, when you know how human beings can be, even the best of them.

23

The following day, Trystan and I took a cab to the Financial District. Jim Kohn's office was on the thirty-fifth floor of a forty-seven-story building. A part of me, maybe the small girl inside, wanted to ride the elevator all the way to the top floor.

The windows in the lobby of Jim's firm looked down on Wall Street itself. This guy definitely was about the image of his career as much as the satisfaction of advising people on how to make their money produce more, on acquiring enough to provide security, whatever number that is for any individual.

The people in the street below truly did look like ants. From that height, their movements along the sidewalk appeared erratic. They plowed forward, dodging left and right so they could maintain their speed and avoid crashing into the pedestrians coming at them. The cars did the same, jerking suddenly from one lane to another.

I turned away from the window and settled myself on a comfortable couch across from Trystan. He was reading the news on his phone, seemingly unconcerned that we'd been sitting there for eight minutes past our ten o'clock appointment. I supposed that was one of the ways that he got these people to trust him. He didn't exhibit any ego.

I'd overheard him on the phone. Meetings canceled at the last minute were met with a casual question as to when it was convenient to reschedule. His tone never grew impatient, he never complained or had any subtle condemnation in his voice when he told a client he'd expected their call thirty minutes, or thirty hours, earlier.

The receptionist caught my eye. "Mr. Kohn is ready for you."

Trystan slid his phone into his coat pocket, stood, and picked up his laptop bag. He gestured for me to go first toward the door to the left of the receptionist's desk.

We walked through and along an interior hallway. Visible through the glass office doors, past the people working on phones and computers, were floor-to-ceiling windows, also looking down on Wall Street and out toward Battery Park and the Hudson River beyond. As we turned a corner, the same massive windows faced the East River and Brooklyn. It reminded me of the building where I'd worked in San Francisco — designed to provide the best view for everyone, even those simply walking along a hallway.

Sharing the view and maximizing it for everyone was the only egalitarian thing about this place.

Jim's office looked like a genuine boardroom for the Godfather. It had two walls of those massive windows featured throughout the rest of the space. His desk was the dimensions of my queen-sized bed. There were couches and armchairs made of buttery dark brown leather, making me think of chocolate. Behind the sitting area was a conference table that sat twelve. An enormous vase of white roses stood in the center, reflected faintly on the polished wood.

There was a sideboard with various types of cocktail glasses and a rack filled with alcohol. Above it was a photograph of the Wall Street bull, taken before the statue of the fearless girl was placed in front of it. There was a door to a restroom which he said had a shower and all the required personal care products. Another door opened into a windowless nap room. Jim explained he could take ten-minute power naps in total darkness and silence, not that there was any noise filtering into his office. With this ability, he'd been living on four hours of sleep a night for decades.

Trystan introduced me. Jim shook my hand with a firm, dry grip, but a very abrupt gesture, almost dropping my hand in mid-air. Trystan and I sat in the two wingback chairs closest to Jim's desk.

On the shelf behind his desk was an eight-by-ten sterling silver frame. The photograph showed Jim standing on a balcony with a tropical sky behind him. A dark-haired woman who looked to be a good twenty years younger than Jim was beside him. Her arms were wrapped tightly around his waist. Her head was turned, smiling up at him with utter devotion, a look of giving herself over to him, retaining nothing of her own. There was something about the photograph that prevented me from looking away from it. Maybe it was the size, not what you normally see in an office. Those tend to be five-by-seven — prominent but not taking over. Maybe it was the expression on the woman's face, a look of utter surrender to a man who seemed the type to demand it and to take advantage of it.

Trystan removed his laptop and placed it on the edge of the desk, and I settled my camera bag beside me. The first photo session would be at the end of our meeting — pictures of Jim in his *natural habitat*. I wanted to laugh when Trystan called it that, but not a single muscle twitched in his lips to suggest he thought this was funny.

Jim settled back in his chair, then lurched forward,

about to shove himself to his feet. "Anything to drink?"

"No, thanks." Trystan and I spoke in unison.

"You sure? Water? Coffee? Smoothie? Scotch? Patrón?"

"No, thanks."

He sat forward still, looking anxious to get up and move or get his own drink. "What happens now? You've analyzed all those questions and plotted my personality onto a graph?" He tried to laugh, but it came out flat and slightly scared. He forced himself to settle back into the chair.

"My staff is coming up with a customized action plan covering areas for development," Trystan said. The areas for development were weaknesses, but according to Trystan, using the word *weakness* was counter-productive. "In the meantime, Alex will start photographing you today, as I mentioned. First, the three of us will do a final review of your expectations, just to be sure we're on the same page before we move forward."

"Sure." Jim gave a quick nod, not unlike his rapid-fire handshake.

Trystan proceeded to ask questions about Jim's employees and his feelings about the status of the business right now. He asked about his best and worst clients, and the reasons for that assessment. He re-confirmed that the main goal was to acquire a greater percentage of *high-caliber* clients.

Jim agreed.

I moved to the edge of my chair. "Can you talk about the details around that, so I can get a better sense of what your aspirations are like, how they affect your life?"

Trystan shot me a hard look. "I think we have enough data, we…"

Jim held up his hand, a police officer directing who

should speak, and when. "It's fine. I appreciate the question."

I settled back, restraining my smile.

"I want more. I've achieved a lot..." he glanced around his office. It took several seconds for his gaze to travel from one amenity to the next. "I wouldn't tell this to anyone but you," he nodded at Trystan, "And now you." I received the same nod. "I have an excellent track record. I want to operate at the elite level, move in that exclusive world. I want to be known as the guy who can make magic happen, and I want the attraction of luminaries. I honestly don't know why. I just do. Isn't that enough?"

"Of course," Trystan said. "There's no need to explain."

There was every need to explain. And I would have thought the guy would want to. He wasn't after more money, he wanted that inside track, to be able to name drop and to hang out with other well-known and well-connected people. Household names. Politicians. Actors. Not just the wealthy, but the institutionally rich whose names have littered American history. He wanted power.

It seemed shallow and pointless. What would having those people as clients do for the enjoyment of his life? He was essentially their employee. It wasn't as if he'd get invited to their parties. He wouldn't acquire the power they possessed.

24

After some more superficial discussion and a PowerPoint presentation where Trystan showed the results of Jim's various personality tests, he left me alone with Jim.

I didn't like Jim. At all.

If you want to hang out with household names, that's fine. But if you're so eager for their attention that you pay an enormous fee to have a guy coach you on how to raise your game to make that happen…well, it made me wonder whether Jim wasn't all that bright, despite his financial expertise. His stated reason for hiring us bordered on pathetic. It was almost as if he was paying for friends. Or at least paying to make himself likable to the people he wanted as friends.

He wanted to be in the cool group, to sit at the popular kids' lunch table.

And now I had to take photographs of him to expose how he came across when he was working at his desk, meeting with clients, giving advice. In this first session, we wouldn't be able to duplicate his true behavior since there were no actual clients, but at least we'd get an impression of him behind that stupendous desk — his typical posture and demeanor.

The desk was walnut. The surface was polished and nearly empty. The only objects in all that space were his computer screen, a wireless keyboard and mouse, and a charging dock for his phone. Near one corner was a wood box with low sides, in the center of which was a red Mont Blanc pen resting on a black velvet pad.

I removed the camera from the bag and settled it on the chair where Trystan had been sitting earlier.

"What do I do?" Jim said.

"Just relax for a minute while I get the camera ready. You can check email or read the news. Actually, it's better if you do. I know it will be difficult, but I need you to not think about the camera, not think about how you look or that I'm taking photographs. You need to ignore me."

He smirked. "That's not feasible." He laughed and let his gaze run over me.

I sighed, trying not to let him see the sudden exhalation. I didn't want to end up explaining to Trystan that I'd had to smack down my very first client for hitting on me. I'd paid careful attention to what I wore — black slacks, a loose pale yellow top, and a jacket that covered my bare arms and streamlined my shape. My heels weren't super high, and I'd worn less makeup than usual. Not that any of that matters. Not that it's about what a woman wears, but we're so socialized to think it does matter, it's hard to stop thinking that way. And at the same time, it's not that a woman can't use clothes to get what she wants.

You dress to look nice, and somewhere, there's an invisible line between deliberately dressing to attract and wanting that attraction taken at face value, not as an invite. From there, you can't help but think... *How much cleavage? How much leg? How high are fuck-me shoe heels, exactly, and how high are classic pumps?*

I'd been hoping my appearance would send a

professional message. Apparently, it hadn't. Or he wasn't receiving.

He gave me a smile that was difficult to read. Leering? I didn't think so. Knowing? Possibly. Victorious? Smug? Curious or inviting, or suggesting the ball was in my court?

I didn't smile back.

I attached the flash, removed the lens cap, and took a few steps away from his desk. He was not checking email as I'd suggested. He was staring at me, a tiny smile still playing across his lips, a glazed quality to his eyes.

I wondered whether Trystan had foreseen this. And from there, my thoughts took a paranoid leap. Had Trystan wanted me for this job so that I could get male clients' minds on me, and on sex, so that I could capture them with their guard down? In fact, did he think my appearance would have an effect on women as well? Creating some kind of self-consciousness, or envy or lack of confidence?

Trystan would call me paranoid. And possibly egotistical.

It sounds obnoxious to consider my appearance in such a flattering way. But the fact is, I was lucky in the genetics department. It's not boastful to recognize that, it's just an observation of what is, and a lifetime of noticing how others respond to my appearance. Drawing excessive male attention and a certain amount of female envy isn't necessarily a good thing. I've definitely used it to my advantage, but sometimes, it's honestly exhausting. Sometimes, you just want to *be*. Sometimes you want to have an interesting conversation with a man you've just met instead of feeling that tension crackling around his skin, seeking a response.

"Why don't we start with you checking your email like I

suggested." I smiled to remove the sting. "We don't want you simply staring at the camera."

He didn't move.

"Jim?"

He smiled.

"Check your email. On your computer."

"I like hearing you tell me what to do."

I snapped three shots.

"Hey."

"Hey, what?"

"I wasn't ready."

"That's the point." He knew that was the fucking point. If this was how he was in his *natural habitat*, I couldn't imagine how it would be dealing with him in public places where he might put on even more of a show, given his desire to attract the attention of the famous.

"Delete those," he said.

I lowered the camera and took another step back. "Trystan explained the purpose of the photographs and video."

"Explain it again."

"We want to see how you hold yourself, what kind of demeanor you project, how you interact with your clients, and with people in general when you're in public places. Since eighty percent of communication is non-verbal, a lot of how potential clients perceive you comes through your posture and facial expressions, and tone of voice."

"Sounds like a bunch of bullshit to me."

"It's the process Trystan has set up. So let's get back to it. If you want this to be a success, you need to trust what he's outlined."

"The provocateur?" He spoke with a drawl, then laughed.

"Yes. He wants to provoke you into being your most authentic self, being the person you are most of the time so you can figure out how to up your game."

"You're pretty full of yourself," he said.

"This isn't about me."

"You gals are all the same. I give you a little visual appreciation, and you get all pissed off. You want to defy the natural order — male and female. Castrate a guy for looking. Someone should assess how you come across. That know-it-all attitude." He smiled as if he expected me to take it all in good fun.

I snapped three photographs.

"Stop it." He brushed his wavy hair away from his forehead.

"I'm here to take your photograph. You paid a lot of money for our insight."

"Isn't that the truth. But I can spare it."

I lowered the camera. "Would you prefer to do this another time?"

"It's awkward, you know. Having someone point a camera at you. Especially a woman who looks like you. Why don't you smile a bit, don't be so fucking serious and then I'll relax. Clearly, you don't have a lot of experience as a photographer."

"I'm not a portrait photographer. My job is to support what Trystan is offering. Insight."

"Fuck it." He stood and walked to the window. He turned toward the glass. His shoulders rose as he inhaled deeply, then remained rigid for a moment, countering whatever relaxation he was hoping to get out of a deep breath. He exhaled and turned. "You're making this very uncomfortable, you know. I didn't think it would be like this."

"Try to stop thinking about me. Why don't you look through your schedule for the rest of the day, work on whatever you'd be doing if I wasn't here. Check your clients' accounts or whatever."

"Janine takes care of my schedule."

"You can't even look at it?"

He returned to his desk, pulled out the chair and sat down. He moved the mouse and leaned toward his computer.

I began taking pictures. He tensed with each click of the shutter.

"That's good," I said. "Now why don't you settle back in your chair as you were when Trystan and I were sitting across from you." I walked over and put my camera on one of the chairs. I pulled it several more feet away from the desk, picked up the camera, and sat down. I took several photographs quickly before he could get too wound up.

I picked up the bag, removed the flash, and reattached the lens cap. "I think I have enough. Trystan said you have a dinner meeting tomorrow and I'll be there to take photographs." I stood.

He stared at me with a look of utter loathing.

"You'll see me, of course, but I'll remain as unobtrusive as I can."

"I don't think that's at all possible for a woman like you."

"Please stop making this about me."

"There's that attitude again."

I gave him a chilling smile. "I'll stay out of the way, and

I'll work to avoid including your client in any shots. You'll forget I'm there after a while, I guarantee it."

I put the strap over my shoulder. Any of the things I would have said prior to him opening his obnoxious mouth were now things I did not want to say — *Looking forward to working with you. It's been a pleasure. Nice meeting you.* I didn't even want to shake his hand. But I had to do something.

I walked to the edge of the desk and extended my hand. "I'll see you tomorrow night."

He ignored my hand. "I can't wait."

I went to the door and let myself out. All the way down the thirty-five floors I wondered why a good-looking man with that much money, and if the photograph was to be believed, a wife who adored him, had to work overtime trying to force me into becoming some sort of plaything in his quest for power.

25

I ended up meeting Victoria and Rafe at a restaurant in Little Italy. They'd abandoned their interest in my preference for Thai. I guess they couldn't stop thinking of pizza so they seemingly decided noodles of any kind would please me, and they could still get their pizza.

The restaurant had a sidewalk eating area, and the evening air was pleasantly warm, but Rafe said he had no desire to become a boiled lobster. The interior was narrow and deep. We were seated at a table near the front. A large painting hung on the wall beside us. It depicted a street lined with Mediterranean buildings featuring iron balcony railings and pots filled with red and pink geraniums, the long legs bursting with flowers spilling over the sides between the balcony rails.

Rafe ordered a shot of Patrón, Victoria asked for a glass of white wine, and I requested a martini. We surveyed our menus, Victoria pouring over hers as if it were the Rosetta stone. Our drinks came, and we drank a toast to new neighbors. Victoria returned to reading the description for each item, murmuring some of them out loud while we sipped our drinks.

Finally, she decided on sharing a pepperoni and sausage pizza with Rafe. I asked for angel hair pasta with clams.

"Good day at work?" Rafe said.

"Different, but okay."

"Just okay?"

I sipped my drink and looked around. We were the only ones in the front section, but the back was filled, lots of late middle-aged people escaping the heat.

He persisted. "Why was it just *o-kay*?"

"Isn't okay an adequate description?"

"Not really."

I took another sip of my drink and told them about Jim. "I'm pissed, but it's my first client. I don't want to make a thing out of it."

"You absolutely should make a thing out of it," Victoria said.

"If he thinks I can't handle men like that, Trystan might change my responsibilities. And I like taking pictures. I like that it gets me away from a desk."

"You can't put up with that. You need to stand up for yourself," she said.

"I didn't put up with it. I think the next time, he'll be more manageable. Especially in front of other people. It's unlikely I'll be photographing him alone again."

"Still. I hate that shit." She swallowed some wine, leaving her lips wet. She licked them and purred her pleasure at the taste of the wine.

"Next time tell him your boyfriend will take him on," Rafe said.

"I don't work that way."

"Why not?"

"I don't need to invent a boyfriend to take care of me. I'll handle it." I regretted mentioning the incident. I didn't need advice from either of them, but especially Rafe, on how to do my job, or how to handle a difficult guy. I surely had more experience at it than he did. I changed the subject to their business, feeding them a steady stream of questions about how they made trades, what the stress was like, and whether they ever got bored. They insisted the stress was manageable since they only worked two or three hours a day, all experienced day traders did.

We ordered a second round of drinks, and a few minutes after that, our food came. The pizza was placed between them. Rafe pulled out a wedge and put it on a plate for Victoria. He picked up another and took a large bite, seemingly oblivious to the temperature, which looked to be quite warm since steam was rising from the place where he'd pulled off the two cheesy triangles.

I twirled pasta around my fork, stabbed a clam, and held it over the plate, waiting for it to cool.

Rafe filled me in on all the cool things about New York. He sounded like a travel guide, a guide that doesn't actually know the cool places, just the places tourists flock to — Times Square and the memorial at the world trade center, the Statue of Liberty and Yankee Stadium and Central Park.

Still, it was interesting. He continued until the last slice of pizza was eaten, and my plate was mopped clean. It was the most delicious pasta dish I'd ever eaten. The light creamy tomato sauce, the fresh Parmesan, and equally fresh clams, made me feel like I was eating something prepared by the gods.

Rafe suggested a third round of drinks.

"Not for me." I nudged my glass away from my plate, wanting to keep myself from mindlessly habitual sips, savoring the last few tablespoons.

"We can get a cab," he said.

"I don't drink more than two martinis at a time."

"Is that a rule?" he said.

"No."

"Then have another one. I'm paying."

"I only drink two."

"So it *is* a rule." He grinned and leaned over the table.

"I don't call it a rule. Two is enough. I like to enjoy them, not just mindlessly slam down alcohol like some high school kid trying to get drunk as fast as possible."

"Semantics," Victoria said.

I didn't reply, and Rafe ignored her. "Why can't you call it a rule, when that's what it is?"

"What difference does it make?"

"It makes a difference because I said it was a rule and you argued with me and it really is a rule and you won't admit it."

"Are we twelve?"

"Why'd you say that?" He signaled the server and ordered another shot, another glass of wine, and another martini, with four olives.

I looked up at the server. "Forget the martini. I'm still finishing this one. And then we're done." I picked up my bag and pulled out several twenties.

"I got this," Rafe said. He shifted onto one hip, tugged his wallet out of his back pocket, flipped it open, slid out a credit card, and tossed it on the table.

The server stared at the card and my cash. "You guys work it out. So no martini?"

"That's right."

She headed toward the bar.

"You're spoiling things," Rafe said.

"You need to chill," Victoria said.

He reached his hand across the table and touched the base of my glass. "Come on, Lexxie."

"Alex," I said. "I prefer Alex. Or Alexandra."

He sat back in mock horror.

"Rafe." Victoria's voice was edged with tension.

"I have it handled," he said.

"You have what handled?" I moved my glass toward me and pulled out the swizzle stick. I sucked off the second olive and let it roll around inside my mouth, enjoying the infusion of vodka and salt before chewing it.

"I have you handled." He laughed. "And I really think you could have used another drink. Then you'd be able to admit that you have rules."

I chewed my olive.

"I told you to chill out," Victoria said. "You're getting too wound up."

"I'm fine." The drinks arrived. Rafe pushed the cash toward me and handed the card to the server. She took it and left before I could argue.

He downed his shot and put the glass on the table with a loud thud. "Everything is fine. Just fine. Right, *Al-ex?*"

I shrugged.

"Dessert?" Victoria said.

I shook my head. Rafe ignored her.

Victoria took rapid sips from her glass, seeming to be as eager as I was to leave. I finished my last olive and the drink. Rafe signed the bill. We went outside and started toward the subway. Rafe dropped back, letting Victoria lead the way. He moved close to my side. "I didn't mean to upset you." He spoke in a low voice, impossible for Victoria to overhear with the noise of people talking as we passed another sidewalk dining area.

"I'm not upset." I spoke in a normal tone.

He touched my arm. "You're so beautiful. It's fun seeing you drink in the flavor of New York City."

"What are you doing?" I moved away. Surely, even if Victoria couldn't see, she would sense what he was doing. I did not want to get in the middle of the two of them. Rafe was good looking enough, someone I might hook up with in other circumstances. But a couple? No thanks. Way too much drama. Even if I found him wildly attractive and my body was longing for a guy, there were too many choices that were better than getting into the middle of someone else's relationship.

I shivered.

"You okay?"

"I'm absolutely fine. How about you?"

He laughed.

I walked faster until I was beside Victoria. She didn't turn to look at me, but there was no vibe that she was angry or jealous. Something was off about these two. Maybe sitting all day in front of constantly shifting charts, making split-second decisions that could drive your fortune up or down in a moment, did something to your relationship. Although what that was, I couldn't say.

26

The office was deathly silent. Stephanie liked coming in early for that reason. Even the sound of clicking keys made her aware of other people, which resulted in feeling she needed to adjust herself — stand up straighter, smile, work more diligently. It wasn't a good thing. She knew that. Her behavior should always be the same. After all, God never stopped watching, so why did she act differently when there were people around?

But she did. She had to avoid coughing because they might find that annoying. Coughing was both a bad habit and the result of chronic allergies — the repeated and regular cough that had plagued her for most of her life. Her sister used to complain about it, as if Stephanie could control the irritation and mucous in her throat. It was embarrassing to think she was causing disgust with a physical response over which she had no control.

When the office was empty, she felt like she owned the entire space. She liked that she didn't have to constantly anticipate someone appearing in her doorway, expecting a smile and a welcome. She could yawn, she could slip off her shoes and free her feet from the pinch of leather.

She could be herself.

There was no one here to make her feel inadequate. There was no one she had to compete with.

Since Alexandra had shown up, there was definitely a

competition. It ate at her, the way Alexandra had stolen Stephanie's chance to do something far more interesting, and more valuable. It didn't matter that Alexandra had no idea she'd stolen it. That job should have been hers. Alexandra had a smugness that suggested she was better than Stephanie. She assumed she deserved the job. She had an air of arrogance that said Trystan was lucky to have her.

Stephanie slipped off her flats and left them beside her desk. Her feet were clean. She'd used a pumice stone to rid them of telltale dead skin that might find its way into the carpet. She didn't use lotion or powder, so there wouldn't be any scent or faint outlines of her toes left behind.

She left her office and entered Trystan's. He kept his computer screen locked, as all of them did. It was required, in order to give the utmost protection to the sensitive information their clients provided. And any sensible person did the same. Your whole life was on your computer. A break-in, even if it was just a junkie looking for cash, or electronics to sell, put your entire existence at risk.

Nevertheless, she always started with Trystan's computer, trying to guess the password. She gave it only a single try during each visit. Unless he used one of those ridiculously long passwords filled with random letters and numbers, she would hit upon the right word or phrase at some point. She had to.

Now, the most important objective had become finding that elusive sheet of paper. Not just any information she could ferret out, but a specific *piece* of information.

Like all offices, this one wasn't truly paperless. She wondered if that day would ever come. Human beings craved their pieces of paper. There had always been a subtle distrust of computers, and now that the reality of artificial intelligence was upon them... Even without developing minds of their own, computers could die, they could freeze, they could get infected with a virus, they could lock you out if your password was typed incorrectly more than three times. It was frightening, knowing you were stupid and helpless without your computer and smartphone.

People even a few years younger than her, like Alexandra and Diana, probably didn't have that same fear. They lived exclusively in a digital world. They'd never known anything else. But they were foolish for doing so. Any sort of global crisis, a failure of the power grid, would melt down the entire modern world.

She sat at his desk and typed ILoveNYC into the box on the screen. It told her the password was incorrect. She knew him. There was no way his password was random. He liked to keep things simple.

Every single time she arrived this early, she allowed herself fifteen minutes to investigate his office. It was like panning for gold. Someday, she didn't know when, she might gain access, or find a few folded sheets of paper that could change her life.

There was nothing wrong with what she was doing.

Some people would say she was invading another person's privacy. But it wasn't private when it was at the office. The computers were locked to protect client information from outsiders. She and Diana and now Alexandra all had access to those files, so she wasn't stepping over any lines in that. If Trystan had other things on his computer, and she had no doubt that he did, that was also related to work, and therefore something all of them deserved to know.

The Bible had nothing to say on the matter of snooping. Not that she could recall. It was such an ugly word. Investigating would be better. She supposed it could be considered a form of lying. Since she didn't tell Trystan what she was doing, she was withholding the truth.

Did that make it a lie?

In her view, it was self-protection, possibly even protecting Trystan from himself. She was hired for this job, paid a salary, and promised opportunities for advancing her career. But no opportunities had been forthcoming, and didn't it show diligence, and courage, and the widely praised trait of going after what you wanted, to investigate what was being concealed? All the career advice suggested those attributes were critical for success.

So what was wrong with looking through his office? He shouldn't be keeping secrets, not secrets that impacted her career, if that's what it was.

If Alexandra was making more money, with no experience, and obviously less longevity than Stephanie, that was wrong. Stephanie had a right to know, and Trystan had a responsibility to fix it. The company was much too small for an HR department. In a larger firm, she would be able to talk to HR about salary equality and job qualifications. Here, she couldn't do that. Trystan had made it clear that salary increases would come once a year, and aside from that, raises were given when there was an increase in responsibility.

But she'd never been allowed that increased responsibility!

She had to understand what Trystan saw in Alexandra. Surely it wasn't just her appearance. He wasn't that shallow.

She knew him well, and he wasn't swayed by that sort of thing. Most of the time, he hardly seemed to notice a woman's appearance.

No, there was something else going on, and she needed to find out what it was.

He might have notes on Stephanie's work. He was always taking notes on a legal pad. Where did he store those pages? Maybe she'd failed in some terrible way that she was completely blind to. Maybe she'd damaged a client relationship. Maybe he didn't realize how competent she was, that she had an inherent ability to make people feel comfortable. He'd rarely seen her with clients. How would he know?

She walked to the bookcase and ran her finger along the edge of the shelf directly in front of her. There were five shelves built into the wall. Three contained books, one contained an old set of DVDs — training materials he'd used years ago when DVDs were still a thing. The other two shelves had decorative objects — a black-streaked glass swan, which he loved because he subscribed to the miraculous possibilities of so-called black swan events. It sat alone on a shelf. The other decorative shelf held a photograph of his twelve-year-old daughter and a clay pot she'd made in a summer class.

Stephanie pulled out one of the books, a thick hardback that told the success stories of Olympic athletes. She thumbed through it. The office was so sparse, this was what she was often driven to — looking through book pages for handwritten notes, folded pages that he'd squirreled away. She hadn't found anything. Yet.

If she could only figure out…

"What are you looking for?"

The book started to slide out of her hands as she turned suddenly. She grasped it more tightly, then closed it and placed it on the shelf.

Alexandra stood in the doorway, a smirk on her face, her hand on her left hip, that leather messenger bag she carried instead of a purse slung over her right shoulder.

Stephanie smiled. She was not guilty. There had been no reason to jump like that, the jitter of a person who's been caught doing something wrong. She was simply looking through Trystan's books. "A book."

"What book?"

She moved away from the shelf. "It's not important. You're awfully early."

"I have a lot to do today."

"More than usual?"

"Yes."

"Why? Because you spent too much time with Jim Kohn?"

"No."

"You were gone an awfully long time after Trystan got back."

Alexandra shrugged. "I had to take pictures."

"How did that go?"

"As you'd expect."

"What does that mean?"

"Do I report to you?"

Stephanie folded her arms. "I'm just interested. We're a team here. We share information."

"Well, there's no information to share. Trystan wanted photographs taken in Jim's *natural habitat*, and that's what I did. I took pictures of him sitting at his desk. Pretty boring, actually."

Stephanie walked toward the door.

"You forgot your book."

Stephanie smiled and paused, waiting for Alexandra to move out of her way.

Alexandra grinned. "What are you up to? Snooping for dirt on our boss?"

"Of course not." She fingered her cross. She was handling this all wrong. She was supposed to be kind to Alexandra. She was supposed to be warm and caring and accept her as she was, and look for open doors for sharing her faith. The woman obviously had a very pagan view of the world.

Stephanie moved past her and out the door. The next time, she'd come in much earlier. And first, she'd check out Alexandra's office.

27

Delmonico's was on Beaver in the Financial District. Jim was scheduled to meet his client for dinner at seven. The client knew about the arrangement for photographs and didn't have any problem if part of her face was captured in any of the images, as long as the photos were only used for Jim's coaching sessions. I wondered how he'd explained the purpose of the coaching to her.

I would be sitting in the back, using a telephoto lens so that I could capture Jim at a table thirty feet away. While I watched him and took photographs, I would eat a salad so I didn't look too out of place. The camera was bad enough. Trystan had made arrangements with the restaurant manager.

I arrived at quarter to seven, ordered a glass of sparkling water, and took my camera out of the bag, leaving it on my lap for the time being. I would order the wine and salad once Jim and his guest were seated.

His guest arrived first, at five minutes to seven. She was seated with her back to me, also pre-arranged.

Jim was late. When he appeared in the doorway, I took several shots of him and continued to snap pictures as he entered the room, striding toward her table. Video would have been better, but I wanted to get a feel for doing this in public before I ventured into that. There would be other opportunities for photographs and video.

I photographed him shaking his guest's hand, pulling

out his chair, summoning the server, and leaning forward, talking fast, using minimal gestures.

This was going smoothly and probably wouldn't take long enough for me to eat a salad and drink a glass of wine, but those were my instructions for not attracting too much attention, so I ordered a Caesar salad and a glass of Chardonnay.

I took a few shots of Jim ordering dinner, and then pictures of him holding out his small iPad so his guest could see whatever information he wanted to discuss with her.

After that, things got a bit dull. I wished I could be slightly closer. I had plenty of shots of his posture — straight and confident, his expression — overly solicitous, and his tendency to talk a bit too much, which I'd shown in a series of twenty shots taken in succession, during which his lips never stopped moving.

I put my camera aside and took a few sips of wine. I scooped up a crouton and a slice of Parmesan cheese, followed by a few pieces of romaine lettuce. The salad was delicious. It made me hungry, and I wished I could order a full meal. The food smelled delicious, and based on the salad, I imagined everything was worth sampling.

Jim and his guest ate dinner rather quickly, ordering only a single glass of wine each, and skipping appetizers, salads, and desserts.

I pushed my empty plate to the side and took more photographs, making sure I got several of him eating, drinking, and of course, talking.

Two cups of coffee were delivered to their table, but a few minutes later, the woman stood. She shook Jim's hand and headed toward the door. Jim flagged the server, and while I was packing my camera, another glass of wine was delivered to his table. Jim stood and walked slowly toward me, carrying his glass. He pulled out the chair across from me and sat down. "How'd it go?"

"Fine. Trystan will show them to you at your next meeting."

"Why can't I see them now? You're right here."

"Because that's not how it works."

"Don't be difficult." He took a sip of wine.

I stood.

"Where are you going?"

"I'm finished."

"You didn't drink all of your wine."

"Your meeting's over, so I'm done." I picked up my glass, swallowed the last of the wine, and settled the strap of my camera bag on my shoulder. "Bye."

He stood. "Hey, not so fast. Order another glass of wine. On me."

"No thanks." I started toward the door.

He came around the table and took my upper arm as if he meant to steer me, not rudely or aggressively, but definitely firmly, in another direction.

"Please let go."

"Have another glass of wine, and we can talk. Get to know each other."

"I already know what I need to."

"What's that supposed to mean?"

"Nothing. I only needed to know a bit about your job and enough of your profile to be able to take photographs."

He stood close. He took a swallow of wine and slid his hand up my arm. His breath was warm and fruity with red wine. "I don't know a thing about you."

"You don't need to."

"But I want to." He was still holding my arm.

"You're my client, this is a business relationship. Please let go of my arm."

"Or what?"

"Or nothing, just let go of me."

"You sound like you're making a threat."

I laughed. "I'm just telling you to let go of me. Now."

He slowly loosened his grip, but his fingers still circled my arm. "Be nice. I want to get to know you."

"Let go of my arm."

He let go and slipped his arm around my waist, pulling me close. He put his face against my hair. "Mmm."

"You need to stop."

"You make it very difficult. You're a tempting treat."

I slid out from under his arm. "Trystan will be in touch." I walked quickly, weaving among crowded tables, headed toward the entrance, keeping my attention forward, fairly certain he was following me. I stopped at the reservations pedestal. "My wine and salad were already paid for by Mr. Vogel. This is for the server." I placed some cash on the pedestal. Before I could turn, Jim was beside me.

I went to the door. The maître d' hurried to open it.

"Don't run away," Jim said.

"I'm not running away."

"You're definitely running somewhere."

"I'm leaving, not running."

"Why not a drink?"

"Because I said no." I walked quickly for two blocks and hailed a cab. As I climbed into the back seat, I turned to look.

He hadn't followed. I let go of my breath and settled back against the seat, trying to decide whether I should mention Jim's behavior to Trystan.

28

I ended up not telling Trystan about his slimy client.

Not yet. It wasn't anything I couldn't handle, and every way I looked at it, I couldn't figure out how telling him would benefit me. I didn't want Trystan telling Jim to back off as if he thought of himself as some sort of paternalistic protector. And I definitely didn't want him showing concern for me, or viewing me as weak. I didn't want him thinking this could damage his reputation and make him second-guess hiring me.

The next morning, I went to a gym that was halfway between my apartment and my office. It was the best choice, based on recommendations from Diana's friends and Yelp reviews.

The set-up wasn't as slick as what I was used to. There was plenty of equipment, but no studios for yoga classes and no swimming pool where I could practice my new skill. I decided I would live without all of that for now. I mostly wanted to get back to regular lifting. Yoga was nice, but not what I needed. If I started craving it, I could sign up for classes somewhere else or do it at home.

The membership fee was reasonable, and it would be easy to run in Bryant Park, walk to the gym, work out and shower, and walk to my office building. I was assigned a locker where I left some body wash and shampoo, as well as an extra hairbrush and hairdryer I'd purchased during a stop at Dwayne Reed on my way to the gym. I stuffed in the small gym bag with workout clothes, closed it, and spun the dial.

It was more and more startling to me how much effort was required to live in New York. There was no trunk where I could leave my things, no quick route for errands. Taking Uber was hardly worth it because of the traffic, so really, walking and the subway were the most efficient. But I felt like everything had to be thought out ahead of time to ensure there was plenty of time for travel. I wondered what it would be like once the heavy rain started. Or when it snowed.

My day was consumed by a lengthy meeting to review new clients, interrupted only by Diana, Stephanie, and I going out for lunch — beet salads for all of us, and sparkling water. We talked about work so it felt like a continuation of the meeting, without Trystan's input.

At five-thirty I locked my computer screen, grabbed my bag and headed out for the gym.

The locker room was as steamy as the air outdoors, not the cool, coconut-scented air I was used to at my gym in San Francisco.

I changed into a sports bra and black Capri workout pants. I went to the mat in the front corner and stretched for several minutes, taking time to survey my fellow members. The stationary bicycles were occupied by five women. The treadmills and elliptical machines were all in use as well. One guy with short dark hair, damp from his effort so far, was using the lat pull-down and a woman who looked to be in her fifties was lying beneath the weights of the bench press, her hands clasped on her ribs as she rested between sets.

I started with the free weights — doing several sets of exercises to work my biceps, triceps, and shoulders. By the time I'd finished, the bench press and lat machine users had moved on, and no replacements had taken over. Three women were waiting for the treadmills, talking and tapping at their phones.

I spent an hour trying out all the machines, even the ones that duplicated work for muscles I'd done with free weights. All weight machines are slightly different, and it takes a few times to get used to the idiosyncrasies. In the end, the workout is the same, but your body has to get accustomed to the grip and the speed with which the weights move on their cables, and even the shape and feel of the bench or seat supporting you.

I took a shower, leaving my hair wet so it would keep me cool as I walked home. I stuffed my sweaty clothes into the gym bag. Laundry was yet another thing that required slightly more effort than I'd grown used to.

After months of walking down a single flight of stairs to use Sean's sparkling-clean high-tech washer and dryer that were rarely in use by anyone else, I now had to descend from the third floor to the basement, past occasional pairs of overly curious eyes, lugging my laundry basket, a plastic container of quarters, and my bottle of detergent. The laundry room had a concrete floor that looked like twenty thousand people had walked over it during the course of its life. The single, twelve-by-eighteen-inch-square window looked out at the sidewalk but was so obscured with grime, it was impossible to see much more than an occasional shadow passing by. There were three washing machines and three dryers, and when they were all going, the noise and the steam were unbearable.

I entered the lobby and combed my fingers through my hair. With the humidity, it had hardly dried at all during my six-block walk. I climbed the stairs. Rafe stood near the railing on the landing, looking down the stairwell as if he'd been tracking each step.

When he spoke, it seemed he had. "I wondered where you were."

I walked around him toward my door. "Don't be keeping tabs on me."

He laughed. "I'm not. I just know you're always home from work by six-thirty."

I felt a mild chill down the center of my back as if a drop of water from my hair had fallen onto the top of my spine and made its way slowly down each vertebra. "You've been standing here since six-thirty?"

"Six-fifteen, actually."

I reached into my bag for my keys.

"Do you want to come in for a glass of wine, or a beer?" he said. "I might even have stuff for a martini."

I doubted he had *stuff* for a martini. Certainly no olives, if he'd just thought of it that minute. And did he even know how to mix a martini? Did he have vermouth in his cabinet? Something about that word *stuff* made me think he had no clue.

"No thanks," I said.

"After a long day? It would be nice to unwind."

He edged closer until he was standing between me and my doorknob. I wasn't quite sure how he'd managed to insert himself into that narrow space. I had the keys in my hand now.

"You're so beautiful," he said. "I imagine you hear that all the time." He laughed. He put his hand on the doorknob.

"I doubt Victoria would appreciate hearing you say that."

He leaned closer. "She's not here."

"Not really the point."

"She gets me."

I wasn't sure that was true. It sounded more like wishful thinking.

"She's very open-minded. She wouldn't have a problem at all if you and I got…friendlier."

I shoved the key in the lock and elbowed his forearm, forcing his hand off the knob. "I'm not interested."

"Are you sure?"

"Absolutely."

He took a few steps back. "I think you're the type who doesn't like an aggressive move. I guess I blew it." He gave me a sad-puppy face.

He was wrong. Aggressive moves are fine, in fact, they're exciting. But not crude ones. And not from a guy who's in a relationship. It was insulting that he thought I was stupid enough to get between him and Victoria, no matter how much she *got him*.

29

Portland

Oddly enough, Mr. B did not immediately run to my parents with a report of my disrespectful, blasphemous behavior. Neither did he speak to me right away. After his stumbling exit through the fake door, he was nowhere to be seen for the rest of the evening. His wife took over, talking to us about the next steps in the program.

When Mrs. B was out of earshot, a few of my friends laughed and gave me high fives for my dramatic debut. They worried I was in trouble. At the same time, they hoped they were wrong and that I would get called up there again. It was so much more fun compared with a lecture about sharing the steps to salvation.

Some of my friends felt this way.

Others told me I was a brat, and others said I was making fun of god's wish that we would draw everyone into his arms. They said I had no feelings and they worried whether I was destined for hell if I kept ridiculing god's instructions to save the human race.

At first, I thought Mr. B might end up ignoring the whole thing, keeping his distance from me, trying to regain his dignity. But I wasn't that lucky. Two weeks later, he was waiting for me at the entrance to the small auditorium when I arrived for evangelism training. He touched my shoulder, crooked his finger at me to follow, turned, and went to the opposite corner of the room. He pulled up a chair and gestured that I should sit down.

"I'm fine standing," I said.

"Sit down."

I put my hand on the back of the chair and bent my leg, resting my knee on the seat.

"I told you to sit down."

"I'd rather stand."

"I don't care what you'd rather do. Until this program is complete, I'm in charge here. You need to respect my authority and submit to the leader God has put over you."

"What difference does it make if I sit or stand?" I had a pretty good idea what difference it made. He only had an inch or two on me. I could look him directly in the eye. And he knew from our scenario on stage that I was a stronger person than he was. He had to have me sitting in that chair.

"I told you to sit down. That's what difference it makes." He folded his arms across his chest, crumpling the lapels of his suit coat so that it looked as if he'd made two little caves for squirrels. A completely random thought, but it's what came to mind.

He gave me a tight, smug smile. "I have all the time in the world. If you want to stand here all night, I can wait."

"Don't you have to lead the training?"

He took a step to the side and leaned against the wall. He curved his fingers over his palm and studied his fingernails. He picked at a hangnail, or something bothering him on the tip of his finger. It might have been a phantom imperfection, something to do while he waited for me to comply.

We stood like that for at least five minutes. I turned slightly and saw Mrs. B at the front of the room, shooting him expressions of confusion and curiosity. It was after seven and the training should have started at seven.

Still, we stood there.

"You're a troublemaker," he said.

"Not really."

Suddenly he stuck out his foot, knocked my foot that was on the floor, throwing me off balance. I fell away from the chair. He grabbed my upper arms and forced me down onto the chair. I struggled, but he placed his hands on my shoulders. He was surprisingly strong for a man with such a delicate build.

"Don't create a scene. You've already made this take far longer than necessary." He cleared his throat. "I didn't appreciate that behavior during our demonstration. First, I gave you an opportunity to be an example to your peers, and you treated it with contempt. Second, you were disrespectful and rude and downright evil. God doesn't take kindly to those who lead his children away from the truth."

I waited.

"I've had time to think about how to handle your bad behavior, and I believe the best solution is to have you up on the stage again."

I wondered whether he was hopelessly naïve, or had a scenario in mind where he would attempt to humiliate me as I'd done to him. I didn't set out wanting or intending to humiliate him. I just wanted to make it clear to everyone that the canned questions were insulting. I wanted them to see how smug their belief was that they could manipulate someone into believing. Or maybe I just wanted to watch him squirm, so it was humiliation after all. I really don't know. He wasn't an awful person, just…smug. Self-important.

"I want you to prepare your thoughts. I'll review what you write and provide corrections and insight…"

"Corrections?"

"Yes. And then, you'll deliver it to the rest of the group. You have two weeks."

"Thoughts about what?"

"Let me finish."

"But if they're my thoughts, how can you correct them? That makes them not my thoughts."

"Let me finish."

I folded my arms.

"Your speech will cover the need for salvation. It will discuss the consequences of turning away from God, and the value of our program for offering people eternal life. You'll do this with enthusiasm so your peers will be excited about learning this very effective process and become better prepared for our outreach efforts."

"I don't think…"

He moved closer, looking down at me, which is what he'd wanted all along. "It's not up for discussion."

"It's not fair."

He laughed. "Fair has nothing to do with it. You need to realize how important this is. You've given the impression this program has no value. And you're wrong. It's critical for saving souls. We're providing the tools for believers to share their faith."

"You can't make me say those things."

"I think I can."

"How?"

"I'll involve your parents if I have to. But I expect your punishment will be far worse if I do. Is that really what you want?"

It wasn't. Did he know that, or was he guessing?

I stood and stepped behind the chair. I gripped the back, feeling the metal hard against my bones, warm now from the weight of my body against it. We glared at each other.

"Have your essay to me by next Wednesday." He turned and walked to the front of the room. When he stopped, I heard Mrs. B begin rattling off her concerns. I couldn't make out her words. But the tone was clear — he was in trouble, just like me.

30

New York City

Stephanie had one valuable thing that would help her begin fixing the injustice that had been thrust upon her, and she hadn't needed to get into Trystan's computer to find it, or even risk slipping into Alexandra's office. She had access to the master schedule. She knew that schedule inside and out. She was responsible for setting up more than ninety percent of Trystan's meetings, and now, Alex's appointments.

The following afternoon, Alexandra was scheduled to videotape a lunch that Jim Kohn had arranged with two new clients, clients for whom he'd be on his absolute best behavior.

Stephanie would be at that lunch. Uninvited, of course. She would watch what Alexandra did, how she interacted with Jim, and most importantly, she would be on the lookout for any mistakes in how Alexandra approached the situation. She would compile a list that could be reported back to Trystan. And she had no doubt there would be issues to report. Of course, she'd have to explain how she'd spent time observing the two of them, but she'd work out the details of that later. For now, she needed access and information.

She dressed carefully for the occasion. Instead of her usual flats, she bought a new pair of high heels, choosing heels that were taller than what she normally wore. She had to be sure she looked chic, that she fit in with the lunch crowd, that she looked like a powerful businesswoman, not an office girl out for a salad and a glass of sparkling water.

The suit she wore was borrowed from Eileen's closet. It was a little tight through the waist, but nothing she couldn't manage if she paid attention to her posture. She applied makeup with more drama than usual — shadows around her eyes, mascara, color on her eyebrows, and blush beneath her cheekbones. She combed her hair back and secured it with a large barrette at the nape of her neck.

Looking at her reflection, she wondered why she didn't put in this kind of effort every day. She always looked fine for the office, nicely dressed, appropriate. But what did they say — dress for the job you want, not the one you have. How would she go about that? As good as she looked right now, was it really the look she needed to have the job that should have been offered to her?

She left her apartment, managing to slip out unseen, dodging the inevitable teasing for getting so dressed up. She hoped no one at the office made a comment.

They didn't. Forty-five minutes before Jim Kohn's lunch appointment, she left quietly without telling anyone where she was going. If she lied and said she was going for lunch, someone was bound to ask her to bring food back for them. Worse, Diana might ask to join her.

She hated spending the money, but she was not taking the subway all the way to the Financial District in heels and a nice suit. She'd be wilted by the time she arrived, and that would make her feel awkward and obvious, everyone staring at her disheveled condition. She took a cab to Harry's and settled at a table in the corner closest to the kitchen, assuming

Jim's table would be front and center. She told the server she had eye strain and asked that the lights in her section be turned down. *There's plenty of light, the full brightness isn't necessary, don't you think?* The server agreed to accommodate her.

The restaurant was filling. She'd been sitting there for nearly twenty minutes, eating her salad which had arrived far too quickly, threatening her plan to nibble one slender strip of raw vegetable at a time, chewing each bite ten to fifteen times. The slow and complete mastication required a lot of intense focus, which helped her feel less conspicuous. It somehow made her feel Alex wouldn't notice her if she weren't giving off a vibe of trying to hide.

Of course, she wasn't really conspicuous. That was inside her head, her own self-conscious fear of being found out. No one was paying any attention to her. The nearby lunchers hadn't even glanced in her direction. They were engaged in their own conversations, their own workplace and romantic dramas, lacking any interest in those seated around them. They sipped wine and looked over the menus for something low-calorie and filling, tempted by the steak or pasta offerings. She poked her fork into a thin slice of red onion and ate it slowly, hoping they weren't late or had canceled at the last minute. Her stomach spasmed at the thought.

31

Finally, she saw Alexandra crossing the street, the camera bag slung over her shoulder. Alexandra entered the restaurant and went to the maître d'. As usual with Trystan's clients, the details of the photography session had been pre-arranged with the manager. Alexandra was shown immediately to a spot that was farther away than Stephanie had hoped for.

Before Alexandra even sat down, Stephanie saw that she'd have to move her chair to the left, pushing it away from the table so she had room around the table leg. She inched her chair into place.

Jim and his clients arrived a few minutes later. The clients were both males, dressed in gray suits with white shirts. One wore a bright green tie, the other had his shirt collar open. They didn't look like the type that needed Jim's help making money, but what did she know.

Alexandra was already holding her compact camera, filming the three men as they settled into their chairs and ordered drinks and food without even glancing at their menus.

As Alexandra sipped wine and shot her film, Stephanie worried there wouldn't be any missteps to report back to Trystan after all. It was a perfectly innocuous task — one that it would be quite difficult to do poorly. She wasn't sure what she'd expected her nemesis to do. Intrude on the lunch, making herself too important by talking when she was supposed to be filming? Stephanie couldn't really remember what she'd expected. It had seemed like such a good idea. Now, she felt foolish and extremely concerned that Alexandra might see her. She was trapped in the corner, unable to leave once she finished her salad, which would increase the risk of being seen.

If she were caught, explaining would be uncomfortable.

She drank some of her sparkling water, hoping the sharp bite of carbonation would stimulate her mind to find a believable reason for being here.

She took a long, focused breath. No one would notice her. But even though it was unlikely, she continued to worry. The most casual glance around the restaurant and Alexandra's gaze might land right on Stephanie. Even with her hair pulled back and her more business-like clothes, she'd be immediately recognizable.

There was something about Alexandra that made you think she could figure out anything you were up to. The way she'd snuck into the office that morning. There had been no sound of the lobby door closing. Alexandra wouldn't have even known Stephanie was in the suite, so why would she open and close the outer door with such stealthy movements? There had been no sense of her presence until she spoke, scaring Stephanie out of her skin.

Alexandra was smart. That was one of the things Trystan probably liked. She was always studying the others with unconcealed curiosity. In every meeting they'd attended together, Stephanie felt the woman's cold gaze on the side of her face. Easily half the time when she turned her head, she found Alexandra looking directly at her.

Stephanie wished she could figure out a way to force

her out of the company. The desire was harsh, and she hadn't wanted to admit it, but there it was. She hated Alexandra, and she wanted her gone. She didn't give a flying flip about considering the state of Alexandra's soul. Let someone else take on that burden. She wasn't required to save every person in New York City.

The fork slipped out of her fingers and clattered on the plate as she went to pick it up. No one looked in her direction. She stabbed a piece of lettuce and ate it. Next, she stabbed a slice of egg. It immediately came apart, leaving crumbs of yolk in the dressing like baby chicks drowning in muck. If she didn't have to continue this charade, she would have pushed the plate to one side.

She took another sip of sparkling water. The glass was already half empty. She continued nibbling at her salad, watching Alexandra. The camera was trained on the three men, and Alexandra didn't seem to get tired, holding the camera steady like that.

Stephanie's plate was empty. There was no more picking at bits of soggy egg yolk to be done. The server whisked the plate away with a flourish, giving her a look that suggested she should be whisked away with just as much speed and finality.

She drank her water and let her attention drift over the people seated nearby. When the glass was empty, she flagged down the server and ordered another glass. With two lemons.

"That's all?" He waited, suggesting she was too stingy to retain the table.

"I guess a slice of the chocolate cake."

"That a' girl." He turned and hurried away.

She thought about the upcoming sugar rush and tried to

view it as a treat to herself. She'd earned it. The afternoon would be spent regretting it, but she'd earned it.

When she looked again, Alexandra was still filming.

The men appeared to be finished eating, leaning back slightly. One had moved his chair away from the table and was resting his left ankle on the opposite knee. A moment later, he readjusted his position, and all three leaned forward. Then, they were standing, shaking hands, slapping each other's shoulders and butting their fists and seemingly every sort of male farewell gesture they could come up with.

Her cake arrived, no water. She took a bite, keeping her gaze on the men.

It seemed to her that alpha male types had to do an inordinate amount of touching. She guessed it was some form of marking their territory, letting the other guy know they were in control, not afraid of aggressive physical contact, suggesting they wouldn't shrink from a fist in their face.

She turned her attention back to Alexandra. She was still holding the camera steady, unmoving in her seat, her wine glass half full.

When Stephanie looked again at Jim's table, the clients were gone, and Jim was seated, finishing his wine.

She waved at the server for the third time in as many minutes. He finally took notice and dragged himself to her table. "I find it hard to believe there's something wrong with the cake, it's our best seller."

Her mouth felt gummy with chocolate frosting. She didn't want to smile, knowing there was chocolate wedged between her teeth. "I ordered a glass of sparkling water."

He snapped his fingers. "My bad."

"With two lemons."

"No worries." He hurried away.

She looked across the room. Jim and Alexandra now stood near the entrance to the main dining area. Her camera bag was over her shoulder. They were standing closer than would be comfortable for most normal people.

The sparkling water arrived without lemons. She nodded at the server and drank the bland water, relieved to cut some of the sweetness that had consumed her and was working toward closing her throat.

As she watched. Jim put his hand on Alexandra's shoulder.

This was interesting. Was there something going on there? Yes, he'd been touchy with his clients. But that was a male thing. Touching a woman, especially one who essentially worked for you, was another matter.

Yet, Alexandra did nothing to dislodge his hand. They remained abnormally close, and she continued looking up at him, listening to whatever he was saying, which seemed to be quite involved, contorting his face into a serious expression, then a smile passing across his lips before quickly disappearing.

Stephanie held the fork a few inches from her mouth, the moist cake clinging to the prongs, afraid to maneuver it between her lips. Even a blink as she put the cake in her mouth might cause her to miss something important. She hardly wanted to breathe, fearing she might miss a slight change in position or a rapid gesture that would tell her more about what was going on across the room.

Jim's hand had moved lower on Alexandra's back, a gesture that suggested they were intimate. The touch was gentle and had an air of ownership.

Stephanie lifted her plate and held it in front of her, eating as if she were standing at a wedding reception without a table in sight, moving each bite into her mouth without looking away from the couple in the doorway.

What would Trystan think of Alexandra flirting with…? Coming on to…? Starting a relationship with…? …A client.

32

The moment my eyes were level with the floor of the landing, I saw the flowers lying on the doormat in front of my apartment. They were wrapped in pale pink paper with a wide yellow ribbon tied into a bow. I was used to the rare bouquet of flowers coming wrapped in thick cellophane with a rubber band around the stems that comes with an arrangement purchased from the supermarket or a street stand.

Inside were two dozen exquisitely perfect yellow rosebuds, just starting to open.

I didn't own a flower vase, which meant another walk to Dwayne Reed. The upside of all these short and not-so-short excursions was that my jeans, which had grown snug while I was in Australia, were much looser. It was headed toward the point where I might need to buy a few new pairs.

I crossed the landing and picked up the bouquet. I lifted the flowers to my nose. The soft petals stroked my skin. The aroma was sweet and mild, but strong enough to obliterate the faint damp and musty smell of the landing.

I put my key in the lock, turned it, and went inside. I placed the flowers on the table while I shed my bag, cotton jacket, and shoes.

The corner of a white envelope poked out from among the stems. I removed it, trying to guess who had sent them. A long-distance gift from Gavin? A gesture of friendship from

Diana? Weren't yellow roses symbolic of friendship? I thought Gavin would send white or red. Or nothing at all. He and I both knew that without proximity, we wouldn't go on together.

I lifted the flap and removed the card.

Please forgive my brutish behavior — *Rafe*

I pulled open the kitchen drawer that held scissors and a wine opener and other miscellaneous items. I dropped the card in and slammed the drawer. It seemed better to hold on to it, for now.

I changed into my comfortably loose jeans, a fitted sleeveless T-shirt, and flip-flops. They weren't the best shoes for walking, but the warm weather persisted, and I wasn't in the mood to wear anything more than absolutely necessary.

Muggy heat that persisted into October was jarring. I was already disoriented from the reversed seasons in Australia — coming from late winter into late summer, and now fall. I wanted true autumn. It was supposed to be fantastic. The best time to be in New York City without summer humidity or winter cold. Diana had informed me I would regret my eagerness for cooler weather once we were slammed with rain and the occasional snow storm.

I grabbed a handful of almonds and popped them in my mouth. Chewing, I let myself out and locked the door.

The walk was nice, the sun moving lower in the sky, but the air still pleasant enough I could look forward to a cigarette and a martini on the roof garden after my errand. As I walked, I let my mind wander over why Rafe would send an apology along with all those obviously expensive flowers. Did he think this would change my perception of him? Did Victoria know?

What was he after, aside from the obvious? I'd never experienced anything like it — a man continuing to pursue me in full view of his long-time girlfriend. This was much different from a drunken pick-up in a bar.

I wove my way through post-work and early-dinner pedestrians, thinking of my own dinner, which was not yet identified. Despite the heat, a slice or two of pizza sounded satisfying and easy. I was starving.

I'd eaten only part of a salad while I filmed Jim and his clients. Once again he wanted to linger over a glass of wine, once again his hands kept finding their way onto my body. This time, I didn't object. Why not let him think he had a chance? I could laugh later. There was one more photo session, and then I'd be done with him. I was still on the fence regarding whether I should mention it to Trystan. Mostly I continued leaning toward saying nothing.

If Jim was put out that I was rejecting him, would he turn on me and tell Trystan that I'd come on to him? If he was the type to do that, I needed to get ahead of the game. But neither did I want uncertainty about what he might do forcing me into overreacting, doing something that would make me look weak, or worse, like a liability.

Definitely pizza. I pushed open the door to Dwayne Reed.

They had a surprisingly good selection of vases, and they weren't bad looking. I chose one that was rectangular with thick, clear glass. I bought a reusable bag so I'd be able to loop the handles over my arm, leaving my hands free to carry the slices home.

The aroma of cheese and chewy dough and meat quickened my pace all the way back to my apartment and up the stairs, flip-flops slapping behind me, making me sound as if I was walking even faster than I was.

I cut the flower stems, pulled off a few leaves, and arranged the roses in the vase before filling it with water. I set them on the table, inhaled their aroma again, then opened my pizza box.

My stomach churned and growled with desire for the cheese and sausage, olives and mushrooms and onions. I ate the first slice right out of the box. When it was gone, I filled a glass with water. I still didn't bother to sit down. I stood with my hip against the kitchen counter and gobbled the next slice.

I drank the rest of my water and mixed a martini. I took a few sips so it wouldn't slosh over the sides of the glass while I climbed the stairs. I grabbed my cigarettes and lighter.

The sky was dark blue, city lights winking on all around me even though the remains of the sun still glowed on the horizon. I lifted my glass toward the skyline in a silent toast and took another sip. I lit my cigarette, inhaled, and blew out a thin stream of smoke.

There was an arrangement of wood patio chairs with a low table between them. Someone had thoughtfully left a ceramic ashtray on it. The stub of a joint and two cigarette butts were still there. I tapped my ash but didn't sit down. I was too keyed up.

I loved living here, loved looking out at the buildings and hearing the hum of traffic, even the blare of horns. I honestly liked all the walking, it just made my days feel packed to overflowing. Maybe that was good. Not as much time for sitting around smoking. Up here, smoking was exhilarating. It had its own sort of quiet.

"There you are."

I turned.

Victoria stood just outside the door leading to the stairwell. "I wondered where you went every evening." She walked toward me. "I've been looking for you."

33

I inhaled and blew out a thicker stream of smoke as if I could keep her at bay by putting a barrier between us.

She ignored the smoke hanging in the space around me and walked up to where I stood by the edge of the roof. She leaned on the half wall and turned, giving me an easy smile. "Can I have one?"

I picked up the pack and handed it to her. She removed a cigarette, and I lit it for her. She didn't smoke it, letting it dangle between her fingers.

"Too bad you don't have an extra one of those." She nodded toward my drink.

I inhaled again and blew out more smoke.

"Am I intruding?"

"It's a public space," I said.

"Well, not really public." She laughed. "Only for the people who live here."

It was clear what she meant by *not really public*, I wasn't sure why she felt the need to explain further. I took a sip of my drink. "Why did your boyfriend give me flowers?"

"Oh. Good. He did get them. I was worried because he kind of blew me off when I suggested it."

"You told him to buy me flowers?"

"Yes."

"Why?"

"He said he'd offended you. That you were upset."

"Neither of those things are true. I would describe it as annoyed."

"Whatever." She finally puffed lightly on the cigarette. She didn't seem to enjoy it much. She blew out smoke in short bursts as if she needed to be sure she expelled all of it. "He owed you an apology."

"I would say he owes *you* an apology."

"Oh, no. Not at all. He said he didn't think you believed him. We have an open relationship."

I nodded. "Is that a two-way street?"

"What do you mean?"

"Open for you as well as for him?"

"Of course." She smiled. "Mind if I have a sip of your drink."

"Yes."

She held out her hand.

"I wasn't saying *yes* you can share my drink. What I was saying was, *yes*, I do mind."

She laughed. "Okay. No worries."

We smoked in silence until my cigarette was gone. With each inhalation, I could feel her wanting to talk, yet quivering with uncertainty over which direction to take. It seemed as if she and Rafe wanted something from me, but what on earth could it be? Possibly I was overthinking, possibly I was paranoid. It might simply be friendship. I didn't mind hanging out with them, as long as they learned to keep some boundaries, but they seemed to have no sense of what that entailed.

"Maybe we can come up here and have martinis together some time," she said. She held her cigarette over the edge of the wall and tapped it, letting her ash drift wherever it pleased, ignoring the ashtray I'd carried to the ledge of the roof.

"From what I've been told, it won't be warm enough for much longer. It could change any day."

"True. But when it's warm like this, you think it's going to last forever."

I took a few sips of my drink and lit another cigarette. "Why do you and Rafe have this so-called open relationship?"

"Life is long. Who wants to be locked into the same person for seventy years?"

I saw her point, but usually, once two people start living together, they accept some sort of long-term situation. Otherwise, you moved out and got your own place. Maybe working together and sleeping together, eating and going out together was too much.

"So you both see other people?"

"We don't date. But yeah, if an opportunity for sex arises and one of us is interested…why not?"

Why not. Still, there was something off about it. My brain felt knotted, knowing that I agreed with her and yet not believing it was quite that simple in their case.

"I can't see pinning someone down," she said. "What's the point?"

"So it's more him than you?"

"What do you expect? Boys will be boys. We can't legislate that, can we." She laughed.

"You can expect someone to respect what you want."

"He respects me."

I wasn't sure he did, but neither did I understand a woman who pushed her boyfriend to give flowers, a very expensive bouquet of flowers, to the woman next door. I couldn't understand a woman who told her boyfriend he'd blown it in his effort to get something going with me. I waited to see if she would say more. She didn't.

I smashed my cigarette into the ashtray. I carried the ashtray back to the table and sat down to finish my drink.

She followed, sitting across from me. "I sure wish I had a drink."

"Go get one. You don't have to stay up here."

"I'm keeping you company."

"It's not necessary."

"So do you want to go out for a drink? Just you and me?"

I considered her invitation. I hadn't gone out at all in the evening, except my dinner with her and Rafe. "Sure."

"Friday?"

"That works." I ate two of my olives. A breeze had sprung up, and it was starting to get cool. The leaves on a small tree planted in an enormous ceramic pot rattled against each other. The sound was quite autumn-like. As if it had heard my thoughts, the tree released four leaves which fluttered to the ground.

"It's awkward, getting flowers from your boyfriend. And now that I know you put him up to it…what's going on?"

"Nothing. He likes you. He acted like a little shit because he's intimidated by you, I think."

Her answer was senseless.

"You seem different," she said.

"Different from what?"

"You don't seem like you're from the midwest at all."

"I'm not."

"You're not so innocent as I thought at first." She gave

me a crafty smile.

I ate my last olive, chewing carefully. "You seem to have a rather biased view of the Midwest. It's not like everyone who grows up there, or lives there, is the same. And it's not like people are a certain way depending on what region they're from."

She smiled, her bright teeth white against her face as the darkness settled over both of us.

34

There hadn't been a single day when Stephanie wasn't the first one in the office. No matter how early I came in, she was there, as if she wanted to keep an eye on me.

When I'd caught her in Trystan's office, she'd recovered nicely, acting as if it was no big deal, acting as if she just wandered in to look for a book. I doubted that. Why did she need one of his books? And if there was something she needed to know for her job, couldn't she Google it, or wouldn't she have already read the book?

I couldn't figure out what she'd been looking for. It was not a book. The place was absolutely pristine — no file cabinets to rifle through, a locked computer, just those few books, and some ancient DVDs.

Her recovery from being startled had been smooth, and I knew she thought she'd hidden it well, but the guilt seeped across the surface of her eyes and gave her lips a strained, awkward twist.

Maybe she had a crush on him and just liked being in his office, touching the things he'd touched, feeling his presence, inhaling whatever scent he left behind.

But if it wasn't a crush, did that mean she also spent time in my office, touching the few things I had there? Did she fondle the polished stones I kept in a small glass bowl? Did she run her fingers along the picture frame that held a photograph of Sydney Harbor, and the other, displaying Tess and me at an outdoor cafe in Melbourne?

I'd thought about trying to beat her into the office, but it wasn't worth giving up my run for a game like that. It felt great to be back to running every single day, lifting weights three days a week. With that and all the walking, I felt healthy and full of energy. Of course, all that energy was fueling my curiosity — about my unsettling neighbors and my nosey co-worker.

As I entered our suite, I heard the tapping of computer keys. The sound seemed to penetrate the walls, echoing around the short hallway, rising up to the ceiling and falling down like rain splattering on a hard surface.

I went to Stephanie's office door. I studied the nameplate on her door and waited for her to look up.

"What do you need?" She continued typing, obviously aware of me the entire time but her rhythm gave no indication she'd been at all startled by my presence.

"I was looking at your nameplate. We both have male names that are modified to become female."

She removed her hands from the keyboard. "I don't."

"Steph is the first part of Stephen."

"It's not pronounced the same."

"I realize that, but it's the same form."

"So what?"

"I was just commenting. That's all."

"And did you want something?"

She'd been working overtime to be friendly when we met for breakfast. Now, her tone and the position of her body were cold and brittle.

"I didn't want anything. Just stopping by to say hello."

"Hello." She smiled. She pushed her chair away from

her desk. She laced her fingers together and stretched her arms in front of her. "I was actually thinking about you."

"Why?"

"We should go to lunch," she said. "Or maybe something else. A gallery. A museum…get to know each other better."

"Maybe."

"You're the one who came by. Now you're too good for me?"

"I didn't say that at all."

"You said *maybe*. It implies that you need to think about it, or that you'll get together unless something more interesting pops up."

"I wasn't implying that."

"It's how you came across."

"It wasn't what I intended."

"That doesn't matter."

"I think it does matter." I ran my finger over her nameplate, feeling the depression where the letters were cut into the plastic.

She glared at me. "Why don't you like me?"

"Why would you think that?"

"Don't answer a question with a question. You didn't disagree, which means you don't like me, and I have no idea why. We need to work together."

"I thought we were working together just fine."

"I feel a chill from you."

"I'll try to make sure I don't give off a chill." I smiled and moved out of the doorway.

As I stepped back, she stood and walked around the desk. "Why don't we grab coffee right now? We could do some window-shopping." She smiled. She lifted her hand to her breastbone and fingered her cross. Sometimes, when she touched it like that, I felt she wanted to impale me with it.

I was probably over-reacting, imagining I sensed something that wasn't there, and yet, it *was* there, shimmering at the front of my mind. "The stores aren't open yet."

"I said window-shopping, silly goose."

Eight in the morning was not the time I was thinking about shopping, even if it only meant looking through windows. At the same time, I did need winter clothes. I was woefully unprepared for an East Coast ice storm.

It wouldn't hurt to wander past fifteen-foot windows populated by plastic women wearing gorgeous coats and cashmere scarves and nice leather boots. I supposed leather boots wouldn't do well in slush and water, but the image gripped me. "Sure."

She secured her computer, and we went out, locking the main door behind us.

"Don't worry." She put her hand on my arm, pressing her fingers into my bone. "Trystan won't be mad if we aren't back until ten-thirty or so. He doesn't mind what hours we're in the office, as long as the work gets done."

I knew this but said nothing.

She let go of my arm. "He's a great boss, isn't he?"

"Yes. So far."

"Do you have doubts?"

"No."

"Then why did you say *so far*?"

"Because I've only been here a few weeks. As far as I've experienced him, he's great."

"But you expect that to change?"

"No."
"You're confusing."
We glided to the first floor in silence.

35

Stephanie and I walked three blocks and stopped at a Starbucks. We ordered lattes. She chose the pumpkin spice flavor, I went for a plain drink. I don't like fruit flavors in my martinis, and I don't like vegetables or candy intruding on the spectacular taste of coffee and cream.

While the coffee cooled enough to sip, we sat looking out the window at the pedestrians hurrying past. Stephanie talked about our clients. She asked who was next on the list for a photography session.

It was odd that she asked me since she did all the scheduling, but I told her. Another financial guy. In fact, his office was in the same building as Jim's. She knew this also but pretended surprise.

We took a few sips of coffee and then headed out. We walked to Fifth Avenue where we strolled past massive plate glass windows revealing stylishly-dressed and dramatically-posed mannequins, some of them headless.

"I can't really afford to shop in these stores," she said. "But I like looking."

We made pretty good money working for Trystan, or at least I did. I assumed her salary was similar, but I didn't push. Maybe she had other expenses I didn't know about. Maybe her apartment was in a more upscale area. Maybe she had an invalid mother, for all I knew about her.

She laughed. "Even if I could afford it, I don't think I

want to spend twelve hundred dollars or more on a coat, right?"

I thought about my very nice salary and my shocking rent. Part of the shock had come from not having paid rent when I lived in San Francisco or Sydney.

Actually paying the deposit and signing the lease had given me a rare moment of second-guessing myself, seeing what I was committing to. It was aggravating, knowing how much I had to lay out every thirty days for electricity, the internet connection, all the things other people had so nicely taken care of for me in the recent past, allowing me to build a very nice nest egg. And still, I was nowhere near the amount of money I needed for my eventual dream of a magnificent home with peaceful gardens and a breathtaking view.

Buying expensive leather boots and a soft, thick wool coat, and other winter accessories, not to mention sweaters and a few pairs of leggings was appealing. Of course, I had a good supply of California-cold-weather clothes, but there's a constant need for updates. And now, there was a need for more warmth, and always, the pure desire.

I wanted the beautiful clothes we were strolling past. But I didn't want to spend my whole salary living in the moment.

I don't want a slow growth of financial resources that takes decades. I want my amazing home and more freedom and control over my life while I'm young enough to enjoy it. That means keeping some of my desires for other creature comforts under control.

I couldn't bear the thought of saving money for thirty years before I had enough to get what I wanted. I was lucky to be paid as well as I had been in all my jobs, but somehow, I needed to get to a place where I could accelerate things. Ideas for how that might happen eluded me.

I turned away from the plate glass window. "How long have you lived in New York?"

"Five years."

"And do you still like it as much as when you first arrived?"

"I love it."

"It's expensive."

"I share an apartment, so it's not horribly unaffordable. Expensive, but I'm doing okay."

I nodded.

"I don't know very much about you," she said. She slowed her pace and turned to look at me. She gave me a hopeful smile.

"There's not a lot to know."

"I doubt that."

I put my hands in my pockets.

"Like, do you consider yourself a religious person?"

I'd been expecting it all this time, yet when she spoke, I was startled. I should have kept my eye more firmly fixed on that gold cross. "No."

Her fingers crept to the icon around her neck. As if the thing had driven ideas into her mind like a stake into a vampire's heart, she began firing questions at me. She wanted to know where I'd grown up, where I went to college, what degree I had, why I didn't have a degree, what I thought of LA, how many boyfriends I'd had, who were my best friends, where did they live, was I close with my parents, what about my siblings?

My brief and vague answers did nothing to stop or even

slow the deluge of questions. She kept on while we walked past stores and looped back, passing the same stores again, this time on the opposite edge of the sidewalk where we couldn't look closely at the enticing displays.

She wanted to know whether I thought lying was okay, and what about shop-lifting? "Do you think it's okay to sleep with a married man?"

"It depends."

"On what?" She stopped and glared at me.

"It's usually too complicated. But I can't say there aren't circumstances where someone would want to do that."

"So you're okay with cheating?"

"Why are we talking about this?"

"I'm trying to get to know you."

"Are you?"

"We work together. I like to know who I'm working with."

The questions continued — about going to church and being afraid of death, about marriage and children…

There was something about the tone of her questions, the constant stroking of that cross, that made me feel I was back in high school, listening to Mr. B's questions about dying that night and being allowed into heaven.

36

Portland

For three nights, I sat with my pen grazing the pages of a spiral notebook, trying to figure out how I was going to write a speech that would hold on to my self-respect and get Mr. B off my back.

My Algebra teacher was fond of Venn diagrams. She talked about them constantly, even when it didn't apply to the segment we were working on. When she talked casually before class about world events or sports, she often invoked the Venn Diagram. She was obsessed with the thing.

I listed the things Mr. B wanted covered — *the need for salvation* and *the value of the evangelism program*. On the opposite side of the page, I wrote the word *skepticism*. I drew a circle around Mr. B's requirements and another around skepticism. There was no overlap.

I tore out the page and ripped it to shreds.

Normally, I would write essays or speeches for school on the family computer, but I didn't want the curious eyes of my parents looking over my shoulders. All of my brothers were in college at this point in time, so no one knew what had happened during my improvised scene with Mr. B.

I filled an entire page with doodles. I tried writing a poem about knocking on doors, selling religious dogma as if it were a new miracle household cleaner that removed stains from carpet and streaks from windows and germs from the bathroom sink. I tore out and destroyed that sheet as well.

I copied the entire Sermon on the Mount into my notebook, imagining I could get away with reading that and calling it my speech. Clearly, he'd never accept it, but it did push my thoughts in a new direction.

The computer was in a small alcove off the kitchen. If I searched for commendable topics or prepared homework, it didn't matter whether my parents passed by and glanced at the screen. I went downstairs and woke the computer. Inside the box at the center of the Google homepage I typed — Jonathan Edwards evangelist.

We'd learned about Jonathan Edwards during Wednesday night Bible classes the previous summer. The summer mid-week classes featured lectures about notable church leaders, supplemented with outside assignments to read some of their books and sermons.

Jonathan Edwards is known for two things.

First, he was the main guy who shaped the first Great Awakening in the United States during the 1730s and 40s — the beginning of the Evangelical church movement. Since Pure Truth Tabernacle was solidly in the evangelical camp, we were instructed to look to Reverend Edwards as a brilliant and anointed man. He'd helped Americans realize the truth of heaven and hell and salvation and damnation and good and evil. His revival theology taught that religious conversion wasn't only intellectual belief in correct doctrine but had to be accompanied by a physical change in one's heart — being born again.

Secondly, Mr. Edwards is famous for writing and delivering a sermon with the heart-warming title, *Sinners In the*

Hands of An Angry God. We'd all been told to read this sermon and given a true-false test on what it had to say.

Google brought up the biography of John E and conveniently linked to his sermon which definitely deserved to be categorized as an example of hellfire and brimstone. In fact, it could be considered the very definition of hellfire and brimstone...

The pit is prepared, the fire is made ready, the furnace is now hot, ready to receive them; the flames do now rage and glow. The glittering sword is whet, and held over them, and the pit hath opened its mouth under them.

I was never sure how this aligned with the loving god we were told about, but that's a story for another time.

I printed the sermon and brought the pages back to my bedroom. My parents never stopped by to see what I was doing and didn't seem to hear the printer whirring and cranking out ten sheets of paper.

I flipped to the final two paragraphs — a full page and a half on their own. I copied that section into my notebook, adding additional paragraph breaks where I thought they belonged. I underlined the admonition to *fly from the wrath to come*, it seemed important. I tore out the pages, stapled them together, and wrote my name on the top line.

There was no way Mr. B would believe it was mine, not after the first sentence. And it wasn't at all what he'd asked for, although a Venn Diagram could be made of his request and the sermon. Giving it to him would buy me another week, and it would put him on the spot. Possibly, if I was very lucky, he might give up trying to punish me and work out a different tactic for asserting his power over me.

I folded the sheets of ragged-edged notebook paper in

thirds and stuffed them in an envelope. I licked it, sealed it, and wrote *Mr. B* on the front.

Wednesday night, I handed the envelope to him. He gave me a confident smile, and I gave him one in return. "I hope you like it," I said.

"Did you pray over it?"

I looked down at my feet as if I were humble and liked to keep my thoughts private, not wanting to talk about my prayer life.

"You shouldn't be ashamed of anything related to your faith," he said. He tucked his first two fingers under my chin and gently lifted my head until my gaze met his. "I'll look forward to reading this."

I turned to go.

He put his hand on my shoulder. "Thank you for doing this without giving me attitude. I'm proud of you for submitting to the will of God. You'll be blessed for this. In the long run, I expect you'll be one of our best teen evangelists. You have a very strong will, and you have confidence speaking in front of others. God has given you some incredible gifts."

I held his gaze, wondering if he would say more, digging a hole for himself before he'd read the speech.

He squeezed my shoulder, then let go. He tucked the envelope into the inside pocket of his jacket. He was more wary than I'd realized.

37

New York City

Victoria suggested we meet in Greenwich Village. I wondered again about the *openness* of their relationship. Did Rafe not know we were going out together? Meeting at the bar suggested she was hiding it from him. Wouldn't it make more sense to take the subway together? I had to go home to change clothes anyway. We would be leaving our apartments at the same time. It made no sense.

But when I opened my front door, the landing was deserted and silent. The stairwell was also strangely empty of people coming and going on a Friday evening.

I got off the subway at the Washington Square station. I walked slowly, feeling the foot traffic surge around me. I wore high heels, black jeans, and a black sleeveless turtleneck. I had on a thin peach-colored sweater, perfect for the current temperature, but probably too cold for when I would emerge from the bar in an hour or three. Still, I hadn't wanted to drag a warmer jacket with me. It was only two blocks to the subway. I'd survive.

The bar was dark and loud. Well, not entirely dark. Bright lights shone on the shelves of alcohol. The tiny tables near the windows were also lit with recessed lights, but the rest of the interior was so dark, it took a moment for my eyes to adjust, even after the dusky light outside.

Victoria was seated at one of the window tables, half a glass of champagne in front of her and a plate smeared with dark sauce, but empty of whatever appetizer it had contained. Along with the plate, the multiple lipgloss imprints on her champagne flute suggested she'd been there for a while.

I slid into the chair across from her. She reached toward the chiller beside her, pulled out the bottle, and moved it toward the empty flute near the window.

"I'm not a champagne drinker," I said.

"Everyone likes champagne." She lifted the bottle higher, poised over the glass.

"No they don't."

"Of course they do. Champagne is how the world celebrates. Besides, it has fewer calories than wine, and a lot less than most mixed drinks. It's perfect."

"I'm not going to drink something I don't like just to cut calories. I don't care about that."

"You're the only woman alive who doesn't love champagne."

"I doubt that." I turned, looking for a server.

"I got this whole bottle. You have to have some."

I turned back to her. I held her gaze. Her wrist wobbled slightly, trying to keep the heavy bottle poised for pouring.

A server arrived beside our table.

"A vodka martini. Grey Goose. Three olives. Straight up."

The server turned away before Victoria could mimic Rafe's propensity for ordering other people's drinks despite their objections.

She topped off her glass. "Why don't you want champagne? You're spoiling the fun."

"I told you why."

She shoved the bottle into the silver canister. "Do you want something to eat?"

I nodded. I picked up the small menu, a single sheet of paper that felt like parchment. "I'll have the stuffed mushrooms."

"Should we share? I can order another plate of egg rolls."

"Sounds good." I returned the menu to the rack.

My martini arrived, and Victoria offered a toast to *Nothing. Nothing at all.* She smiled.

While I sipped the martini, she told me the story of how she and Rafe had met which was standard stuff — a bar, an instant attraction, witty flirting. The last part was difficult to imagine.

From the story of their moving in together, she segued to the place on the Upper East Side they were planning to buy soon, and her father who had had a stroke at a young age and needed round-the-clock care. She was so lucky she could afford it, she said. She told me about her plans to decorate her new place and how they would have a dedicated office with cutting-edge equipment instead of a living room littered with computers, a router, and backup drives.

"Isn't the Upper East Side kind of pricey?"

She smiled. "Yes."

"Sounds like your gambling is going well."

She laughed. "I know you want to believe it's gambling, but it's not. We have a lot of data models to help us make decisions. Of course there's some risk, some guesswork, but no more than any other business where you have to forecast sales, where you can't predict how customers will behave from one quarter to the next."

I shrugged. "It still sounds like gambling."

"That's probably because you've never seen it in action."

"Could be." I moved the olives around inside my glass. I lifted the glass to my lips and took a sip. I hadn't realized how tense I was after the morning's grilling from Stephanie. It had hung over me all day like the lead blanket they place over your body when the dentist takes X-rays. A cold weight, pressing down, feeling as if it's suppressing your breathing, retarding the functioning of your organs.

"It's miraculous. It really is. Scooping up small profits from a hundred different sources is fun. You feel like you're gathering all these tiny pebbles, and before you realize it, you have a beautiful jar filled with only the things you want."

"If you want to collect pebbles."

She sipped her champagne. "You should come by and see our set-up. If you come when the market's open, I can show you how it works."

Despite my views of what she was doing, the offer was intriguing. She was right. I didn't know much about it. And buying a house on the Upper East Side? When they were in their early thirties, possibly younger? Those places were worth millions.

I popped a stuffed mushroom into my mouth.

I was not inclined to sit in front of a computer all day, watching charts shift their colored lines, telling me what was up or down, trying to guess when I should buy or sell. It sounded like a recipe for a headache. I wanted to find a way to accelerate my income, but I wasn't going to go in for a pyramid scheme or day trading or any of the other supposed ways to quickly rake in cash.

If I wanted to do that, I might as well learn to play high-stakes poker. From what I've heard, it appears to require more skill than what she and Rafe were involved with. All she was doing was guessing when things would dip and rise and trying to stay ahead of that curve.

Still. A house on the Upper East Side. Full-time care for her father.

I barely had enough to buy a house in the midwest, where she kept insisting I'd be right at home. Even affording that was unlikely. Maybe a summer cottage, with a sagging roof and weeds crowding the porch, peeling linoleum and wind knifing through openings where the house was pulling away from the window frames.

"You're curious, I can tell," she said.

"Can you?" I ate another mushroom and took several sips of my drink.

"Are you sure you don't want some champagne?" She nudged the empty glass closer to my martini glass.

"Stop it," I said. "That's one thing you and Rafe have in common. You don't seem to know what a boundary is."

She smiled. She pushed her hair off her forehead, even though it was too short to truly fall across her brow. It seemed like a gesture that lingered from a longer hairstyle. She reached across with the fingers that had been in her hair and grabbed a mushroom. I pushed the plate toward her so she could reach more easily.

"Why are you so opposed to day trading? Do you have some religious hang-up about gambling and you're projecting it onto day trading? Which is not gambling. I don't know how many times I have to say that."

She hadn't said it all that many times, and it absolutely was like gambling. Not unlike betting on a sports team. Sure, it's not the same as spinning a roulette wheel or tapping buttons on a slot machine, but it's closely related.

"Well, *do* you? Despite the midwest thing, you don't come across as religious."

"I'm not."

"Then why are you such a prude about a decent and honest way to make money? Do you think everyone working in finance is gambling? Lots of people make a lot of money in the stock market. It's how America works. It's how the entire world functions. You invest in businesses, and you make a return on your investment. It's not even remotely like gambling."

"Traders and fund managers study economics, they delve into the details of the businesses they choose to invest in. They don't just guess."

She took a long swallow of champagne and re-filled her glass, following that with a few more sips. "Do you want to order more food? Or go somewhere else?"

"This is good. I could go for more mushrooms. And some of those tempura long beans."

We ordered both, along with bruschetta. I ordered another martini. We talked about movies and TV shows. She talked about baseball. Then she launched into the detailed plans for decorating their new home.

Hearing about paint colors and custom furniture, draperies, and luxurious bathroom remodels made me more curious about how exactly they were making all this money. It sounded too good to be true. And it sounded unstable. Your income could sky-rocket and then crash, remaining bottomed out for weeks or months, possibly even years, because so much seemed to depend on timing. If you missed your timing and couldn't get your rhythm back, then what?

At the same time, I needed a more lucrative income. That home living in my fantasies was no closer than it had been three years earlier. I wanted a life that was beholden to no one. She made it all sound so good. Except for the aroma of gambling, and the thought of sitting alone at a computer half the day every single day of the week.

The appetizer plates were empty. One olive lingered in the bottom of my glass. Victoria emptied the rest of the champagne into her flute. "I will be so glad to get out of that apartment and have some room to breathe!" She sipped her champagne. "Just wait until you've been there a year or two like we have. Three years! The noise…oh my god! I don't think I've slept through the night since I moved in."

I ate my final olive.

I couldn't decide whether the change in her tone from friendly to smug was caused by drinking an entire bottle of champagne, or a desire to make herself better than me. I could have gone either way. But with her boyfriend lusting after the girl next door, I was inclined toward the second.

38

On the surface, everything about Pete Torkenson echoed Jim Kohn. Their offices were located in the same skyscraper. They had the same glamorous and slightly seductive type for a receptionist. They had the same palatial personal space, and they dressed in similar ways, which I suppose is true of everyone who works on Wall Street. It's true of any part of the business world.

Any man, really.

Women have a fantastic advantage over men when it comes to clothing.

Men can choose slacks and a jacket, in an array of approximately five colors. They have two or three shoe styles with minimal variations in the sole and laces and cut of the leather. They have a few options for facial hair and a rainbow of colors for neckties, and that's *it*.

Women get thousands of shoe styles, they can choose dresses or pants, leggings or capri pants, heels or flats. We get jewelry for our necks and wrists and fingers and ears. I would be truly bored if I were a man. How do they bear it? Looking into those uniform closets every single day of their lives? On the weekends they have a few more options — sandals or athletic shoes. If they work in some industries, they can get away with an earring or two, a bracelet or hair dyed in a primary color.

I suppose most straight men don't care about those

limitations. Maybe they don't want to express their creativity and their personality in their appearance. Maybe they're happy with gray, blue, and black, the occasional dark brown, or a beige for summer. I've never asked a guy. I suppose I should.

There was one feature that suggested Pete was not at all like Jim — his smile was genuine.

Within minutes, I knew he was a nice guy. When I shook his hand, my enthusiasm for my new job was restored. This could be exciting and satisfying, helping people who deserved to find all the success their hearts desired.

Pete's grip was warm and firm, with no attempt to hang on too long, driving the other person to squirm her way free. It wasn't the kind of handshake some men have where they attempt to fondle your wrist or stroke your thumb, looking for a read on whether you might be interested in sex. Men offering those handshakes don't see a human being, they see a female body they want to strip naked. Every move is geared toward determining if, how, and when.

He settled behind his desk, almost as large and just as bare as Jim's. Trystan and I sat in the armchairs facing him, also nearly identical to the arrangement in Jim's office. Maybe every executive office in the entire forty-seven floors was designed the same way — a corner space, over-sized, lots of non-work comforts like alcohol and a full bathroom, and the massive desk with chairs for the supplicants.

Trystan went over the assessment tests Pete had taken and explained my role in greater detail. Trystan asked Pete to review what he was hoping to gain from hiring us. Of course, Trystan had detailed notes from his initial interview with Pete, and I'd read the notes from that interview. Unlike with Jim, Trystan wanted me to hear it in Pete's own words. Maybe he'd come around to my way of thinking. This kind of exchange would give me a sense of the guy that wasn't just words on a page, filtered through Trystan's perception. It gave me an opportunity to study his face and posture while he spoke about what he thought was lacking in his professional life. This was supposed to guide the direction I took with photography and filming.

"I'd say my primary goal is to balance my strengths and weaknesses," Pete said. "I'm naturally conservative, in all areas of my life, really. That bent has controlled my professional life. Ultimately, it hurts my clients. Part of investing is taking measured risk. I'm overly focused on sure bets."

I wanted to laugh. Even a successful fund manager talked about making bets. Victoria was deluding herself if she believed what she did required intelligence and skill without any sort of luck or chance.

Trystan nodded. "You respect money."

"Yes. But you can respect money and take risks at the same time. It's a different kind of respect. I believe I'm doing a disservice to my clients by playing it too safe, remaining ultra conservative in all situations. I need to have a stronger vision, and I can't let downside concerns drive all my decisions. I can't let an over-developed sense of caution dictate how I advise my clients. I tend to see all downside and I low-ball the upside. I'm truly shocked when the upside is better than anticipated." He laughed.

Trystan encouraged him to continue talking, to provide a summary of his life story.

Pete was the oldest of five children, so from the start, he was set up by the gods of birth order to have a greater than average sense of responsibility, at least if you believe that sort of thing. He laughed when he said this, which suggested he absolutely believed it. The belief in fluffy forces directing your fate didn't seem in keeping with a business and economics background — guidance and insight should come from logical thought and analysis, spreadsheets and economic principles. Those are the forces that determine outcomes.

His parents divorced when he was thirteen. He was given responsibility for cooking dinner before his mother arrived home from work, often not until seven-thirty in the evening. There were no complaints from his siblings that their meals rotated between spaghetti, frozen lasagna, tacos in pre-formed shells, hot dogs, and fish sticks.

Because they were on a tight budget, Pete never owned a car, forced to bum rides from his high school buddies. He went to a state college that was decent, but chosen because it was affordable, not because it offered a platinum education and the associated networking advantages. His success had been achieved without that leg up.

His mother was Catholic, careful with money, and kept her thoughts to herself. She insisted their family problems remain within the family.

"She always quoted the Godfather." Pete laughed. "Never let anyone outside the family know what the family is thinking." He grinned. "Yeah, all those things fed into a conservative view of the world, or…cautious might be a better word."

As he had with Jim, Trystan left me alone with Pete for the initial photographs.

When the door closed behind Trystan, Pete turned and looked at me. He was quiet for a moment, which stretched into two. Finally he spoke, his hand still on the door handle as if he needed to orient himself to the room. "I'm not too sure about the photographs."

"You should have expressed your concern to Trystan."

He laughed. "It's part of the deal, right? But I don't see how it helps."

I unzipped the bag and pulled out my camera. I attached the flash.

"Seeing that camera thing makes it more threatening."

"I really wish you'd brought this up with Trystan."

"Jim said it was absurd."

"Jim?" I knew who he meant, but I didn't want to stick my foot in it.

"Jim Kohn. I told him what sort of services Trystan provides."

I nodded.

"He said the girl taking photographs was...invasive."

"Was I?"

He shrugged. "Just repeating what he told me."

"Well, why don't you try it out for yourself. And trust all aspects of the program Trystan designed."

"He seems to know what he's doing," Pete said.

"That's what all our clients say."

"Except Jim."

"Did Jim say that?"

"About the photographs," he said as if that offered clarity.

I removed the lens cap. "I shouldn't talk about a client, but..."

He let go of the door handle and walked toward his desk.

I turned slowly. "The results are more useful if you aren't self-conscious, trying to perform."

He laughed.

A lot of his laughs had a nervous, rough edge to them, so it seemed he was quite self-conscious. It would be hard not to be, with someone pointing a large lens at you and snapping photographs when you were simply sitting or standing with nothing much to do, not even the distraction of posing as if for a head shot. Knowing your flaws in posture and facial expressions would be scrutinized and analyzed would make it worse. Still, they'd signed up for it.

"Try to relax and forget I'm here. Sit at your desk and check your email. That should be enough distraction to put me out of your mind."

He did as he was told. I snapped quite a few photographs, pleased when I saw the manufactured smile begin to fade, the email capturing his mind, pulling him away from the camera and away from me.

39

Stephanie sat at her desk, hands idle in her lap. Her ears and all her attention were tuned to the main door of their suite. When she heard the click of the handle, she ran her fingertips across her cheeks, pressing gently to calm herself.

She heard Trystan's footsteps, soft on the carpeted floor, heard the rattle of his keys as he dropped them into his pocket. She felt the change in temperature as he moved toward the hallway, his body tracked in her mind.

Timing it perfectly, she rose from her chair, coffee cup in hand. She reached the doorway to her office just as he did. "Hi, there." She lifted her cup. "Heading for a refill."

He nodded.

"Can I get you some?"

"I'm good." He moved around her.

Instead of crossing to the break room, she circled around him, walking beside him to his office.

He glanced at her. "What's up?"

She took a quick, sharp breath. "I've been debating this for a while, but I really think I need to tell you something."

"Out with it."

"Can we sit in your office?"

"I thought you wanted coffee?"

She laughed, which turned to a giggle. She felt her face redden. The conversation had been all worked out in her mind. But feeling the intensity and the reality of his presence, which had not been worked out in her mind — because how can it be? — was making her nervous. It was impossible to anticipate the reality of another person. She could imagine a conversation, plan all of her thoughts and the order in which she'd reveal them, but she could never get the sense of that other presence ahead of time — those eyes and his heartbeat and the sound of his breathing and…She took a deeper breath. "Yes. I do. But then, do you have a minute?"

"Sure." He continued to his office.

She hurried to the break room, filled her mug with stale coffee, and dumped in cream without bothering to stir it. She scurried down the hall, sipping the coffee to keep it from sloshing out. As a result, she seared her upper lip and the tip of her tongue. Great. That would make it more difficult to remain cool and business-like, feeling that hot swollen tongue touching her teeth, bumping against her tender lip, affecting the sound of every word she uttered.

Once she was seated in the chair facing Trystan's desk, she took another sip, resisting the urge to screw up her face in disgust at the thick, sour taste.

"What can I do for you." He smiled.

He didn't turn to his computer or glance down at his phone. She loved that about him. He was one of the most attentive people she knew. When she talked to him, she felt as if she was the only person in the room. Of course, in this case, she was, but even when others were nearby, his attention was solidly on the person in front of him. You never felt he was thinking about what interesting things might be waiting in his inbox or spilling across the web — other work issues, new clients, messages from friends or his daughter, world news…Everyone else seemed to have their minds in three places at once. Trystan, when he looked at you, was all yours.

"I feel uncomfortable telling you this, but I think it needs to be said." She fingered her cross, looking to God for strength as she usually did.

He waited.

"I think Alexandra is having an inappropriate relationship with Jim Kohn."

Trystan's face was a mask. He didn't register shock or disgust or even disbelief. Had he already known? If he had, he'd be less inclined to value her loyalty, her willingness to turn on another woman for the good of their business. But she wasn't turning on another woman, not really. She was being truthful. She was thinking of their clients, and their reputation.

What would people think if they knew someone was flirting with, or seducing a client? Or whatever you wanted to call it. No one would sign up for their services. They'd be considered sleazy at best, and unethical at worst. Or was that the same thing? She wasn't sure. Unethical seemed worse than sleazy though.

"Why do you think this?"

"I saw them. Touching."

"Saw them where?"

"When she was filming his lunch."

"How did you see that?"

She didn't like the question. It was clear what was behind it. He was turning on her, considering whether she was trying to make trouble. But she wasn't stupid. She'd worked this part out in her mind. "I had a meeting with my attorney." She swallowed the lie. "It's right near Harry's where they were meeting."

Trystan nodded.

He was off track. It didn't matter how she'd seen them. "They were *touching* each other."

"Touching, how?"

"She was giving him this look…" Her face grew warm, exactly as she'd hoped it would, telling Trystan she was embarrassed. She'd decided not to start with Jim because this was on Alexandra. Trystan needed to see it as her fault, her misstep, her poor judgment. Her slutty-ness.

Trystan smiled with a vague, absent look in his eyes.

"Jim had his hand on her lower back. She was leaning into him."

"It could be innocent enough."

"It wasn't."

"You don't know that. I'm more troubled by your reaction."

"What? Why?" She touched the arms of her cross with her thumb and forefinger, pressing against the hard crossbar, trying to steady herself. This was not the response she'd imagined during the night when she lay in bed, eyes closed, trying to conjure up the feel of his presence so she could fully practice what she'd wanted to say. She felt as if she'd gone far off the track.

"People, even colleagues, occasionally touch one another. It's a human response. And you know full well that what we're doing here is very personal. Our clients invite us into their lives and allow us to see their vulnerabilities. There's going to be an emotional connection at times. In fact, I expect that and I'm concerned about our effectiveness when there isn't a deep connection."

She stared at him. He was full of crap. She was so sure

of it, she almost thought that other ubiquitous word that was so disgusting. "You don't think there's something a little...I don't know...off about her? She almost seems...evil."

Now, his expression changed. Dramatically. She'd made a mistake, and she was immediately aware that it might be one she couldn't recover from. Why had she said that? Used that word? People didn't talk in those polarizing terms. It was considered impolite, unhip, old-fashioned.

"Is there an issue I should be concerned about?"

"What do you mean?"

"I don't want any kind of backstabbing or pettiness here. I've made that very clear. I won't tolerate it."

"I'm sorry, I just..."

"Please treat your colleagues with professional respect. And don't go reading into situations you know nothing about. Seeing things that aren't there. It makes you sound unstable. Understood?"

She nodded.

He lifted his chin toward the door, then turned his attention to his computer.

She went out, closing the door quietly behind her. As it closed, she realized her coffee mug was still on his desk. But so what? He could take it back to the break room. He'd practically chased her out of his office. And he'd made her feel like a troublemaker. She was not.

Alexandra *was* evil. Stephanie could feel it, and Trystan's response proved it. That woman had cast some kind of spell on him. Not as in actual witchcraft, but she was manipulating him. Evil was not too strong of a word at all.

40

After my photo session with Pete, I grabbed a hot dog from a street vendor and ate it on the subway. It wasn't the ideal ambiance, even for a street dog, but I was starving. It was one-forty-five, and all I'd had for breakfast was a cup of oatmeal before my run at five o'clock.

I was so hungry, I wasn't very neat about opening my mouth for each bite, and several pieces of sauerkraut dribbled out of the bun onto my skirt. I picked them off with a napkin and wadded it into a ball, hoping I didn't end up smelling of pickled cabbage.

When the hot dog was gone, the woman seated across from me smiled. She had gray hair, and her face was heavily powdered, making her skin take on the appearance of crumpled paper when her mouth curved into a smile. "Hungry?"

"Famished."

"You sure enjoyed it." She turned her attention back to the smartphone in her left hand, and I spent the next three stops admiring an old woman for her tech savvy, even if smartphones don't technically require that much savvy. She wasn't put off by something new and completely unfamiliar, something that hadn't existed until she was in the final stretch of middle age. She tapped and swiped and pinched with the best of them.

Every step of the three-block walk from the subway to

the office was pleasant — it was a clear, breezy fall day. The damp, heavy heat of late summer had been brushed away. Everything looked and smelled clean, glistening in the brilliant light.

My phone buzzed as I entered the lobby. I pulled it out. A text from Trystan, asking whether I was free for a drink after work. I texted back that I was, and then spent the eighteen-floor ride wondering why he wanted to meet after hours.

At five, he sent another text saying he wouldn't be ready until six-fifteen. I texted back a thumbs up. I'd spent the afternoon uploading and sorting photographs of Pete. I was adjusting the lighting and selecting the photographs that would be most useful to Diana, based on a matrix she'd developed. Fiddling with it for another hour was fine by me.

When Trystan finally appeared in my doorway, Diana and Stephanie were gone for the day. We left the building and walked without talking much, keeping a rapid pace. He'd chosen a tiny bar that had upholstered stools with backs and only three tables. He said it was his go-to spot for a quick drink after work.

Our drinks had been ordered but not served when he jumped right in. "Are there issues with Jim Kohn?"

"What do you mean?"

"Just what I said — are there issues?"

I longed for my drink, for the distraction of swirling a stick of olives around the glass, stroking the stem, doing anything to aid my thinking about how to answer. I really did not want to complain about a client.

"I'll take your silence as a *yes*."

"Don't take it as anything."

"Then why haven't you answered the question?"

"I was trying to figure out what you meant by issues. It's an ambiguous word. It could mean anything, don't you think?"

He gave me a knowing smile.

Our drinks arrived.

He lifted his glass toward me but said nothing. He took a sip of his gin martini and placed the glass on the cocktail napkin. "Jim spoke to me. He said you might be upset."

"About what?"

"Why don't you tell me."

"If he thinks I'm upset, it's on him to explain why he thinks that."

"So you didn't have any kind of altercation with him?"

"No."

"Nothing physical?"

I shrugged.

"Yes or no?"

"Nothing that I can recall."

"He seemed to think it was a big deal. He seemed to think you were *very* upset. He was concerned. He was concerned I might drop him as a client."

"Why would you do that?"

"If you refused to work with him."

"I have no problem working with him."

"None?"

"He's not my favorite person, but I respect what he's accomplished. And I can see that you might be able to help him get what he wants."

"That's not a ringing endorsement."

"We're supposed to like all of our clients?"

"No. But it sounds as if things aren't going as well as they could. I want to know what made him apologize. He's not the kind of guy who easily admits to a mistake."

I took a sip of my drink. A *mistake*. Not how I would have characterized his behavior.

"You need to be straight with me. Our work is based on openness. In fact, in the interest of openness, Stephanie also suggested there might be a problem between you and Jim."

Before I could answer, the front door was flung open, and a group of seven or eight people flowed into the bar as if they'd just been released en masse from a cage and couldn't wait another moment to get their drinks. They were laughing and talking, almost shouting, as they surged toward the bar.

"But don't get distracted."

"I'm not."

"You're watching them instead of answering my question."

"What does Stephanie have to do with it?"

"She saw you when you filmed him at Harry's."

"How? Did she put a recording device on my camera bag?"

He laughed.

"I'm serious. Did she follow me?" I thought of that gleaming cross — a woman on a mission. The necklace was a beacon. I couldn't imagine her being anywhere in the vicinity without that emblem drawing my attention to her. If she'd followed me, she must have been careful to remain out of my line of sight.

"She had an errand in the Financial District. It doesn't matter how she saw you."

"It does matter."

The noise around us was making it difficult to talk in normal tones. This wasn't a subject that leant itself to raised voices. He looked at me, his eyes boring into mine. "I need you to tell me if there's an issue."

"There's no issue."

"Stephanie said he was touching you."

I shrugged. "It was nothing."

"I want to make sure everything is okay."

"It's fine."

"Then why did Jim want me to offer you an apology?"

"I don't know. If he thinks he has something to apologize for, he should speak to me."

"You're my employee."

"Yes, I know that. But if he thinks he offended me, he should speak to me."

Trystan picked up his drink and took a long, steady sip. "I'm trying to watch out for you. I don't want you to be uncomfortable. If anyone behaves inappropriately, you need to bring it to my attention."

"If there's inappropriate behavior, I can take care of myself."

"You can't keep me in the dark."

What did he think this was? A bartering session between two men about the feelings of a woman who was incapable of handling her own interactions? I took several long, slow breaths. I considered how I might change the subject. It was difficult, when he'd brought me here for the sole purpose of offering another man's apology, of letting it slip that my co-worker was following me. An *errand*. It was a large city. The odds of her having an errand on that day, in that area, were slim. I was surprised Trystan believed that.

It sounded as if Stephanie was as wary of me as I was of her.

He leaned closer. "I'm serious. I need to know everything that's going on. Everything."

"Got it." I was hungry. How long was he going to keep repeating himself? Did he think I wasn't listening? No matter how many times he said it, I had no intention of telling him about my experiences with Jim.

"I'm concerned that I can't trust you if you're keeping things from me."

"I'm supposed to report every word I say, every word they speak to me? Every time his arm bumps mine?" I laughed.

"I need to know I can trust you."

"You can."

"I don't know if I can. You still haven't told me what's going on."

"Because there's nothing going on."

He narrowed his eyes, then turned suddenly and signaled the bartender. "Do you want another drink?"

"No thanks."

"We're not finished here."

"I'm good."

He looked back toward the bartender, held up one finger, and pointed at his drink.

We sat in silence while the bartender made a show of mixing Trystan's drink. When it was placed in front of him, he took a long swallow — quite a lot, for a martini. Without turning to face me, he said, "It's crucial that I know I can trust you to be honest with me, and to be discreet at the same time."

"I'm not having sex with Jim if that's what you're worried about."

"I'm not."

I ate my last olive. It was time for me to leave, but he didn't seem to be anywhere close to wrapping up.

"Jim mentioned something else," he said.

"What's that?"

"He had the impression you didn't think the photographs were all that necessary."

"That's what *he* thinks. He's projecting."

"You didn't say anything to undermine what you're doing?"

"Of course not."

"You need to understand..."

I sort of wished I had another drink, but I was starving. I wanted to get out of there and get some food. Dinner did not seem to be on his mind. If I had another drink, I'd be tipsy *and* even hungrier.

I asked the bartender for a glass of water with ice. He filled a glass and placed it beside my empty martini glass. I picked it up and drank half the water before setting it down again.

"You have to keep this to yourself," Trystan said.

"Sure."

"I have your word?"

"I said, *yes*."

He sighed. "The photography is more for show. There's nothing that important to be gained from photographs, or video, in helping people improve their performance. Performance is a mental game. But the photography is one of the things that differentiates us from the average life coach. It gives the appearance that we're elite. It allows us to charge more."

"So it's bullshit?"

"I wouldn't put it like that."

"Then what would you call it?"

"Getting insight into their behavior helps with their own self-reflection — feeding their mental game. But you have to sell it to them."

"Okay."

"You didn't strike me as someone driven by ethics. It's why I thought you'd be good for the job."

"So it's a bullshit job?"

"Stop using that word."

"What word should I use?"

"This is why I needed to hire someone myself, instead of using outside photographers…to keep things close to the chest. Right?"

"Okay."

"Diana understands that. Stephanie doesn't, so you need to be absolutely discreet."

"I will."

"And you need to sell the idea to our clients. If they have doubts or objections, you need to talk it up."

"So more bullshit?" I smiled.

He glared at me. He took a few sips of his drink, then pushed it away. He pulled out a black AmEx and signaled the bartender. When the card was taken, he turned back to me. "I'll talk to Jim again, and let him know everything is okay."

"You do that." I smiled.

41

Besides mine and Victoria's, there were two other doors that opened onto the landing of my floor. Rafe and Victoria always seemed to be coming or going, but I hadn't seen a glimpse of the others. I didn't even know who lived there. I wouldn't recognize them if they sat beside me in a restaurant.

When I arrived on my floor after my drink with Trystan, carrying a bag of Indian takeout, the door closest to the stairs opened. A man with a shaved head stepped onto the landing, closed the door, locked it, and turned. His face was as polished as the rest of his head. He was tall, over six feet, his forearms tattooed with an intricate design, all in black. He wore a black T-shirt and faded blue jeans. He smiled. "Hi. I was wondering who moved into Nick's apartment."

"3A?"

"Yep. That was Nick's."

I moved toward the railing and transferred the bag of food to my left hand. I held out my right. "I'm Alexandra."

"Nice to meet you, Alexandra." He took my hand with a warm, firm grip but without trying to control the handshake. "Kent. How are you liking 3A?"

"It's nice. I like the French doors. Do all the apartments have them?"

"Just the one-bedrooms."

"And yours is…?"

"Two-bedroom. There are two of each on every floor."

I remembered this from the landlord, but I didn't realize only the lucky one-bedrooms got the French doors. Those doors made me smile every day. I loved the openness of them, the funkiness of them, the uniqueness, at least relative to any place I'd ever lived. Maybe in New York, they were common.

"Nick loved that place. It has the most interesting view on this floor, if you can call it a view." He laughed.

"Why did Nick leave? Did he find a better view?"

His friendly expression retreated. "Not really sure of the details."

I waited, assuming he would offer a few of the details.

"Did you just move to New York?"

"Yes."

"Welcome, then. I see you have dinner, or rather I smell that you have dinner, so I'll let you get to it. Good meeting you." He started down the stairs.

"Same here."

I went into my apartment and scooped my food onto a plate. I poured a glass of water and a glass of Chardonnay. I propped up my tablet. I brought up a news site to keep me entertained while I ate, and to keep my mind off the former occupant of my apartment, along with the unknown and seemingly complex details of why he'd moved out.

It was an innocent question, asking why someone had moved out of an apartment he loved. The closing up of Kent's face was sudden and severe. Avoiding the details he did know made me think there was something I should be aware of.

The apartment was nice. I'd only seen a single roach, despite the horror stories I'd heard of New York and its roach population. The noise was what I'd expected with living in the middle of the city that claims it never sleeps. Apparently, it was too much for Victoria, but I found it exciting, reminding me constantly of where I was living.

While I placed jasmine rice and butter chicken into my mouth, I read some political news, which quickly bored me. I scrolled past the leading headlines and found the summary of an article about something Stephen Hawking had written right before he died. It was a theory of parallel universes. The idea was intriguing, but it didn't sound like the kind of parallel universes people fantasize about. I wallowed in the stew of celebrity gossip and then scanned reviews for some of the top New York restaurants.

The Indian food was fantastic. The meals I'd eaten with my co-workers were very good, but I wanted to try something fabulous. I wanted to eat at well-known restaurants and feel myself melt around exquisite, world-famous dishes. I wanted to experience all the city life I could. I had no idea how long this job would last. I hoped at least a year. Maybe New York would turn into my permanent home. It was hard to say. In the meantime, I wanted to feel like a real New Yorker.

Despite my very specific dreams of the kind of home I want, I'd never given much thought to where it would be located. I'd always pictured something with a lot of property around it, but what about a penthouse? That could provide a different kind of life, one that might be equally comfortable. I'd focused on owning property because it would be fantastic to go running where there was no one else around, but was that realistic? Would I own property with enough space for a five- or six-mile run? It wasn't likely.

I jotted down a list of restaurants I wanted to try. I was

pretty sure I could get Trystan to take me to one of them. Maybe a team dinner. It was a bit of a toss-up. Eating out with him and Diana would be great, but Stephanie would of course be invited.

I sipped my wine and thought about what Trystan had said.

Was she stalking me as prey for her evangelistic efforts? Or was she trying to sabotage my job? I couldn't understand why she would tell Trystan that she'd seen Jim's hand on my back. It had nothing to do with her. I would have thought she'd use her knowledge as a way to get close to me, to try to work her way into my mind and turn my thoughts toward god and my eventual destination.

I refilled my wine glass, slid my arms into a fleece jacket, and grabbed my cigarettes.

The landing was deserted. I locked my door, and instead of immediately climbing the stairs to the roof garden, I stood for a moment studying Victoria and Rafe's door. I took a few steps toward it and knocked. I waited for a few seconds, then knocked again.

After a moment, I turned away and headed toward the stairs.

On the roof, I looked out at the city and sipped my wine. It was too windy for a cigarette to be enjoyable.

I wondered whether Nick had ever stood at this spot and enjoyed the view. I wondered why he'd left and why it seemed to be a complicated secret. I imagine there's a never-ending flow of people moving in and out of apartments in any large city, especially apartments like mine that weren't the upscale type that owners held onto for decades. But Kent had made it clear there was a reason with a lot of details, and I couldn't help wonder whether the next door neighbors and their open relationship had anything to do with it.

42

Stephanie was losing her footing. Trystan's refusal to give credibility to her concerns about Alexandra was insulting. A deep, rushing sense of shame filled every pore of her body. He might as well have smacked her face and accused her of lying. He certainly implied it.

She would never lie. She was not a liar. Lying was offensive to God. There was that small lie about seeing Alexandra and Jim during a visit to her attorney, but that wasn't a lie that mattered. Why she'd been there was irrelevant. What she'd seen was important.

The more she thought about the encounter between Jim Kohn and Alexandra, the more she realized that Alexandra was bad news. Trystan should have seen that from her description of what had happened, but he'd cut her off before she finished speaking. He'd only worked with Stephanie for five months but he'd always trusted her judgment. At least she'd thought he did. Now, he was almost dismissive of her. Was he close to deciding he didn't need her? Why pay three full-time salaries when all she did was schedule meetings and help Diana enter data into the system?

Of course, Diana, and now Alexandra, were too good for those tasks, so maybe she was still needed. Her job was secure because they wouldn't lower themselves to menial work. She was useful but not valuable. She was on a lower tier, in both her salary and her status.

She shoved her key into the lock and opened the door to their suite. It was so unfair. This woman had dropped into her world out of nowhere, stolen her job, and turned Trystan against her. She had no idea how to win back his respect. He'd taken her observation and turned it into something that painted her as a busy-body. He'd suggested she was catty, trying to create a problem where none existed.

As the door eased closed, the motion-sensor light came on, but the rest of the space was dark, cool air blowing out of the vents. She went to the hallway and turned on the lights, then went immediately to the break room.

She'd had a cup of coffee at home, but a second cup was definitely required. It was six in the morning, still dark outside. The building felt quite empty around her — hundreds of offices on the floors below her, dark and silent.

Once the coffee was brewing, and all the lights in the break room, hallway, and her office were burning, she felt slightly alone in the world.

She'd never been in the offices before dawn, but it was necessary if she planned to go through Alexandra's office without being caught.

Every moment of her morning was carefully planned. She would look through Alexandra's office until six-thirty, then drink a cup of coffee and get started on her work. A few minutes before Diana made her usual seven-forty-five appearance, Stephanie would send a text message inviting her to lunch.

If she approached Diana once she was in the office, Alexandra or Trystan were likely to overhear. It wasn't that she'd never gone to lunch with Diana, but now that this third wheel was here, it could no longer be a casual thing. It had to be a group event, or you felt you were deliberately excluding someone. She didn't like to be unkind, even with such bitter feelings churning inside. She needed to make people feel included. Trystan had emphasized that very point.

While the coffee dripped, she hurried to her office, dropped her purse on the chair, and went into Alexandra's office. There was nothing that stirred obvious interest. All of their offices were designed for tranquility, with minimal décor and none of the usual office clutter — filing cabinets, trays of paper, canisters of pens and pencils. Nearly everything was stored on the computer and its various backup systems, including one located at Trystan's home to offer additional security, or so he said.

She pulled open the single drawer on the left side of Alexandra's desk. It was empty. That alone was meaningful. No one kept their drawers entirely empty. There was always something — an unfinished bag of chips from the vending machine, or a flyer someone had handed you on the street, announcing a play or film that looked interesting in that moment, but that you promptly forgot about.

In her own desk drawer she had a supply of dried noodle snacks, ready to eat as soon as a cup of boiling water was added, a few candy bars, the flyers she was always collecting, a handful of matchbooks…she couldn't recall what else, but it was occupied. So was Trystan's. And she was certain Diana's was as well.

She closed the drawer. She walked to the wall opposite the desk and studied the photographs. The first, of Sydney Harbor, seemed pretentious. She got it. Alexandra had lived there for a few months. But that didn't make her Australian, it didn't make the place such an important part of her life that it was one of only two photographs selected for her wall. She was exaggerating her connection because it was glamorous.

The other picture of a woman with dark hair, her cheek pressed up close to Alexandra's, both of them grinning like idiots, puzzled her. Was it a sister? Alexandra had dark blonde hair with rust-colored streaks, so it was impossible to know her true color. There wasn't any obvious resemblance, but lots of sisters didn't look anything alike.

She lifted the photograph off the wall. She carried it to the desk and undid the clasps holding the photograph inside the frame. The back of the photograph was blank, so no help there. She put it together and re-hung it.

The bookcases were empty of books. When she'd commented on it, Alexandra said she read ebooks and didn't need a bookcase filled with dead weight she had to lug everywhere she went. Stephanie wondered if it was because she was woefully unqualified for her job and didn't want to advertise that by displaying books about photography for beginners or pop psychology.

She walked out of the office. There was nothing to be uncovered there. It was sterile, despite the supposed personalized touch of her photographs.

She settled in at her desk and began inputting the results of tests taken by two of their new clients. Reading the answers to the extremely personal questions was always interesting. She found herself lost in someone else's world. It was the best part of her job, reading about other lives, so different from her own. Often, she wondered how she would answer each question herself.

The next hour and a quarter raced by, and it was almost too late when she sent the text message asking Diana to go out for lunch. Diana was in the elevator already.

Her phone buzzed less than five minutes later, just as she thought she heard the distant chime of the elevator arriving on the eighteenth floor.

43

It shocked her that Diana texted back immediately. *Lunch sounds great.*

There was no accompanying suggestion that Stephanie should also invite Alexandra. There was no hint that she'd said *yes* just to be nice. Somehow, those simple words sounded like genuine pleasure. A message from a friend, almost.

For the rest of the morning, each time Stephanie looked at the time, it seemed that only five or ten minutes had passed when she'd expected thirty or forty. She found herself re-reading every word she typed, unsure whether she'd gotten it right. It would be so much easier if the tests their clients took, and the comprehensive profiles they submitted, could be done electronically. But Trystan was a strong believer in pen and paper for these exercises. He thought the connection between the slowly moving hand and brain was stronger. He believed the laborious pace compelled their clients to consider each answer more carefully. There was no easy delete key that could be held down, wiping it all out in a fraction of a second. Of course, if he didn't have that belief, her job responsibilities would be cut by two-thirds, and the job itself might be non-existent.

It was only eleven-fifteen. She continued reading and typing responses into the forms.

Then, without warning, it was noon, and Diana was standing in her doorway, purse slung over her left shoulder, the strap cutting between her breasts, and the purse fitted against her right hip. "Ready?"

They walked to an Irish Bar where Stephanie had made a reservation before she even suggested they go to lunch. It was an ironic choice since neither of them drank alcohol, but the food was delicious. Stephanie had been confident that Diana would say *yes* because she was the sort of person who always wanted to be nice. It was that same trait that twisted Stephanie's stomach into a knot during the entire walk, worried that Diana would suddenly text Alexandra and ask her to meet them.

Stephanie still couldn't relax when they were seated at the table, menus open in front of them.

Diana ordered a kale salad with chickpeas and avocado along with an iced coffee. Stephanie ordered baked macaroni and cheese with garlic bread and sparkling water with lemon. She hoped the heavy, creamy comfort food would settle the roiling in the pit of her stomach. They talked about work and the weather and Diana's brother who was moving to the UK for a tech job.

Stephanie let Diana's lament over missing her brother fade. She remained silent for a few minutes, long enough to make a change of subject seem natural, sensitive to Diana's feelings about her loss. "Now that you've worked with her for a while, what do you think of Alexandra?"

"She prefers to be called Alex."

"Right. A boy's name modified to fit a girl."

Diana didn't point out the similarity with Stephanie's name, for which Stephanie was grateful. Neither did she offer her opinion of Alexandra.

Stephanie speared several pieces of macaroni. "What do

you think of her?"

"She's nice."

Stephanie laughed. It was the wrong reaction, but she couldn't help herself.

"Why is that funny?"

"She's a lot of things, but nice is not how I would ever describe her."

Diana shrugged. She didn't ask how Stephanie would describe Alexandra and still didn't offer any information.

"I think Trystan rushed into hiring her. He didn't vet her," Stephanie said.

"How do you know?"

"I don't know the specifics, but I get the sense he decided on the spur of the moment."

"He has good instincts. He hired us, right?" Diana laughed. She put the straw in her mouth and sipped her iced coffee.

"I'm concerned."

"Well, you should talk to Trystan about that, not me."

"I wanted to bounce it off you. I need your viewpoint before I do too much."

"Too much? That sounds ominous."

"I get a vibe that isn't…well, it isn't good."

"I hope this isn't about you getting impressions from a supernatural source. You know I'm not into that."

"No. This is fact. Something I saw."

Diana ate several forkfuls of salad before responding. "What did you see?"

Stephanie leaned across the table. They were surrounded by strangers, but she felt the delicate subject matter required a lowered voice. "I saw her with a client.

They were..." She straightened, unsure how to describe it. Suddenly, *touching* seemed the wrong word. That word had slid from her mouth, and Trystan acted as if it were nothing, completely normal for a woman to be touching a client, or rather, allowing him to touch her like that. Giving him that look. It was a look that Alexandra gave Trystan and had even given to Stephanie. Something that was pure...she wasn't sure how to describe it. Hunger was the word that came to mind.

Diana took a few sips of coffee and nibbled at a piece of kale. She seemed perfectly fine to wait, not at all curious about what Stephanie had to say.

Stephanie longed for Diana to plead with her to share the information, longed for the deeper connection that came from discussing a shared concern, longed for the kind of friendship where you could confide your observations and weren't challenged or criticized for them. The other person understood your feelings and even admitted to similar feelings of her own. "They looked like they're having an affair."

Diana laughed. "Really? How do you *look* like you're having an affair? You saw them going into a hotel?"

"Not exactly."

"Well, what? I like Alex. I think she knows how to handle herself professionally. I don't want to gossip about her."

Stephanie saw that Diana's interest was waning. There was only half a second to make up her mind about how far to take this. "They were in a restaurant." That was the truth. The rest of the words came out in a rush as if she'd been planning them all along. "He had his hand on her leg, sliding it up her skirt. Way up her skirt. Not like exploring and seeing what she would do, but like he'd done it before. And she was looking at him like she wanted to tear his clothes off and have sex on the table."

Diana laughed.

"Why do you keep laughing?"

"Because I think...I don't know what I think. I suppose...if they are, it's none of my business. Or yours." She took a long swallow of iced coffee.

"That's terrible for us. Having our co-worker sleeping with clients."

"If you think that, you should talk to Trystan. Or better, talk to Alex. Not me. Is that the only reason you invited me to lunch? I thought you were being friendly."

"It's not the only reason."

Diana plucked a piece of kale off her plate with her fingers, ate it, and nudged the plate away from her.

"Aren't you eating the rest?"

"I've lost my appetite."

"I know what you mean. The thing is, I already did talk to Trystan. And he...he didn't seem concerned."

"Then that's the end of it."

"Not if you talk to him also."

"Not going to happen."

"Why not?"

"First, I didn't see them. Second, I don't think it's our business."

"But what about our reputation?"

"I don't see how it would hurt. They're adults. It's probably not the best idea. I would never do it, but she's from California. Right?" She smiled.

This was not going as Stephanie had planned. She'd

assumed Diana would be shocked, and upset. She'd assumed their shared reaction to the scandalous information would draw them together. And she'd assumed Diana would want Trystan to know. "It would really be good if you mentioned it to Trystan. I think you're underestimating the impact on how our service is perceived. And that could affect our jobs."

Diana studied her. "I don't want to get dragged into that kind of backstabbing."

"It's too late. Trystan thinks I'm making trouble and…"

"There you are. I don't want to be making trouble."

"But she's the one that's making trouble. I need you to back me up."

"There's nothing to back up. I didn't see them. But even if I had…"

"If you don't mention to him that you're concerned about her, I'll tell him what you did." She gave Diana a slow, confident smile.

The look that spread across Diana's face would be enough to get Stephanie through the rest of the day, possibly the rest of the week.

44

Portland

When I saw Mr. B's face, I knew he was preparing for an epic battle with me. He was not going to drag my parents into it or get any other outside help. He was going to beat me single-handedly, prove that he had power over me. I knew this because instead of a face contorted with rage, he looked at me with the most pleasant smile I'd ever seen cross his lips.

The lips smiled.

The eyes remained cold.

It's a cliché, but it's a cliché because it's true. A smile without the accompanying warm feelings and amusement and joy glowing in the eyes is something deadly. The first time you recognize it, you understand why it's said that the eyes are the windows to the soul.

Many people think they can get away with that lifeless smile. They don't understand that some will recognize it for what it is. They think they're fooling you into trusting them, they think you'll let down your guard and see only good intentions based on a manufactured turn of the lips and friendly exposure of the teeth.

It takes practice to make sure the eyes are in sync with the smile. And only people like me realize it's necessary.

While some fail to recognize those smiles that lack the accompanying good intention and warmth coming from the inside, radiating through the transparent material of the human eye, many know them in an instant. Those people feel a chill and become subconsciously wary. They don't always know why.

And so I've learned to make sure the look in my eyes lines up with my smile, when necessary. If I want to blend in with my emotionally-driven fellow human beings, that skill is a requirement.

Mr. B had no idea I saw his rage simmering in those hazel irises he turned on me. He didn't know I could see the desire to hurt me in the hard black dots of his pupils.

"I almost phoned your house," he said. "But I decided this would be better taken care of in person. Come with me." He walked along the side of the auditorium and out through one of the doors that led to a corridor lined with offices and two-person conference rooms. He pushed open the door of a tiny conference room and gestured toward the nearest chair.

When we were both seated, he placed the envelope on the table between us. "This is plagiarism."

"What is plagiarism, exactly?"

"Passing off another's writing as your own."

"I don't think I passed it off as my own."

The smile tightened, the eyeballs almost jittered with the effort to maintain that smile. "Your name is at the top of the page."

"So you would know who it was from."

"You thought I was ignorant of the remarkable Reverend Edwards?"

"No. But I thought his words fit what you wanted."

"I made it quite clear I wanted *your* thoughts."

I smiled, making sure my eyes were filled with innocent

confusion. "You said you were going to edit it, so I didn't think you really wanted my thoughts."

"Don't play games with me."

I crossed my legs. I folded my hands in my lap. He turned away, unable to hold up under my steady, unblinking gaze. He was a little scared, I think, but even more angry that he couldn't seem to get the upper hand. And he never would, because I understood him and he didn't have a clue about me. He pegged me as another defiant teenager that he had to browbeat into submission to himself, as god's appointed authority.

He was afraid he was failing in his mission, that Pure Truth Tabernacle was failing, that I was headed for the torment of hell, into the hands of that furious god. It was his job, and on his conscience, to prevent that from happening. But despite all his training and the carefully-crafted questions that formed the basis of his program designed to lead someone easily and unthinkingly into repentance, he had no idea how to do that.

You can't force a human heart to believe something it doesn't want to. Something it can't believe. People try, but history is full of rebellious hearts that burned strong in the face of shunning, torture, prison, and death.

Not to make too much of myself. I'm not some heroic martyr.

I was just a girl who wanted to be true to myself.

And now, I'm a woman who wants the same.

Mr. B wanted to break me.

He tapped the envelope. "Did you think I wouldn't recognize this?"

I smiled.

"I want an answer, not that cat smile you think can seduce anyone."

"Is that what you believe? That I'm trying to seduce you?"

He blushed, and then the rage in his eyes grew more intense, if that were possible. He fought to make the blush recede, but he couldn't get control of his body, and the more he battled the heat of his blood, the redder his face grew. "There is a deep-rooted thread of evil in your heart, young lady."

I re-laced my fingers in my lap.

"Your disrespect for God and the authority of your elders is disheartening."

"Disheartening?" I laughed softly. I don't think it was the word he intended. He was underplaying it to try to calm himself.

"Terrifying," he said. "A girl of your age should be pure in heart and mind. You behave like a woman who's been hardened by the world. It makes one want to weep."

He looked very far from weeping. I supposed it was a new tactic. He thought he could tame me with pity instead of battling against my will. Maybe he was afraid I was trying to seduce him. Or maybe he was the kind of man who thought seduction was every woman's primary purpose. A man who believes women are put on this earth to make life difficult for men, to tempt them with desire and outwit them and cause them to abandon their principles and their rock-solid faith in an angry and just god.

"What do you have to say for yourself?"

"I don't know what you want to hear."

"I don't want to *hear* anything. I want you to explain

why you took a famous, life-transforming, world-changing sermon from a man of God and turned it into a lazy homework assignment. You put no thought and no effort into this. You didn't search your heart to find out what God wants you to say to your peers."

"I don't think god wants me to say anything to my peers."

"You're wrong. Very, very wrong."

I smiled. I unclasped my hands and tucked my hair behind my ears. I was tired of sitting in a rather hard chair, watching him stare at me as if he wanted to fling himself over the table, put his hands around my neck, and press his thumbs into my windpipe. He wanted to hold me up as an example of his tight relationship with God that gave him the power to turn human hearts in the direction he wanted.

"I want an answer. Did you do this to defy me? Or to test me, thinking I'd never read these inspired words?"

"I already told you. After you said you would edit whatever I wrote, I figured you wouldn't like anything I had to say. You said I should talk about why people need salvation and this sermon explains that point of view."

"Don't be smart with me." He pushed his chair away from the table. "You're not going to win by being coy. The assignment remains the same. I'll be waiting for your essay next week, and then we'll talk about what I'll expect of your behavior on stage, in front of your peers."

"But you still won't like anything I write."

He stood and picked up the envelope. He moved around the table until he was standing over me. His voice grew deeper, filled with the volume of self-appointed authority. "Then I suggest you spend some time on your knees and find out what you should be writing. Not what your fallen nature wants to write, not what your unrepentant soul finds amusing." He slapped the envelope on my forearm. "You might start by reading this entire sermon. Really reading it and understanding what it says, and praying over what it means for you."

He walked out of the room before I could say any more.

45

New York City

Now I found the roles reversed.

I was waiting around for Victoria or Rafe to show up. I hung over the railing and looked down at the staircase in a perfect square, turning at each half flight. I was lingering, sipping wine, waiting. I longed to light up a cigarette out there, but it was forbidden, and I still didn't know who occupied the one remaining apartment. It could be someone who cared very much about cigarette smoke. And the landlord had been very firm that if you were reported, you were out.

The role reversal wasn't all bad. I preferred that I was lurking outside their door rather than knowing they'd been watching my patterns, seeing me go up to the roof garden when I wasn't aware, feeling they might follow behind, watching me when I ran, remembering how Victoria had inserted herself into my photography class.

I wanted to see one of them because I needed to know why my predecessor had left. I wanted to know why the circumstances were *complicated*. I had to know why there were so many details that some could be unknowns.

For three days, neither Rafe nor Victoria had entered or exited their apartment. At least not while I was around. I'd spent time counting the black and white floor tiles, then counting the posts in the railing. I'd walked down the stairs, counting the number in each flight. I'd taken pictures of all four apartment doors and compared them with each other. They were identical, even the slightly askew brass numbers and letters fixed at eye level, a peephole directly above.

I'd knocked on their door more times than I wanted to admit. I hoped they hadn't been at home, ignoring me, because if they were, they'd think I was slipping off balance. I didn't mind Rafe thinking that, but I kind of liked Victoria. I liked that she was ambitious about money. I liked that she didn't back down from her confidence in day trading when I insisted it was gambling. It was, but she didn't cave.

Kent hadn't been around either. I was starting to feel like the mystery occupant and I were the only people living on the third floor.

Finally, I finished my wine and abandoned my loitering.

The next day I was carrying two bags of groceries up the stairs, filled with greens, fresh trout, and a small bag of wild rice. I'd succumbed too many times to pizza by the slice and hotdogs from street vendors.

As I turned the corner to start the flight from the second floor to the third, the sound of voices wafted down the stairwell. One of the voices belonged to Rafe. I wasn't sure, but I guessed the other might belong to Kent. I quickened my pace, taking two steps in a single stride.

Rafe stood on the landing, leaning against the rail, his back to me. Kent faced him, gesturing wildly and smiling with enthusiasm that equaled his gestures. Rafe wasn't saying much, just laughing from time to time.

Kent stopped talking as I passed between them. I placed my groceries on my doormat and turned.

"What's up?"

"Talking about the game last night," Rafe said. "He saw it live."

"Nice." I shoved my hands into my pockets and walked toward them.

Rafe looked at Kent. "You two've met?"

Kent nodded. He pulled his phone out of his back pocket and glanced at the screen. "I need to head out." He nodded at both of us in turn. He hurried down the stairs and was gone before I could say anything.

Rafe turned his attention to me. "Haven't seen you in a while. Working? Or did you find a boyfriend?"

"Mostly working."

"Mostly?"

"Yes."

He grinned.

I smiled back. "I rang your bell, but you weren't there."

"Oh? Missing me?"

"No. I was looking for Victoria."

"Well, we're connected. A pair. It's hard to get one of us without the other."

That didn't sound very open to me.

"Why were you looking for her?"

"Just wanted to see if she was up for a martini on the roof."

"It's too cold."

"Not if you wear a coat."

He shrugged. "I'll take a martini."

"This was the other night. I'm getting ready to fix dinner now. I should get my food inside."

"I wouldn't mind dinner, either."

"You and Victoria?"

He grinned. "No."

"I thought it was hard to get one of you without the other."

"Yeah. Hey…did you like my flowers?"

"They were nice."

"That's all? You can't say you liked them?"

"I did. I just don't want you to make something out of it."

"Why would I do that?"

"You already are."

He moved closer. "Why don't you like me much?"

"You're with Victoria."

"We're flexible."

"I'm not hooking up with you, so stop pushing."

"You seem a little lonely. Shut inside that apartment all night, every night. I think I hear you crying, through the walls. In here." He pressed his hand against his chest.

I moved closer to my door and picked up the grocery bags. "I was talking to Kent…"

Rafe frowned.

"He said the guy who lived in this apartment before me…"

"He was an asshole. Good riddance. We're glad to have you living there."

"But you're moving soon."

"Not that soon."

"Victoria made it sound like you are."

"Not in the next month, or whatever."

"I was wondering about the previous tenant, Nick…do you know why…"

"I told you what I thought of Nick. What's there to wonder about? He's not here anymore."

"Kent made it sound as if there was a problem and I just wondered if there was an issue with someone in the building, or noise, or the landlord?"

"Nope. It's paradise here."

"So you can't tell me anything about Nick."

"I don't *want* to tell you anything about Nick." He moved away from me.

I unlocked my door and pushed it open.

"What are you making for dinner?"

"Trout."

He made a face.

"Talk to you later."

"So you aren't going to give me a second chance?"

"No. It's for the best."

"No martini?"

"No."

"Maybe with me and Vic both some time?"

"We'll see." Even that simple response was more than I really wanted to offer. I should have said no, but sometimes, an open-ended false promise allows the conversation to wind down. I didn't want to stand there for another half hour, talking in circles. He wasn't going to tell me about Nick. I was hungry and a little tired.

Inside my apartment, I put away the groceries, opened a bottle of Chardonnay, and gave myself a very generous pour. I took the glass to the living room window and looked out on the dark street. I took a sip and thought about the buildings around me, pressing close, so many people. I couldn't comprehend the number of people packed into the tiny island of Manhattan.

It wasn't too much to believe that Rafe and Victoria might have chased Nick away. I wondered whether Rafe would ever stop pestering me and why Victoria wasn't bothered by his behavior. Although I'm quite casual about who I have sex with and what it all means, I'd never met a couple who had a relationship like theirs. It could be Victoria was a masochist of some kind. An emotional masochist who wanted to suffer as her boyfriend lusted after other, better-looking women. Maybe something happened between her and Nick, and this was payback on Rafe's part. Payback that Victoria wanted to hurry to its conclusion. I just happened to be in the wrong place at the wrong time.

46

Trystan and I were seated in Jim's palatial office, all three of us acting as if the fabric of our relationship was as smooth as silk. There were no pulled threads or wrinkles or spilled wine leaving a permanent stain.

Jim had shaken my hand with a firm grip but avoided eye contact. Trystan's demeanor was polished and unchanged from our last meeting with Jim. There was no hesitation suggesting he wondered about Jim's behavior or was suspicious of an apology that appeared to be disconnected from reality, or that his trust in me was wavering.

We were there to review the photographs and film I'd taken. We'd already reviewed all of the images with Diana, and now we'd offer her insights as well as Trystan's. Knowing this part of the process before I'd found out the entire photography effort was a bit of a con, I'd looked forward to it. Now, I felt a bit like I was on stage, performing for both Trystan and Jim.

My nerves were alert, primed to sell the value of the photographs, ready to follow Trystan's lead. In some ways, knowing the photographs were a sideline, I was even more intrigued. It didn't reduce the pleasure of taking them, catching people unaware, uncovering frowns and grimaces and facial tics they didn't know they had. Now, I had the extra challenge of making sure they believed what we were selling.

"If you'll open the shared file Alexandra provided the

link to, we can view these on your large monitor instead of the laptop," Trystan said.

Jim gestured toward the TV mounted on the wall opposite his desk. There was a small couch and two armchairs arranged around it. "I'll bring it up on the large screen so you don't have to crowd around my desk."

We moved across the room and seated ourselves near the screen. Jim picked up the remote, powered on the screen, and navigated to the shared file. Trystan had told me on our way over that he would provide comments on the photographs. I was to wait until he was finished before offering any additional thoughts. He said not only was I new, but he needed to rebuild Jim's confidence in the usefulness of the photography.

One by one, we moved through the shots from that first day in Jim's office, then to his dinner meeting. Trystan pointed out that Jim had a tendency to scowl, asking Jim to try to recall which topics of conversation made him adopt that expression. He explained how it made him look angry, which might stir up unrecognized fear. He suggested that even though clients obviously wanted him to be serious about money, it was off-putting. At the same time, he wouldn't want to over-correct to a constant smile. But he needed to be aware of what his thoughts were when that scowl appeared, and work to soften it.

From there, Trystan analyzed Jim's posture — good, except when eating; his gestures — good; the effect of his smile — warming; and his habit of rubbing his jaw which Diana had decreed neutral. Then he added that even though it was neutral, it happened with alarming frequency, which Jim would see in the video. He might want to think about better controlling those kinds of activities as they could sometimes project anxiety or even dishonesty.

Clients wouldn't be aware of their reactions to these minor physical habits but might be inclined to doubt what he had to say, they might view him as lacking confidence. At the same time, his body language when seated at a table was aggressive, and that was also problematic.

Listening to Trystan, I wasn't sure this was going to build confidence in the elite quality of what Jim offered to his own clients. I couldn't imagine having dinner with someone and trying to think about what my hands were doing with my face, what kinds of habitual expressions I was making, and whether or not I leaned too hard on the table.

We watched the video. Trystan made a few more comments about the volume of Jim's voice and his tendency to talk over his clients, sounding too eager to explain, not devoting enough time to listening.

Jim didn't say much. When the video ended, we sat for a moment in silence.

Trystan's phone buzzed. He reached into his pocket and pulled it out. "I apologize." He looked at Jim. "It's my daughter. I need to take it."

Jim waved him away. "There's a conference room on the opposite side of the lobby. Take your time. I've scheduled ninety minutes for this."

The moment Trystan was out the door, Jim turned to me. "So. What are your thoughts on my expressions and posture and tone?" He grinned.

"In line with Trystan's."

"That's it?"

I thought about my duty to sell. "I noticed when I was

filming you, and even that first time I took photographs, you're hyper-aware of other people looking at you."

"Anyone would be, having a camera tracking them, a woman picking apart their appearance."

I kept my face neutral. "That's true. But I think you need to avoid seeing yourself as performing. These photos were just for you, so who cares what they looked like? Yet, you were very concerned about my presence."

"Good point." He turned off the TV. "And how is all this supposed to help me?"

"Trystan explained that."

"You explain it." He settled back in his chair and stretched his legs out. The toe of his left foot came dangerously close to mine.

I kept my gaze on his face, willing myself not to look at his feet, letting him know I was aware. "People react to a lot of different stimuli. Most of the time, we don't even know what makes us like or dislike a person at the first meeting. We aren't aware of how a way of talking or a facial expression makes us trust or distrust someone. And we…"

"Why do I have the feeling you know exactly what things make you trust or distrust someone?"

I shrugged.

He nodded. "You give the impression you know what I'm thinking."

"This isn't about me, Mr. Kohn."

"Jim," he said. "And what do I do with all this information about my face?"

"These are tools to increase your awareness. Getting new clients isn't solely about your fund management record."

"And my platinum references. My ROI stats."

"People are still going to respond on a gut level. You're competing with a lot of very good investors and fund managers."

"Don't I know it."

"It looks like you're pretty successful. Why do you need more prominent clients?"

"Are you questioning my goals?"

"No. Just curious."

"Ahhh." He smiled. His foot moved slightly, bumping the toe of my shoe.

He didn't excuse himself or move it. I left my feet right where they were, hoping that whatever was coursing through his veins would be unsettled by the willing presence of my feet, by the lack of retreat, halfway hoping he would overstep the line and I could put him back in his place.

"As people acquire more wealth, their goals shift," he said.

"I get it. You can only have so much money."

"Not exactly. More is always welcome, and something you never stop pursuing. But other things rise to the surface. Their appeal and intensity grow."

"You want to be the popular kid."

He smirked. "I've always been the *popular kid*."

"A charmed life?"

"Yes. One of the lucky ones, I guess you could say."

It was clear he wouldn't say that at all. It was his attempt at humility. He didn't view himself as *lucky*, he viewed himself as superior. He acted if he'd created his own brain cells and sculpted his own frame, grown his own hair and eyes and straight patrician nose and perfectly aligned teeth. Possibly he believed he'd looked down from heaven, sitting beside god himself, and selected the man and woman whose genes would give him better than average looks and brains, and then provide a more-than-comfortable childhood and plenty of money for a platinum education.

I crossed my legs. "Do you have any siblings?"

"Why do you ask?"

"Curious. Again."

The door opened, and Trystan stepped into the office. "Apologies."

"No problem," Jim said. "Alexandra and I were getting better acquainted."

Trystan smiled as if we were his two favorite children and he was pleased that we'd finally kissed and made up. He settled into the other chair, placing his phone on the table. "I'm glad you're connecting," he said. "I want you both to feel comfortable and familiar with each other at Jim's dinner on the nineteenth. It's a long time to be taking photographs, which can be tense in itself. Because so many of the guests are the type of people you're targeting as clients, there can't be any friction."

"Oh, we're absolutely connecting." I kept my gaze off Jim's foot.

He hadn't felt any impulse to move it for Trystan's sake. This made me think the apology, whatever it was, had been nothing but a maneuver to make sure he had the first and final word with Trystan.

"She's quite sassy, isn't she?" Jim grinned at Trystan.

Trystan smiled. "She says what she thinks."

I leaned forward and looked at Jim, then Trystan. "Does she?"

Trystan acted as if he hadn't heard. "That's why I hired her."

"Good call," Jim said.

I took a long, slow breath. Would either of them figure out they were talking about me as if I were a new car, added to a stable of expensive and collectible vehicles? Apparently not, or the conversation would have stopped after the word *sassy*. The word *sassy* would never have come up.

"She's working out well," Trystan said. "Exactly the person I needed to make our clients feel comfortable being the subjects of such extensive photography. It takes a girl with confidence and class, and Alexandra has both of those qualities."

"I agree," Jim said.

I, on the other hand, felt something begin to burn like a thin strip of smelted iron running through the center of my body, but I had the class to keep it to myself. For now.

47

The next photography session with Pete was at a dark and seductive cigar club where he was giving an after-dinner talk about what the financial markets looked like for the remainder of the year. Fifteen men and four women, clients and prospects, had been invited. They would be seated in a private room, eating the fattest steaks and largest baked potatoes you could imagine.

Smoking was actually allowed indoors, in the bar only, cigars only. The aroma of cigar smoke wasn't unpleasant when I passed by that room. It made me long to step outside for a cigarette.

For this occasion, I'd purchased a tripod, paid for by Trystan, of course. It was set up in the back of the room. The lens would be focused on Pete's face for most of the evening, with occasional shots framed to show his entire body.

We'd decided on photographs rather than video because Diana really wanted to get into his micro expressions, frozen for analysis, rather than working with video, which reveals something else entirely.

Pete was nice enough to invite me to arrive early for my own steak dinner and baked potato. There was a subtle go-around with the server when my dinner arrived with bacon sprinkled on the potato. Crumbled bacon on baked potato never makes sense to me. If I want bacon, I want a nice thick, crisp strip to savor its flavor uninterrupted, not lukewarm or cold, chewy crumbs. I'd also passed on the offer of sour cream, cheese, or chives. The heavenly taste of unsalted butter and perfectly cooked potato was enough. It's the simple things that are the most divine sometimes.

The server resolved things nicely with a fresh potato, even though she initially thought she knew better than I what I'd ordered.

I stood by my camera as the guests arrived and were seated. I sipped sparkling water with lime and snapped away while Pete made the rounds greeting his guests. I didn't do a lot to ensure careful framing, simply made sure his face, whether from the side, three-quarters, or straight-on, remained front and center in my lens. While Pete spoke, I used the remote to take snap pictures.

When the meal was over, people lingered, drinking coffee and wine, drifting around the space, presumably to network and discuss their reactions to Pete's forecasts. I wondered how these people consistently made money, living off such confident assertions about what would happen in the future. No one knows the future.

There's not a single person who knows with any degree of certainty what will take place thirty seconds from the current moment in time. Ask anyone who's been in a car accident or lived through any other sudden, catastrophic event. It's fast. You can't think. Life changes in a heartbeat, as they say.

Everyone wants to believe they can look at trends and data, they can study the current situation and analyze past patterns and project a reasonable guess at what's coming. And I suppose most of the time it works out. So they continue believing they can predict the future.

But look back on your life. Has it taken the direction and turns you expected? Even if the larger framework was what you anticipated, and set out to achieve, there are things you never anticipated. When I was fighting with Mr. B or sitting in church, arguing in my mind with the preacher, I never in a hundred thoughts saw myself living in New York City, working with a probable religious zealot who was trying to mess with my fantastic job.

It makes us feel secure if we believe we know the general shape of the future. Knowing provides a feeling of control. No one wants to feel helpless in the hands of fate or god or the whims of other people. It's the worst feeling in the world.

So, people try to predict. They make elaborate plans. They think by painting a hundred variations of a scenario, one of them will come to pass, and they feel more confident they truly are in control.

I prefer to face each new event as something exciting. An adventure. A surprise. Freedom from the boredom of predictability. If you know the future, what is the point of making your way through life?

When all the guests were gone, I put the lens cap on the camera and detached the camera from the tripod. I tucked the camera into the bag and zipped it closed. I folded the tripod. As I slung the bag over my shoulder, Pete approached me. "How about a drink before you take off?"

And there you have it. I didn't predict that.

I hesitated only for a moment. The offer was friendly enough, with none of the creepy undertones that emanated from Jim.

I followed him to the bar. I ordered a martini, and he ordered a shot of whiskey. We sat at a small table in the corner. Cigar smoke wafted through the room, but it wasn't unpleasant. They must have had an incredible ventilation system, allowing a light aroma but no sense of suffocating in thick, lingering smoke and the odor of tobacco, damp from sucking gums.

With very little prompting, Pete talked about his wife and kids. His dog. I asked about predicting the future, wondering why he felt so confident. He said the past was the best predictor of the future.

I smiled and sipped my drink.

He returned to the topic of his wife. She'd been offered a promotion in her job at a healthcare company. She would be traveling one week out of the month. He wondered how that would be with his career and the kids. Both were in elementary school with a constant need for rides to and from their after-school activities. He complained about school schedules and the constant teacher-training days that played havoc on career couples. "I'm not complaining though. Truly, I'm thrilled for her. She's wanted it, and she deserves it."

I pulled an olive off the stick and popped it in my mouth. After letting it roll around for a moment, I chewed and swallowed. "Have you ever met Jim Kohn's wife?"

He laughed.

"Why is that funny?"

"I shouldn't have laughed. No, I've never met her."

"Why did you laugh?"

He picked up his glass and downed the remainder of the whiskey. "I shouldn't have."

"But you did, so you have to explain."

He gave me a warm smile. "I don't have to explain. Professional courtesy. My apologies. Enjoy your drink." He pushed out his chair. "If you decide to have another, or want to order a dessert, ask them to put it on my tab." He extended his hand.

I hesitated, then took it.

"Looking forward to seeing the photographs. Have a good evening." He turned and walked quickly out of the room, taking his instinctive laughter and his secret with him.

48

I stood by Diana's desk, looking out the window at the wall of windows across the street. I was waiting while she downloaded the photographs of Pete from my camera. She was chattering about how good the images were, laying it on somewhat thickly about how brilliant I was at capturing people in exactly the right moment as if I knew seconds before how their micro expressions might shift.

She'd paused about halfway through and adjusted a few of the photographs so they appeared in black and white. She said if I ever got tired of being confined to executives and other ladder-climbers, I could set up my own studio. It sounded fun, but I imagined there was a bit more to it than just putting up a web page and announcing you were a world-class photographer worth twelve-hundred dollars an hour. Although thinking about that potential hourly rate for a high-end artist did give me a moment's pause.

"How did you get so good at this? Trystan said you didn't have any background in photography."

"I took the class he arranged for me."

"That's it?"

"Yes."

"What all did they teach you?"

"Mostly about the camera. And lighting. The shop owner is really into lighting. I only have one session left. It's about composition."

"I think you have that down."

"Thanks."

"Composition is probably more about an aesthetic eye than anything."

"Probably. But I'll still show up. It's interesting. I'm sure I can learn a lot more."

She glanced at the partially-closed door and turned her chair to face me. She lowered her voice. "Sudden change of subject — is there a problem between you and Stephanie?"

"Not that I know of."

"She seems…I don't think she…"

"We're water and oil."

"Why?"

"I'm not religious. And she…"

"I'm not religious either. This is more than that."

"What happened?" I sat on the windowsill.

She scooted her chair closer to the window. "She seems to think there's something going on with you and Jim Kohn."

"There is."

Her eyes widened. She pulled her head back slightly.

"Not that. He's a little… well, a lot…full of himself. And more than a little misogynistic."

She laughed. "I've never met him, but there are some things in his personality tests. And his profile…" She nodded. "I can see that."

"He came on to me, but it's nothing. I have it handled."

"Are you sure? Stephanie told me she saw him with his hand up your skirt."

"Not true."

"I think she told Trystan."

"Why would she lie about something like that?"

"Stephanie's…different. Out of place in the world, is how I would describe it."

I nodded. Why would Stephanie tell a lie that could be easily found out? Was she not very smart, or didn't she care if she was found out?

Her attack on my position here was not what I'd expected. I thought she wanted to befriend me, set her sights on me for conversion. I thought she wanted to beat me over the head with that giant cross. Maybe this was her first step in some strange plan of evangelistic fervor that was more modern than the questions Mr. B had shoved down our throats, that filled fat binders with questions which assumed every person would answer the way the proselytizer wanted.

Two or three possible answers were assumed as if the human mind can only take three possible paths when confronted with any kind of question. It was absurd. It's why everyone got frustrated with the program. No one answered the way you expected. Mr. B should have learned that the first night he questioned me on the stage.

She folded her arms. "She's always been a bit odd, but since you were hired, she's gone a little over the edge."

"How?"

Diana shrugged. She wheeled her chair back toward her computer. "I don't know why she wants to create problems. This is such a great organization. I love what I'm doing. I thought she loved it too. Did anything happen?"

"No. We had breakfast together. I caught her snooping in Trystan's office. That's it."

"What was she looking for?"

"No idea. She tried to pretend she wanted a book, but it was obvious she was looking for something."

Diana smiled. She twisted her earring through the hole in her lobe. It was a thin curved bar that had a silver chain dangling in front and behind, a turquoise stone on each end. I studied the earrings, trying to figure out how they went into her ear. They looked light and not the kind of earrings that make your neck ache or get in the way when you put your phone to your ear. They looked like the kind of earrings I might like.

A line of creased skin formed between her eyebrows. "Just watch your back."

"I will."

"I wish I had."

"What do you mean?"

She sighed. She looked down at her hands. She twisted the ring on the middle finger of her right hand, turning it around so the black onyx stone was underneath, then rotating the wide silver band until it appeared on top again. "Look, I guess I should tell you the whole story."

"There's a story?"

She laughed, then glanced at the door again. She spoke in a whisper now. "I did something stupid. She caught me. She's very sneaky, and I don't think I fully realized that. I thought she was just quiet."

"I can't believe you'd do anything stupid."

"We all do once in a while, right?"

"Maybe." I thought of the dead man's telescope I'd stolen and all the hassle it had taken to get it out of my life once I realized my mistake. "Yes. I wouldn't say stupid things. Impulsive."

"But sometimes it's more than impulsive. It's…what I did wasn't right. Unethical, really. And she said she'll tell

Trystan if I don't express concern about you to him."

I turned and looked out the window. Curiosity bloomed when she said she'd done something unethical, because I couldn't see that in her at all, but the moment she added that last bit, my thoughts went elsewhere. What was wrong with Stephanie? I didn't do anything to mess with her. We hardly even interacted except for casual hallway chat after that breakfast and our impromptu trip down Fifth Avenue. What the hell?

I stared at all those windows facing our building, wondering what dramas were going on behind each one. Millions of people and millions of problems, petty and huge. "Are you going to?"

"No. I don't have any concerns." She smiled. "That's why I'm telling you. You should talk to her. Find out what the issue is and see if you can get her to back off."

I turned to face her. I almost asked what she'd done but decided to leave it alone. I'd find out eventually.

49

As Diana said, we all do stupid things from time to time.

Two martinis are my limit. I know that. But that night at Jim's dinner party, I had three. It's one of those things that sometimes happens, despite your best effort at predicting how an evening will go. It was a serious lapse. I knew who Jim was, but allowed the lure of nice vodka to overwhelm my good sense.

His house was more of an estate than a house, located about an hour out of the city. Mansion would be a better description than house. The place was complete with a security guard-manned gate and a horseshoe-shaped drive. The ancient trees and lush gardens seemed to stretch for acres in the early darkness of an October evening. Inside, there were more staircases and bedrooms than I could count on my several forays out of the dining room to look for a bathroom while also exploring the monstrosity of a house.

The house I'm building in my mind will be spacious and well-appointed, but I cannot see why anyone would ever need twenty bedrooms, unless you have large weekend parties, which I suppose some do. It's not a world I've ever lived in.

Speaking of a world I hadn't experienced, Jim had sent a limo to pick me up. Just me. All the way from Midtown, along roads sheltered by dark trees, I nestled into luxurious leather and the silence of a well-insulated vehicle. Outside of my window, I watched stars slowly appear, scattered across the sky once they were no longer fighting with city lights.

The recognizable faces at his party were as astonishing as the house. Faces that everyone knows. Faces that flow through Twitter and Facebook and news feeds every week, sometimes every day. Those who were known to everyone talked to each other as if there were an impenetrable and invisible wall between the known and the unknown, the known breathing that rarefied air everyone talks about. The others formed smaller groups, occasionally glancing around to see whether they were noticed.

I was surprised that Jim had been able to get some of these high profile people to attend. If he had so much pull that people whose lives are lived on a stage were willing to make time for a party with no particular purpose, then why did he need Trystan to help him up his game?

They were happy to drink his wine and eat his food and socialize, but did they trust him with their money?

No one seemed overly troubled by the divide between big names and no names. I found it fascinating and would rather have spent my time photographing that division, but I was supposed to be capturing every possible expression that crossed Jim's face, not taking celebrity photos. It required a lot of focus, and I should not have succumbed to martinis.

But the moment I walked in the door, I was met by a man in a tuxedo who asked what I'd like to drink.

I explained my role.

"I know who you are, Alexandra." He extended a lightly tanned hand. "I'm Joe. I'm happy to take your drink order."

"I'll have sparkling water with lime."

"Is Pelegrino suitable?"

I nodded, smiling at his formal speech, taking in his

height — well over six feet — eyes that exuded warmth and a slight twinkle in the pale gray, and his broad shoulders, and thick light brown hair. He was a man made for the well-cut tuxedo.

"If you desire anything else, at any time, let me know." He winked.

I hid a second smile. "Thank you."

"For future reference, what is your favorite drink?"

When I told him I liked vodka martinis, he rattled off the list of available vodkas. I might as well have been in a high-end bar in the city. I caved. I asked for a martini with Ultimat and three large olives.

"I'll have that for you right away." There was no suggestion he was amused by my child-like desire for excess olives.

I went out to the patio where heat lamps kept the air pleasant enough that a sweater wasn't required. There was a cushioned teak patio chair, large enough for two people and perfect for me and my equipment. It was at the far corner of the slate patio, looking out over a vast lawn, a pale blue, backlit swimming pool, and a forested area beyond that. I wondered whether Jim owned the forest or his property simply backed up to a greenbelt.

Joe brought my drink and moved a small table close to my chair so I could reach it easily. He asked whether I would like oysters or a few crab legs with chili sauce. I opted for the crab leg. That too appeared on my table with a tiny silver fork and a linen cocktail napkin. I hadn't known they made cocktail napkins out of fabric.

I ate the crab leg and took a sip of my drink. It was perfect. I wondered whether Joe had made it himself. The superbly mixed drink didn't bode well for the rest of the evening. But I managed to persuade myself that the alcohol would help me relax, stop my constant analysis, and help me take pictures that came from instinct rather than a calculated plan. It sounded plausible. I'd only had a single sip at that point.

The evening flowed flawlessly. I ate three crab legs and took it slowly with my martini. Eventually, Jim and his guests moved into the dining room. I took a few photographs during the salad course and then wandered out so he could eat his dinner and talk without knowing the camera was snapping every flick of his tongue and stray drop of sauce on his upper lip. Later, I would be able to stand just outside the door and capture more shots without him noticing.

I climbed the wide curving staircase and wandered around the second floor, but didn't venture to the third. I tried counting the bedrooms but was sidetracked when I came upon a workout room that was as large as some private gyms. It included its own shower, jacuzzi, and steam room. It featured floor-to-ceiling windows offering the same view as the patio.

Downstairs, I wandered through sitting rooms and the kitchen and a smaller staging room for the caterers. I saw the living room and a library and finally ended up in Jim's office.

It too had built-in shelves of books, as if the library wasn't enough. The shelves here were filled with money management books. Of course, there are thousands of books on any topic, probably tens of thousands, but seeing so many in the flesh was overwhelming. I found it hard to believe he'd read all of them, but when I pulled one off the shelf, it had a few clear plastic sticky tabs marking pages that contained notes scribbled in ink.

I replaced the book and wondered whether I should embark on a self-improvement course. Maybe I'd reach my goals more quickly if I had more knowledge and a bit more direction to my life rather than following whatever happened to present itself at any given moment.

Below the books was a series of cabinets, the top of those functioning as a wide shelf where a collection of at least twenty-five framed photographs were displayed. It wasn't the cluttered jumble of frames and photos you sometimes see. There were a lot, but they didn't crowd each other.

All of them were pictures of the woman who was framed in his office. I saw her sitting on a beautiful chocolate brown horse in full riding gear. I saw her holding a tennis racket and a golf club. Others showed her holding a champagne flute, a tiny dog, a cosmo, a signed copy of a bestselling novel, and a pair of flippers for snorkeling.

Mostly, I saw her with her arms wrapped around Jim Kohn.

And lastly, I saw an enormous diamond on her left ring finger. So, she was his wife. Or still a fiancée.

I picked up one of the photographs.

"Do you need anything?" I replaced the photograph and turned.

Joe stood in the doorway. His face lacked any readable expression. He didn't appear to be chastising me. He truly seemed to want to know if I needed anything.

He looked at the glass in my hand. "Another martini?"

"I shouldn't. I haven't eaten much."

"We have a place set for you." He led me to a small

room with a TV, more books, and an impressive array of magazines on a credenza. I sat at a table covered with a white cloth. In the center was a single white taper, nestled securely in a silver candlestick holder.

Thin strips of rare beef, an arrangement of baby green beans, and creamy wild rice with pieces of dried cranberry were arranged on a white plate. I sat down, and Joe placed a white napkin across my lap.

As I picked up my fork, a glass with icy breath on its sides, containing a lovely martini with four large olives was placed beside the unused wine glass. I didn't object. I should have.

50

That second martini went down smoothly, faster than the first. The food was delicious, and the sting of the vodka and vermouth was a nice complement to the sweetness of the wild rice and those delicately buttered green beans.

When I finished eating, I returned to the dining room where they were just starting dessert. The catering staff was carrying in plates of chocolate cake as well as trays of cheese and fruit, flatbread and salted nuts.

It had reached the point that I did not see how Jim could be persuaded he needed any more shots of his facial ticks. There are hundreds of variations, of course, but in my mind, it was a hard sell to convince the man that every single one of them mattered.

On the other hand, he desperately wanted these people as clients, so maybe the persuasion wasn't all that difficult. Desperation is a persuasion of its own. He needed something to cling to that would get him believing he could achieve what he was after.

I was having a good time simply watching these people whose faces I knew from television and the news. Seeing them eat and laugh and behave like normal human beings was oddly fascinating. It's easy to think they aren't real people when you see them packaged and clipped by the media.

The media is supposed to be perfectly unbiased, but that's an impossible feat. No one is unbiased. We all have opinions. We wouldn't be human beings without them. I can't imagine seeing every thought you try to express chopped up into something that will sound provocative or provide click bait, something that people can argue with as if that's all you had to say. Editing you and then persuading the world that's the sum of your thoughts. If you really want to know what a politician or a celebrity thinks, you need to listen to a long interview, and even those get interrupted by the interviewer looking to gain recognition for his or her own sparkling witticism. It's hard enough to know a human being face-to-face, filtered through the media is impossible.

My thoughts distracted me from keeping my camera on Jim. Of course, I'd had to sign a non-disclosure, spelling out that I couldn't sell, reproduce, distribute any photographs of the house or Jim, or take a single photograph of anyone else, including staff and caterers. Occasionally I let the lens of my camera drift toward one of the public figures just for a moment, thinking they wouldn't know if I snapped a photograph. I could keep it to myself.

The caterers were walking around the table, offering after dinner drinks and pouring coffee. Jim looked as sharp as he had when the evening began. I realized he hadn't touched a drop of alcohol. I had to give him credit for that. But now, he was accepting a beautiful cut crystal glass from Joe, partially filled with gold liquid. He must have decided it was time to let down his guard. He raised the glass to his guests, thanked them for a terrific evening, and took a long, greedy sip.

The others toasted in return, insisting all the thanks should go to him.

He took another swallow of the gold stuff. His face

looked triumphant. I didn't need a course in micro expressions to read that. I took several shots, closing the distance with each one.

Joe appeared at my side, carrying a tray with a gorgeous martini. Four olives. I picked it up and took a sip of brain-chillingly cold liquid. As it flooded my senses, I nearly sighed with pleasure. I'd been there for several hours and didn't feel overly tipsy, but still. Three martinis is a lot. I took another sip. It was so good.

Soon the guests were pushing back their chairs, murmuring good-byes, piling on more thank-you's, and moving toward the doorway. Joe was handing out coats and purses. The front door stood open, and two valets had begun driving cars up to the front steps. A few limos in the mix were sucking their occupants into the black cars and away into the equally black night.

I packed up my camera and asked another staff person for my coat and bag. While I waited, Jim crossed the entryway and stood beside me.

"Will you stay for a few more minutes? I'd like your take on the evening," he said.

I caught a glimpse of the red flag. I heard a distant warning. Deep inside, below the hum of the martinis. But three is a lot. I ignored the faint warnings. "Sure. No problem."

"Would you like a drink while we chat?"

"No thanks."

"Just a glass of wine."

"Okay. Why not."

As the guests continued to depart, I followed him to the office.

He stopped at the doorway. "I'll be right back."

I returned to the photographs I'd been looking at earlier. I picked up several in turn, studying each one, trying to figure out what the story might be. Jim didn't wear a wedding ring, and there had been no hostess at the opposite end of the table. Instead, one of his best clients had been seated there.

The last photograph, partially covered by a duplicate of the one in his office, showed her wearing an enormous black hat that covered most of her face. Her dress was scooped off one shoulder. Most interesting of all, in that sole photograph, she wasn't wearing her diamond ring. It looked like a cover shot for a magazine. Then it struck me that aside from the photographs with Jim, most of the images looked like they belonged in a model's portfolio.

"I should get rid of them."

I turned.

Jim stood a few feet behind me. He held two glasses of red wine. He handed one of the goblets to me. He clinked his glass against mine. "To new expressions."

Clever toast. I smiled and took a sip. "What should you get rid of?"

He nodded toward the cluster of photographs. "The pictures. But it's too painful." His eyes looked glassy, with something else beneath the surface that I couldn't read. Too bad Diana wasn't there to help me.

"Why?"

He sighed. "She's beautiful, isn't she."

"Yes."

"My wife."

"Oh. I thought…"

He held up his hand to silence me, an overly aggressive gesture. I was simply being polite.

"She left me."

"I'm sorry to hear that."

"Clearly, I haven't let go." He gave me a sad puppy look. The expression didn't quite match his tone of voice.

My impression was that he wanted me to feel sorry for him. My impression was that he'd definitely *let go*, but he liked showing off photographs of his hot former wife, for some inexplicable, and possibly sick reason. "I'm sure you will at the right time."

"Why don't we sit down."

Instead of walking to the chair he went to the window seat near the front of the room. "Sit here. You need to see this." I took a sip of wine and followed.

He opened the drapes, and I looked out on a garden I hadn't seen earlier. It was decorated with hundreds, possibly thousands of fairy lights wrapped expertly around trees, strung across freeform metal sculptures, and rising toward a pole at the center of the garden where they joined. It was breathtaking.

"It's amazing," I said.

"I find it very soothing."

I took a sip of wine and put my glass on the windowsill. I leaned forward to get a better look through the side panel of the bay window.

Then, Jim's hand was on my leg, sliding up under my dress. Instead of pushing him off, instead of registering shock, and yet not being at all surprised, my first thought was of Stephanie. Did she have some kind of weird psychic ability that had allowed her to foresee this? Of course she hadn't. My mind raced. I didn't believe in that sort of thing. Possibly she had a good read on Jim from his profile, and the leap to him doing something like this hadn't been a big one. But those three martinis buzzed in my brain, and it took me a minute to sort myself into reality.

In that half second while my thoughts raced in absurd directions, his mouth moved onto mine, and his hand left my leg and slid down the front of my dress.

I gasped as much as I could with his wet, insistent mouth on mine, his tongue trying to force its wormy way past my lips. His fingers were hot and damp as they touched my skin, moving quickly inside my bra, grabbing my nipple, and pinching hard.

I tried to wrench my head away from his mouth, but his other arm was locked around my neck in a way that prevented any movement. My whole body was in the grip of his hands and mouth, and I couldn't turn or make any intelligent sounds.

Without any flexibility in my upper body that would allow me to push him off, I resorted to my legs. I lifted my leg as high as my short dress would allow. I slammed my high heel into the top of his foot.

He cried out. He quickly released my mouth and upper body. "What the fuck?" His voice was a bellow, and I wondered if Joe would come into the room. Or maybe this was a common thing, and he was paid well to ignore alarming sounds from Jim and his guest.

"Get off of me!" I stood and started toward the door.

"Wait. I thought…"

"Wrong."

He was suddenly standing closer, but several feet away,

careful to keep distance between us. "I misread your signals."

"No, you didn't. There were no signals."

"That dress." He looked at my legs. They weren't over-exposed. Nothing was. It was a typical little black dress, more conservative than many.

"It's a dinner party."

"I shouldn't have."

"Stephanie will be in touch to schedule a meeting with Trystan to review the photographs."

I went to the entryway, picked up my camera equipment, and went outside. Fortunately for me, the limo had been waiting directly in front, moving into position when the other guests left. For a moment, I considered calling an Uber but then decided against hanging around for possibly an hour before it arrived. I climbed into the back. I would enjoy the ride home at Jim's expense.

Inside the dark, silent car, I opened the tiny fridge. I peeled off the foil and popped the cork on a split of champagne. I filled a flute with bubbling liquid and took a sip.

When the limo finally stopped in front of my apartment, there were two empty half bottles discarded on the seat.

51

Portland

Any one of my brothers would have been happy to talk to me about the situation with Mr. B. They loved giving me advice. Mostly, their advice revolved around my perceived flaws.
You take things too seriously.
You fight battles you can't win.
You're stubborn.
You always have to be right.
They were happy for me to call them at their dorms and talk about anything. They were curious to hear what was going on at home. They wanted the gory details of my disagreements with my parents. I'd been a source of entertainment for them over the years. After each story, they jumped in with their insights regarding *how I was.*

Still, I liked talking to them. I laughed at their advice, repeated during every phone call, and with each brother — Eric sounding like Jake who sounded like Tom.

The house was empty without my brothers. And life was more difficult without the distraction they'd provided. Now, my father was laser-focused on getting me to traverse the *last mile*, as he called it. As if I were a project he needed to complete to perfection and he was very unhappy with the progress so far. In a way, I suppose children are projects. But only for parents who forget that each little bundle of joy has her own DNA and it can be molded, but it definitely cannot be modified.

There was no one to talk to about my next move with Mr. B. I had to figure it out myself, and there was no obvious solution. I was not going to write something I didn't believe. And he was not going to back down until I produced a speech that he deemed appropriate for me to deliver, looking out into the darkness, seeing the whites of my friends' eyes and hearing the impatient shifting of their bodies on folding metal chairs.

Finally, I wrote what I believed. It was the only way.

The next week, I brought it sealed inside an envelope. He didn't smile or thank me when I handed it to him. He simply pinched his fingers around the envelope, holding only the very edge as if whatever was inside might stain his hands.

While we acted out the next role-playing exercise outlined in our binders, Mr. B slipped out of the room. A moment before the end of the twenty-minute role-playing, he returned. It seemed he'd set an alarm to be sure he was back in time to prevent any goofing off before his final lecture of the evening.

I'd managed to skate through role-playing by always volunteering to be the prompter in each group I was assigned to. The others forgot what to say quite often because we were required to deliver the lines word-for-word. Mrs. B moved among the small groups, her narrow figure draped in a white dress, appearing like some kind of specter in the poorly-lit auditorium. Her jaw-length blonde hair was almost white, and her pale, make-up-free skin completed the impression.

Mrs. B never said much. She smiled vacantly at the high

school kids who were often daydreaming during her husband's lectures. She occasionally led the short opening prayer. She stuck close to Mr. B's side. When he was talking one-on-one with an eager student who wanted to save the world from their sins, she stood slightly behind him, stroking the sleeve of his coat and nodding with barely perceptible movements of her head. She always wore pale clothes — usually white, with the occasional beige, soft baby yellow, and washed-out pink. The colors were so low-key, her dresses and sweaters looked white until she moved directly under the beam of a fluorescent light.

The first time she'd actually looked me in the eye was after Mr. B chastised me about my submission of *sinners in the hands of an angry god*. Long shadows covered her brow, and her eyes peered out at me, looking more frightened than angry that I had the gall to defy her husband.

Mr. B crossed the room, heading directly toward me. Mrs. B followed, trotting to keep up. She looked worried. Every few steps, she reached out as if to grab his coattails.

"Please come with me." He curled his finger and then pointed toward the side door.

Off we went to one of the two-person conference rooms.

"Sit down."

I sat. I'd already fought and more or less won that battle. It would only drag things out if we spent ten or fifteen minutes arguing about the position of my body.

He slapped the envelope on the table. It made a surprisingly loud smack on the wood veneer. The edge of the folded pages slid out. "Do you want me to bring your parents into this?"

"Not really."

"Do they know you're an unbeliever?"

"Probably."

"Have you been baptized?"

"Not really."

"What the hell does that mean?" His face turned red as he realized a curse word had slipped out, suggesting the word had lived inside his head for some time. "You either are, or you are not."

"My father shoved me into the water."

"Did you repent and open your heart?"

"No."

"Then you were not baptized. Why are you even here?"

It was a strange question, given that his whole purpose for being there was to ask people questions that led them to change their lives. Didn't he think he should be trying to convert me instead of yelling at me for not being converted? "My parents belong to this church. They want me to be here."

I don't know why he'd never spoken to my father. I suppose he didn't want to admit his failure. I suppose he thought he could control me with threats and was unwilling to give up that belief, just as he wholeheartedly believed that threats of damnation brought people to their knees.

He took a deep breath. I could see him trying to calm his feelings, could almost hear the words he was silently whispering, pleading with god to pierce my heart. "I'm deeply concerned about you."

"I'm fine."

"We never know when life will come to an end. It can happen quite suddenly."

I had no doubt that it could, but I was not going to spend my life thinking about my death. I would worry about it when the time came. If I didn't have a chance to think before my heart stopped beating, then so be it. Who knew what might come after. Maybe all the dead are in another dimension, laughing at how desperately we cling to life. Or maybe there's nothing. Or maybe god is on his throne, and I'm in big trouble. I smiled.

"This isn't funny." He was quiet for a few minutes. He moved toward the door. "You're not using this as an excuse to escape the work required in this course. You will still do the role-playing. You will still make the evangelism calls. But you will not be doing it with your friends where you can poison their minds or turn this into a joke. You'll be visiting unbelievers with my wife. She's offered to take you under her wing."

I didn't need a wing to cower beneath, but making visits with his wife might be interesting. More interesting than listening to the other kids parrot what they'd memorized from the pages of those huge navy blue binders, stamped with a large white cross and a white flame, the name of the course arching across the top.

Once it was over, I might have some entertaining stories for my brothers.

52

New York City

Despite my three martinis and the equivalent of an entire bottle of champagne to dissolve the feel of Jim's hands and mouth, I was awake at five-thirty the following morning.

I'm used to pushing through alcohol and cigarettes to run or lift weights the following morning, but I wasn't up for either. Instead, I dressed in jeans and walking shoes and a long-sleeved T-shirt. I brushed my hair into a ponytail, put on a white hoodie, and went outside.

Carrying a large bottle of water, sipping as I walked, I headed to Central Park. It was a ten-block journey that I covered rapidly. Juggling the water and long, quick strides were easy because the sidewalks were deserted at six on a chilly Saturday morning.

When I reached the park, I continued along Central Park West to Strawberry Fields. I spent some time contemplating the mosaic memorial to John Lennon — *Imagine*. As the sun rose, I finished my water. I stood and walked to a small secluded area where I did a few yoga poses that were manageable in jeans, on concrete, wearing shoes — mostly variations on the warrior pose.

I walked home and made scrambled eggs with cheese and tomatoes, green onions and salsa. I cooked up four strips of bacon and two pieces of wheat toast with butter. I brewed three cups of coffee and drank all of them.

By the time I'd showered, I felt like myself.

I tossed the roses left by Rafe. Their brown-tinged heads had been permanently bowed for over a week. They'd lasted longer than they should have. As I stuffed them into the trash, the stems snapping, the petals falling away from the hips like sloughed-off skin cells, an idea began to take shape. The memory of those roses might be useful in the near future. I took out the trash and spent what was left of the morning smoking on the roof. It was deserted. The sky was crisp and clear, and there was no wind. I felt transported and relaxed.

That afternoon was my final photography class.

As I walked out of my building and turned toward Eighth Avenue, Victoria appeared beside me, emerging from the alcove leading into the building next door where she'd obviously waited for me to emerge.

"I thought we'd walk together," she said.

I shrugged.

"That's not very friendly."

"Late night. I'm tired."

"Oh. Did you meet a guy?" She shoved her elbow at my upper arm and giggled with far too much enthusiasm.

"Work. Theoretically."

"Why do you say that?" She hurried to keep pace with me. "Don't walk so fast."

"I like walking fast."

"Whatever." She scrambled until she was a few steps ahead of me. "Why did you say *theoretically*?"

"It was a dinner party. I took photographs. So a party, but work."

"Oh. Did you meet any interesting guys?"

"I was working."

"That doesn't mean you can't meet people."

"In this case, it does."

She pestered me with questions the rest of the way to the photography store. Inside, Leon was helping a customer. He gestured toward the back, indicating we should wait for him in the classroom. I was unreasonably annoyed. The class was scheduled for one o'clock. It was three minutes to one. He should have someone covering the store so he could be ready for us.

We trudged to the back. I sighed and sank into a chair. I wasn't as restored as I'd thought. The memory of three martinis that left me slightly off-guard and slowed my reflexes swam behind my eyes. The memory of Jim's hands and mouth ate at the inside of my throat, making each breath feel like something I had to work to draw into my body. I wanted to put him in his place. I *needed* to put him in his place, but I wasn't sure whether I should do that permanently. It was risky. It would be a lot of work. Right now, I didn't feel up to it.

"You're in a foul mood," Victoria said.

"I told you I had a late night."

"Big deal. You've never worked late before? Or did you party and you're not telling me?"

I unzipped my bag and removed my camera. We didn't normally use the cameras until Leon finished his instructions and lectures on art, but I wanted to touch the solid weight of it. I wanted to feel the heft of metal and plastic against my fingers, I wanted to have something to manipulate and adjust. I wanted to think about the power it had to unsettle people, to capture what was inside of them, inadvertently revealed in a photograph.

Sure, the same can be done with any smartphone. But not with such intimate results. The lighting that Leon loved to talk about was difficult to control with a phone camera. And more importantly, the expensive, well-crafted Nikon was able to observe people from a distance. It took fragments of their lives that they had no idea they were yielding. Just as some indigenous people believed, a camera actually does steal a piece of the soul because it captures and exposes the eyes and the shape of the mouth in a way that allows closely held thoughts to seep out. And with a good telephoto lens, the subject never knows that a portion of their life has been preserved and can be analyzed and might ultimately be used to betray them.

A smartphone is busy with too many things — connecting to friends and relatives, exploring the entire world. It brings every piece of information humankind has ever considered or discovered into the palm of your hand. It sends your thoughts to a single person, presumably for their eyes only, or it blasts your words and images around the globe, to be re-tweeted or shared with strangers. A camera does one thing.

"Why are you ignoring me?" Victoria said.

I looked at her, waiting for her brain cells to connect, recalling that I'd mentioned twice I was burned out. It was five minutes after one. No Leon.

"How is work going for you?" Victoria said.

"Fine."

"Still liking it a lot?"

"For the most part."

She tipped her head to the side and gave me a semi-smile. "Even when you love the work, there's always the people. They're not all lovable, am I right?"

"You're right."

"Problems with your boss? It's so frustrating to not control your destiny. Your money is in his or her hands. Your career is subject to someone else's whims. Really, it feels like your entire life is being controlled by someone you hardly know."

"I don't look at it like that." As I spoke, I wasn't sure if that was true. Usually, I know when I'm lying. But those words came out, and I wasn't sure where they'd come from or whether I meant them.

"Good for you." She laughed softly. "I had a boss once who showed up in my office every morning a few minutes before the time I was supposed to start work. When I came in, he wrote the time on my whiteboard, and beside it, in red, he wrote how many minutes I was late."

I laughed, grudgingly happy she'd shaken off my mood. "I guess he didn't have a lot to do?"

"That's how middle management is in a big company," she said. "Micro-management is their forte."

"And that's one reason I like working for smaller companies."

"Or for yourself. Which is the best of all," she said.

"But a lot of pressure. It's all on you, right? Rise or fall by your own effort."

"That's the greatest thrill of all. Even more than loving what you do, to be honest. At least for me it is." She unzipped her bag and removed her camera.

She was right. Maybe someday I'd give more thought to

that. But for now, I did like what I was doing. And I liked having a predictable paycheck. I liked playing mental games with my co-workers and the people I reported to. Soon, our work with Jim would be over, and although I was sure there would be more like him, they would be in the minority.

53

The door opened, and Leon stepped into the room. He didn't apologize for being late — thirteen minutes past one. I felt like writing it on the whiteboard, but there was no red pen.

He launched into a lengthy commentary on what great students we'd been, and although he needed more students to supplement the shop's income, he'd enjoyed teaching a group of two. We'd asked perceptive questions, and we were quick to learn, and we had a natural talent for photography.

How on earth he would know that, I had no idea. He hadn't reviewed any of the shots we'd taken.

He folded his arms. "For our final class today, I'm going to talk about composition."

I already knew that. I sighed, hoping I'd get something out of this last class after dragging my unwilling body out of my apartment.

"Along with lighting, composition is the key to good photography." He went on to cover some pretty basic things about framing, simplicity, and the rule of thirds. He talked about breaking a subject or scene into nine segments and how to think of each one, training your eye to see both detail and the supporting elements. He made it sound as if the physical world existed only as a prop for a photograph. He had us experiment by taking photographs of the table and chairs.

"Such simple objects," he said. "But with a skilled eye,

they can become meaningful in themselves. Have you ever considered the nature of a chair? The simplest object can become a work of art, with the right photographer."

I hadn't ever considered the nature of a chair, and I saw his point.

He talked some more. We asked a few questions, mostly to be polite, I think, since his lecture was pretty clear. He recommended a few books.

While Victoria was asking him to repeat the titles and then suggesting he write the titles and authors on the whiteboard, my mind wandered to composition and Stephanie. If I had a shot of Stephanie in Trystan's office, it might make her back off. She'd been shot through with guilt when I caught her. There was no way she wanted Trystan to know she was the sort of person who invaded his personal space, who spied on her colleagues. Or that she'd betrayed his trust, even if there was nothing to find.

But she was there so early. Short of coming in at four in the morning and hiding in my office, how on earth would I get a picture of her? It might take days to catch her at it.

As part of his list of book recommendations, Leon wrote the name of photo editing software on the board.

I smiled. Stephanie had made up a story about me. Why not conjure up my own photograph? All I needed was an image of her and an image of Trystan's office.

54

Monday morning I ran for six miles along streets that were empty when I began at five but filling quickly by the time I returned to my apartment building.

The day ahead was fairly easy, without a lot of desk time. Trystan and I were scheduled to meet Pete at his office to review photographs from his speech at the cigar club. The meeting was set for nine-thirty, so there was no point in going to the office first. Trystan had told me to take a cab and submit the receipt for reimbursement. He'd ordered me a credit card that would allow me to charge what was necessary. I couldn't see what that would be, beyond the occasional cab and the photo editing software, if I figured out a legitimate need for it.

I wore a skirt and sweater with a short jacket and moderately high heels. There's something about the Financial District that makes you feel you should dress up. I don't have a lot of nice pants, I'd rather wear jeans. If I'm getting slicked up, I like to wear dresses or skirts. As long as they're well-cut, they're more comfortable.

Some women who want gender equality seem to think a woman should dress like a man. They believe that because men don't expose their legs or bare arms or toes in the business world, women should also refrain. I don't get it. I love dresses and skirts and girlie shoes and make-up. Maybe men should dress like women. That would be just as equal.

Sure high heels are sometimes painful, and bad for your feet over the long haul, but no one can deny they look great.

When I exited my building in high heels and a skirt, I was certain I'd look like a financial expert myself. My hair was tamed into a sleek bob instead of the tangled waves I'd been wearing since I had it cut to the middle of my neck. My make-up was understated, and my lip gloss was a conservative buff color.

This was the first time I'd gone directly to the Financial District from my apartment, so I allowed extra time, choosing to pad what Google maps told me. Far too much padding, as it turned out.

I arrived at ten after nine. I paid the cab driver and entered the lobby. I seated myself on one of several minimalist off-white leather couches. They were scattered throughout the spacious lobby, arranged with similarly styled chairs and glass tables. Potted plants provided the illusion of privacy in each sitting area.

I put my camera and bag on the floor beside me and looked around the lobby. Most people were entering or leaving the building. Only a handful were seated, waiting for appointments.

On the table in front of me was an array of newspapers — The New York Times, the Financial Times, The Wall Street Journal, and a bunch of others. There were papers in French and German, Chinese and another-character-rich language I wasn't sure about. Maybe Korean.

I picked up the Wall Street Journal and scanned the front page. I smiled behind the paper, wondering if I still looked like a girl from the midwest, or Portland, for that matter. I hoped I looked like a woman who had millions at her fingertips and was delving into the Journal for insight into the financial under-pinnings of the global economy.

"Slumming?"

I lowered the paper.

Standing in front of me, looming over me actually, was Jim Kohn.

"We don't have an appointment, do we?" He pulled out his phone and tapped the screen.

"We have other clients in this building." I wasn't sure why he was pretending ignorance. Pete had referred him to us.

"Ah." He slid the phone into his pocket. "Then why are you sitting in the lobby? Soliciting new business?" He winked.

I folded the paper and placed it on the table. It doesn't happen often, hardly ever, but I was shocked. He was so calm and easy. Had he completely forgotten Saturday night? But even if he had...*Soliciting?* His meaning was clear, but if I called him on it, he would deny it. He'd turn it into something I'd done inside my own head.

He smiled at my hard stare, unfazed. He took a step back and looked down, his gaze lingering on my legs.

I uncrossed them and stood. I moved away from the couch and gave him a smile designed to melt him. And he melted, I could see his face change. I could see the bravado fade and a glimmer of hope flicker in the corners of his eyes.

"By the way," I said. "Thank you for the roses. It wasn't necessary, but so appreciated." I continued smiling, making sure the heat inside of me bled to my eyes, to be misinterpreted by him.

If he hesitated, I didn't catch it.

"Of course, of course. I understand I was offensive.

I'm a feminist kind of guy. I understand women. Probably more than you realize."

I was sure he didn't understand a single thing about women, or human beings, for that matter. He understood money, and he understood what he wanted and how impressive he was, but his understanding of humanity stopped at the surface of his own skull.

The images of Rafe's yellow roses came into my mind, beautiful no matter how they'd irritated me. I saw the brown petals falling away like torn scraps of paper. I saw the broken stems as I'd put them in the trash, but the thorns had been as sharp as ever, even in death.

"Women are suckers for roses." He grinned.

"Yes, we are."

"I'm glad there's no bad blood between us."

I smiled.

"I respect Trystan," he said. "And I value what he's doing for me. I would hate for any misunderstanding between the two of us to interfere with that."

"That would be a shame," I said. I glanced toward the door. It was close to nine-thirty. I was confident Trystan would arrive before the half hour.

As if I'd drawn him with the intensity of my desire to punch Jim Kohn's mouth, the revolving door turned, and Trystan entered the lobby. I lifted my hand and waved.

Jim turned. "Ah. The man himself."

I picked up my bag.

"Good talking to you," Jim said. "I'm glad we're on the same page. I'm looking forward to lots more productive photography sessions."

"I think the photography phase of our assessment is

complete, but check with Trystan."

Trystan was beside me now. "Check on what?"

"No more photographs of Jim, correct?"

"That's right."

"I'm disappointed," Jim said. "I think I was finally getting the hang of relaxing in front of a camera. It's a skill all on its own."

"We should head up," Trystan said.

Jim ignored him. "It's made me realize, I've underestimated what it takes to have a modeling career. Maybe those girls have more talent than I gave them credit for."

Perhaps I'd been right that his wife/fiancée was a model. It explained the flamboyant hat, the exquisite hair and makeup, the photographs with every imaginable prop.

But none of that mattered. Hopefully, I was now done with him.

55

The temperature had dropped to fifty-five, but there was absolutely no wind, so the roof garden was pleasant. I wore a wool coat and had a scarf draped around the back of my neck, just in case. I had the entire garden to myself.

The trees had lost their leaves, but they looked strangely elegant against the lights of the surrounding buildings. They gave off a sense of unyielding pride even though this was what they'd come to. They accepted the seasonal change with grace, everything exposed, nothing useful to offer hungry birds or over-heated humans. They stood still and silent and genteel.

A martini sat on the table in front of me, the liquid just below the rim as I'd only taken a single sip. I was, however, on my third cigarette. It didn't bode well for the next day's run, but right now, I needed to calm myself, and that's one of the best ways I know — the slow, lazy inhalation and exhalation of smoke.

My mind was drifting, not yet latching onto anything specific regarding Jim. During the cab ride back to the office, Trystan had worked on email while I thought about the things Jim had said. I thought about the kind of man who took credit for sending flowers he hadn't. It seemed cheap, in an odd sort of way. As if he saw a chance to make himself look good without spending money. It was also risky. How did he know the actual sender wouldn't come to light?

I took a sip of my drink. I tipped my head back and looked up at the sky. There was a thin covering of clouds, blurring the edges of the three-quarter moon and hiding most of the stars.

"Can I bum one of those?"

I sighed. I lowered my head. Rafe stood near the doorway that led from the stairwell to the garden. I hadn't heard it open, lost in the silent, endless depth of the night sky. "Help yourself."

He approached the sitting area and took the chair across from me. He picked up the pack, removed a cigarette, and pulled a lighter out of his jacket pocket. He flicked the wheel three times before he got a steady flame and was able to light the thing. He held onto it and blew out a thick cloud of smoke. "You seem sad," he said.

"Not at all."

"Vic said you're having issues at work."

"Did she?"

"Are you?"

I inhaled smoke and blew it out. I picked up my glass and took another sip.

"Can I have a taste of that?"

"No."

He nodded and sat back in his chair. "Fair enough."

The darkness settled around us. Traffic sounds seemed to fade, although maybe my senses were simply consumed by the guy across from me. I hoped he wouldn't linger beyond two cigarettes.

"Smoking isn't good for you," he said.

"I'm aware."

"But you do it anyway. Calculated risk?"

"You could say that."

"Less than ten percent of casual female smokers actually get lung cancer," he said.

"Is that right."

He inhaled, held it for a moment, and let out a stream of smoke. "Yep."

I continued smoking. I took another small sip of my drink. I considered eating an olive, but I forced myself to be disciplined.

"You're sure you're not sad?"

"I'm not."

"Lonely? It must be hard to come home from a shitty day at work and have no one to talk to."

"How do you know I don't have anyone to talk to?"

"You live alone, right? I haven't seen anyone there. Not even a weekend guy."

"You seem to think you know who comes and goes from my apartment."

"I'm not spying on you."

I thought of Victoria's interest in a surveillance camera. It had seemed like a ploy to stalk me to my photography class. But maybe not. Maybe she already had one. Maybe it was for both of them to keep a watchful eye on their neighbors.

"I'm not," he said.

"Good to know."

I stubbed out my cigarette and let it fall into the ashtray.

"Are you having another?"

"Maybe."

He picked up the pack and held it out to me. I took it and placed it back on the table.

"You like to fuck with people's heads, don't you."

I laughed.

He grinned. "You can trust me, if you want to talk."

"I doubt that. You hit on me right in front of your girlfriend. Not what I would call a demonstration of trustworthiness."

"Try me."

"No thanks."

"Vic is fine with it. I told you."

"So you did."

"And she told you. Right?"

"She did."

He put out his cigarette, picked up the pack, and pulled out another. This time, he got the flame right on the first try. "I'm not a bad guy."

I ate one of my olives.

"Vic is a strong woman," he said. "She knows her own mind. Knows what she wants. We were best friends before we hooked up."

"That's nice."

"It means we get each other."

"So I've been told." I removed a cigarette from the pack and lit it. I'd only avoided it to refuse his offer. It was stupid and childish and only hurt me when I wanted one. He couldn't have cared less. I inhaled the sharp smoke and blew it out. I wouldn't mind sitting on the roof all night. I wished I'd brought up supplies for a second martini.

If I asked, he would gladly run down and get another glass and the vodka and a shaker, if they had one. Despite his occasional creepiness, he wasn't unpleasant to be around. It occurred to me that, at times, the creepiness almost seemed like an act. He was easy to talk to, or not talk to, as was the case at that moment.

"I like that Vic wants her own money," he said. "She doesn't want to be beholden to any guy. She and I are total equals. I don't know what I'd do without her."

That last part surprised me.

"You seem like the same kind of woman. You want life on your terms."

"Don't all women?"

"Not in the same way."

I didn't feel like giving it much thought. I didn't feel like thinking at all, which made the easy back-and-forth relaxing, like swatting badminton birdies with Tess. No goal, no score.

"I'm sorry your job has you down."

"It'll work itself out," I said.

He nodded. "Lots of times, that's true."

We smoked in silence, the minutes slipping by, but not uncomfortably. I'm not uncomfortable with silence, but most people are. It was nice to smoke, knowing he wasn't squirming for something to say. Sometimes, I like watching that squirming pressure people feel to come up with fresh topics, to find a witty comment or tell a story that will interest the other person. I even like hearing people drone on about a boring part of their day simply because they're compelled to fill the space with sound.

It did bother me that he'd known I was on the roof. I hadn't seen a camera on the landing, and it was crazy to think they'd go that far to keep an eye on me. Were they able to hear my front door from inside their apartment? Or had he knocked on my door and then simply guessed because Victoria told him I liked spending time up here?

Although we'd fallen into an easy conversation for the

first time, there was still something odd about both of them. I couldn't shake that impression, but I couldn't figure out what it was, beyond their very casual approach to sex outside of their relationship. If that was even true. When either one of them mentioned their supposed freedom, it didn't have the ring of truth.

56

The Spirit of God was telling Stephanie that Alexandra had an ulterior motive. But despite that impression, Stephanie couldn't think of a reason to say *no* to the request. It was the eagerness with which Alex had approached her. And the smile that seemed almost sisterly. Even Alex's tone of voice had been adjusted to carry a slightly pleading quality. It was completely unlike her.

Stephanie couldn't understand the reason for the request. After hesitating for half a second too long, she still couldn't think of a way to say *no* without appearing self-conscious, insecure, unfriendly, rude. "Okay. Sure," she said. "Outside?"

"In your office is fine."

"That seems boring."

"My photography instructor said good composition can make a mundane object take on a new kind of life. The essence of it is revealed. Something ordinary becomes a work of art. During our class, we photographed a conference table and chairs. How boring is that? Plus, the focus is on you, not the setting." Alex laughed. "Should we get started?"

Stephanie shrugged. She pushed her chair away from her desk. The finicky back wheel jammed, and the chair stopped abruptly, forcing the seat to make a sharp turn away from the immovable wheel. She stood quickly to avoid falling to the side, feeling more off balance. "Okay."

Alex left and returned a moment later with her fancy new camera, already out of the bag, the flash attached, the lens cap removed. It looked as if she'd been confident that Stephanie would say *yes*. The certainty with which her reaction had been judged irritated her. She almost wanted to say she'd changed her mind. It wasn't too late.

"Stand on the other side of your desk. You can put your hand on it and put your weight more on the right so you won't be so stiff."

"I'm not stiff."

Alex smiled. It was a smug expression. It suggested Alex saw through her and absolutely knew she was stiff. And she was. She felt awkward and lacking in style around Alex. She felt faded and middle-aged. She felt out of step with the world, even more than usual.

"Think about your boyfriend," Alex said.

"I don't have a boyfriend."

Alex laughed. "I bet you have a crush. Think about him." She raised the camera. The shutter clicked several times in succession.

"Wait. I wasn't ready."

"This is about composition. I'm framing you with a partial of the window."

"But I don't want to have a crazy look on my face."

"No worries," Alex said. She moved the camera and made herself cross-eyed, sticking out her tongue and dragging it to one side.

Stephanie sighed.

Alex adjusted the lens. "Now some close-ups. Tell me when you're ready."

"What does a close-up have to do with composition?"

"I want to get your neck and that amazing cross. You have a beautiful neck."

"Do I?" Stephanie touched her throat. She'd never thought about her neck before, never considered that a neck could be beautiful or ugly. It certainly wasn't a feature people tended to point out. And it almost implied that the rest of her was not all that attractive. Who focuses on your neck?

The camera snapped.

"I wasn't..."

"It's okay. I didn't get your face."

"That's weird — taking a picture without my head."

"I told you, it's about practicing composition."

"I don't think that's what Trystan expects from the photographs. It's to capture people's expressions and posture."

"Composition still matters."

Stephanie couldn't see why. She felt Alex was using her, but she couldn't see why that would be either. It was a strong impression, very strong. The Spirit again. It was almost a warning. Composition did not matter at all for Trystan's purposes. Diana needed pictures of people to label their micro expressions before she handed them off to Trystan for review and feedback to their clients. That was it. Photographing their clients had nothing to do with art.

Alex continued to direct Stephanie's movements around the office, standing near the window, then in front of the shelves, and finally, standing near the old-fashioned coat rack. Alex gushed about the coat rack, tossing out flattering words about Stephanie's *excellent* taste, about *quality* objects, about the meaningful nature of furniture that survived for decades or centuries.

It sounded like a bunch of baloney to Stephanie.

After twenty minutes, Alex declared the project finished.

"When can I see the pictures?"

"These are just for my education."

"But they're of me, I should be able to see them. You should delete the ones I don't like."

"This is practice for my class. I told you that."

"I should still get to see them. And have the right to veto."

"No."

"It seems like you misled me."

"I said they were for my class."

"But you didn't say you'd be keeping them."

"I didn't say you could have them."

Stephanie pressed her thumb and middle finger against her brow bone. The conversation was like something out of Alice In Wonderland. The initial feeling returned — she should have said *no*. She'd given in because she hated to be rude, hated to be difficult or uncooperative, a poor sport. But now, Alexandra would have all these pictures, and Stephanie didn't know whether they were flattering and had no idea where they might end up. "I don't want you showing them to anyone."

"The class is over. I *told* you, they're practice."

"Why don't I believe you?"

Alex laughed. "I don't know."

"I feel like you're not telling the truth."

Alex turned her camera on its back and pressed the cap over the lens. "You sound a little paranoid."

Stephanie glared at her. Alex had a way of turning

things inside out. Trying to have a rational discussion with her made the pressure above Stephanie's eyes increase until she felt as if someone had placed a cast-iron hat on her head, pressing it down firmly because it was too small.

They continued throwing words at each other. Stephanie kept her voice low, not wanting to attract the attention of Diana or Trystan. Alex followed her lead, but the words grew more vicious, couched as they were in a soft, gentle tone. Stephanie began to say things she would later wish she hadn't. It was another thing about Alexandra, she pushed you until you cracked.

57

Portland

This is what I wrote for Mr. B, the undelivered speech that got me assigned to teaming with Mrs. B, making calls on church visitors who were ripe for the picking, if we simply asked the right questions in the right order.

I used my most beautiful cursive handwriting, a skill I'd practiced a lot when I was a child and into my teens.

Keyboards are the thing now, but I love cursive writing. I like the feel of my hand moving and the flow of ink onto paper. I always wanted a beautiful, impressive signature. I want gorgeous, loopy letters that let people know I care about my thoughts when I put them onto a sheet of paper, even if it's a sticky note.

I wrote in red ink...

No one needs salvation. Not one single person needs to repent for the way they were created. It was outside of their control. How can it be required that a person repent for something they didn't do? Feelings of lust and hate and envy arise naturally. Should they be over-indulged? No. But there they are, planted in the human heart by god himself, if that's what you believe. Actions might require repentance. I can see that, although not for petty things like teasing or gossip.

But repenting for your thoughts? I don't think so. The human mind was created to think and desire and crave. It's not some self-

inflicted defect. It's the way we are.

How can a creature, supposedly crafted by god be labeled as something that's stained from the inside out? Filth covering their heart and permeating their brain? It makes no sense.

What kind of person looks at a baby with its soft, sweet skin, its large curious and confused eyes, and says — that child is wicked. All of them are wicked. Their tiny toes and fingers, miniature fingernails and noses are said to conceal a heart full of bad things and a mind that's bent on doing evil. I don't accept that. A little baby is simply gazing at the adults surrounding her and wondering how she got here, unsure about how she's supposed to survive without the ability to walk or feed or clothe herself.

I refuse to believe that a superior being created the entire universe, but now looks down on children and insists their parents shove them under the water, forcing them to say that most of their thoughts and many of their words and quite a lot of the things they do need to be wiped out, their insides washed clean. Why? So they can become perfectly fake robots speaking only the allowable words mimicked from the Bible, feeling only supernatural love, and never fucking up?

And the consequences of not nearly drowning your child? Flames licking at her soul for eternity?

A being who created mountains and the sky and eagles and dolphins and lions, along with an infinite array of human beings is now going to send their souls to a place where suffering will never end?

There's a collection of letters and books written by a bunch of men who claimed god spoke directly to them, and those words must be followed to the letter? What made those guys so special? Have they actually thought, really thought hard, about some of the stuff in that book? It's contradictory and boring, full of killing and obscure rules, sprinkled with some good stories and decent poetry.

There's no need for a binder full of questions and answers that we *can use to manipulate people into believing what the people in this church believe. There's no need to visit people under false pretense, acting as if you're interested in their lives, and then hitting them over the head with threats of eternal suffering.*

Thinking back now on what I wrote, I wonder if I'm hypocritical.

I don't think some invisible being would choose to speak through a handful of men and condemn his creation to eternal anguish simply for being human. At the same time, I work diligently to remove from the earth human beings who believe the other half of the human race exists for their pleasure, use, and abuse.

They should repent. Most of them don't.

So I'm doing the same as this Biblical god, his thoughts and directives crafted out of thought-provoking stories and bits of history, a lot of ridiculous dietary laws and bloody dissection of animals and incomprehensible predictions for the future of the planet and its occupants. I've appointed myself as one to decide who deserves punishment.

But I don't believe I'm sending them to suffer endlessly. I like to think they'll wind up in some other dimension where their minds will be opened to see the truth.

I have no handbook or scripture to tell me this is correct, but it makes sense to me.

58

New York City

  Learning to use Photoshop was not easy. I spent every evening for an entire week sipping tea and fiddling with the little tools, watching YouTube videos to help me along. Before I started my self-training, I'd stayed late one evening and taken thirty or forty shots of Trystan's office. This left me with choices. The more I thought about my creative endeavor, the more I wanted to work up several images of Stephanie prowling all over his space.

  I'd caught her in front of the bookcase, but I had no doubt she'd gone through his drawers, possibly tried to unlock his computer. That was close to impossible of course, but the impossible doesn't stop people from trying. Besides, there are enough people that use silly passwords. In his case, she might easily guess it could be his daughter's name or even *provocateur*.

  Combining two images into the amusing mashups you see all over the internet — the heads of political figures welded onto bodies doing something else entirely — is not quite as easy as it looks. Eventually, I got it to work. It required lots of careful, delicate movements of my hand to blur the images of Stephanie's body and make her look like she was standing in his office. It required duplicating images and discarding lots of failed attempts with a loud crunch in my laptop's trash.

A photography pro would figure out my carefully constructed image was fake. Most people who studied the image might figure out it was fake. But Stephanie would be guilty enough to not look too closely. After her initial shock, she might see that the outfit she was wearing was not one she'd worn when she went through his office, but that initial shock was all I needed. That and her fear of Trystan's response. He would have no reason to question the validity of the photo.

I still wasn't sure how I would present the images. Maybe showing them to Stephanie would be enough. Trystan never needed to know. Stephanie would feel guilty, panic, and then tell Trystan she'd lied.

First, I needed to run them by Diana. If she were willing to go along, it would ensure Stephanie would withdraw her threat to Diana. The only problem was, I'm used to handling things on my own so that I'm free to adjust my plan in an instant. Involving Diana would disrupt that flow. But I needed to show her. To shut Stephanie down, Diana needed to know what I'd planned.

During those evenings spent learning how to manipulate images, I'd thought back over my misleading photoshoot with Stephanie.

Her rage had been palpable from the beginning. I could see she didn't want to do it. At the same time, she didn't want to come across bitchy. As I snapped photographs, I came to see that rage was simmering inside of her all the time. It hadn't been as obvious before, but it was there, driving her thoughts and everything she said. It was part of her awkwardness. I didn't think all of it was directed at me, although quite a bit bled onto me.

Perhaps she was angry at god himself. Sinners aren't the only ones resting in angry hands. A fair amount of anger that permeates billions of human hearts is directed right back at god.

That was the other thing about giant crosses like hers. Often, people who wear them don't seem all that happy. Not that I have experience with hundreds of cross-wearing fanatics, but I have some. She fit the profile — mildly bitter, wanting something from everyone, and angry she wasn't getting it.

I hadn't been sure what made her angry at me, but after I refused to show her the photographs, she began to let loose, in a low, soft voice, which in itself was a little frightening. She begged to see the pictures I'd taken of her. I understood that her vanity was getting the best of her, worried I'd taken too many without a warning and fretting that she'd shown her bad side. I didn't have to look at the results to know she was worried I'd captured the red, swollen zit on the edge of her jaw. She worried I noticed that her eyeshadow was a little sloppy and that I'd seen the narrow streak of gray hair above her ear.

Yes, I'd gotten up close. That was my job. As I told her, I was practicing.

Most people get uncomfortable with a camera in their face. Until the camera shoves its nose at them, they think they're hiding their flaws from the world. They don't want those rough spots recorded and digitized and reproduced for eternity. The less comfortable someone is in her own skin, the more concerned she'll be when there's a camera documenting the imperfections. Stephanie was at the far end of that discomfort scale.

Her voice had taken on a whining tone — "I don't think you're doing this for practice. I think you want to...I don't know what you want."

"My photography instructor said the more photographs you take, the more the skills get embedded in your muscle memory, and the better you get at capturing the right image."

Stephanie laughed. "That sounds like a bunch of baloney."

"I don't think it is. It's true for sports and playing a musical instrument. Why not taking photographs?"

"Your job doesn't require practice or an expensive class. You could do what you're doing with a cell phone."

"Not true."

"The only thing you need is the telephoto lens so you can sneak up on people."

"I don't think Trystan would like hearing you label it as *sneaking up on people*."

She glared at me. She ran her finger lightly over the zit, staring at me, seemingly unaware she was touching it, inflaming it with every stroke of her finger, dragging oil and dirt across the infected area. "You act as if you're a professional photographer and you're not."

"I'm not *acting* like anything."

"You don't have some special talent or skill that makes you a good fit for that job. Anyone could do it. I could do your job."

"But you're not. And Trystan bought the camera and signed me up for the class. So obviously he thinks it's important that I improve my skills." I moved toward the door, tired of arguing with her, still unsure why she was so angry with me, why she was effectively slamming Trystan at the same time. They were just photographs. What difference did it make to her?

"He didn't hire you because you're a great photographer," she said.

"Obviously not."

"Then stop acting like you're a brilliant artist. You think you're so good at something everyone on earth knows how to do. You were taking those pictures of me like you think you know me, like you could get me to reveal my true self."

"Are you worried about revealing your true self?"

Her hand jerked involuntarily as if she wanted to scratch my face, but all she did was emit sounds of disgust.

I stepped back into her office. I put my hand on her arm as a show of sympathy for whatever was roiling inside of her.

She shook me off. "We aren't friends, no matter what he wants. He hired you because you're aggressive. Just like them — the clients. That's all, so don't go strutting around like you're going to win an award for your photographs." She turned away from me. "I think we're finished. I have work to do, so please leave."

I did.

It was increasingly clear that my concern over the meaning behind that large cross was misplaced. She had other things going on, and rescuing me from hell was not even on her list, for now.

59

Cold weather had come on with a vengeance. It was too cold to suggest getting an ice cream after work. Coffee didn't sound appealing when the winter sky had already turned toward night as I left the office. I wanted to warm myself with a martini, or a glass of wine. So I asked Diana to join me at a bar that specialized in hot chocolate drinks, where she could order hers without a punch of alcohol.

If she'd said no, I would have adjusted. Talking to her was more important than the beverage selection. But she agreed to my suggestion. We sat at a table barely large enough for our two drinks. I had a glass of Malbec, and she was drinking hot chocolate topped with a rather large puff of whipped cream.

After the ritualistic conversation about work and our latest clients, I leaned forward and put my hand on the base of my wine glass. "I have a favor to ask."

"Sure. Anything."

"Don't say that before you hear what it is."

She laughed. "I seriously doubt it's anything I'll have to renege on."

I placed my phone on the table and pressed the button to unlock it. I pinched my fingers to enlarge the photograph already in place for viewing. I turned the phone toward her.

She picked it up and enlarged the photo some more. "Stephanie? Is this from when you took...oh, wait. That's

Trystan's office."

I reached over and swiped to the next photo. Stephanie's head was turned toward the camera, guilt spread across her face.

"When did you take this?" She placed the phone on the table.

"The other day, in her office. But I modified the background."

"Why? What's going on?" She scooped some whipped cream off her drink and put the spoon into her mouth, licking it as if it were an ice cream.

"I caught her prowling around his office a few weeks ago, hours before the rest of us came in."

"Okay."

"I did this with photoshop. I thought I'd show it to her, force her to back off."

"I don't think that's a good idea."

"What she's doing isn't right."

"It's almost like you're blackmailing her," she said.

"I don't like her making up lies about me. And I didn't think you liked being threatened."

"Yeah, but… I see myself as an honest person…I *am* honest. I'm not perfect, but I don't want to use a lie to manipulate her."

"A lie to counter her lie."

"True." She picked up her mug and took a sip of chocolate.

The aroma wafted toward me. I wished I had a square of chocolate to go with my wine. It smelled comforting. "She needs to leave me alone."

"Why don't you just tell Trystan the truth?"

"I did. But she needs to tell him she lied. It's easier to make something up than to argue that something isn't true. There's always that seed of doubt, once you hear something, you wonder. He'll be thinking of it every time we meet with Jim. He'll always have that tiny question in his mind. She needs to tell him she lied."

She turned her head, looking at the people seated around us, laughing and telling stories. I wondered if she was thinking it would be nice to enjoy her hot chocolate without discussing blackmail. Although that word was a little over the top. I just needed Stephanie to stop trying to damage me. I wasn't trying to do anything to her.

It was important that no one believe anything had happened between Jim and me. I wasn't certain of his fate yet, and even if his death looked like suicide, or drug use gone awry, or an encounter with the wrong people, I didn't want any offhand comments suggesting I must be glad he was gone. That kind of connection does not make for a tidy conclusion.

And I like things tidy. My home, my workplace, the parts of the world that touch me, and murder. No blood. No brain matter, no skin cells and hairs that have silently fallen off my body.

If he ended up dead, I wasn't sure how any of them would view it, thanks to Stephanie's lie. I was sure he deserved it, but not as sure I could pull it off. Cleanly.

I'd already told Diana too much. If Jim died, this conversation might come to mind. Would she find anything odd about it? Would the things I'd said ring true? "This isn't just for me. I don't mean to sound self-important, but I want to do it for you. You're worried about what's not right, but it's not right for her to drag you into her lies."

"Like you are?" She smiled.

"Not exactly. And she's using one mistake to try to hurt you. I don't like that." She hadn't volunteered her mistake. I imagined it wasn't too terrible, but a secret is a secret. Stephanie had no right to threaten her with it.

"I don't need a savior."

"It's not like that."

"It sounds very much like that. I know you're trying to be nice, but I don't need you to rescue me."

"Okay. Then I'm doing it for me." I smiled. I picked up my glass and took a long swallow.

As I put it down, she moved her mug toward the glass and clinked them together. "To being honest. But also to being self-serving, and all those qualities we aren't supposed to praise."

I laughed.

"What's the favor?"

"I just need you to be aware, to back me up if she comes to you."

"Let me think about it," she said. "Send me the photo, and I'll look at it more carefully. I'm not entirely sure it shows what you think it shows. It could appear innocent, and she'll deny it."

I texted all three images to her.

She finished her chocolate. "It's still not right, but…"

"What she's doing is worse."

"Yes." She pulled a twenty out of her purse and placed it on the table. "I need to head out. See you tomorrow."

I knew she would do it. Stephanie needed to be put in her place, and Diana saw that. She just needed to work her conscience around with a bit of self-justification.

60

Our meeting with Jim would be longer than usual because there were nearly two hundred photographs, taken over the course of three-and-a-half hours at his dinner party. Diana had reviewed every single one, noting the micro expressions he was most prone to, adding a summary of how those subconscious thoughts, bleeding into his lips and eyes, might be hurting his efforts to gain the confidence of people he desired as clients.

It had taken her several days to sort through them and make her comments. The process sounded beyond boring to me, but she said she loved it. She was proud of her skill at reading those fine, involuntary shifts in a person's face. She'd taken a course to learn how to do it accurately. Trystan's belief that the photography was a semi-con didn't seem to bother her. She was absolutely confident in the value of her insights. She made me more excited to capture the best images I could, the flashes of emotion that people want to hide from a camera.

Some expressions are easy to read.

But there are adjustments to the face that most people don't recognize consciously. The problem with those expressions is that we know what they mean and we react on a subconscious level, an animal instinct that reads the haughty attitude or the disgust or the fear. It's part of the explanation for why we respond to people with emotional reactions that don't fit the situation.

Our meeting was scheduled for nine o'clock *sharp*. Jim had emailed the insulting directive to Stephanie, who typed it into the group calendar, all caps, in red font, with two exclamation points. 9 a.m. *SHARP!!*

Diana was supposed to upload the photos to the shared folder on Tuesday night, but she'd sent an email that evening. She had a migraine. She needed to take her medication and go to sleep. She would get them uploaded by six a.m. at the latest.

Trystan and I met in the lobby of Jim's building and took the elevator to the thirty-fifth floor. The receptionist waved us past her desk. The second hands on the three clocks mounted behind her desk were sweeping toward the top of the disk. Nine a.m. in New York, 2 p.m. in London, 10 p.m. in Tokyo.

We walked through the open door.

Jim stood behind his desk. "Let's get started." He crossed the room and took his seat near the large screen.

Trystan opened his laptop and synced it to the screen. He tapped a few keys and moved his fingers across the trackpad.

A moment later the folder with Jim's name and company logo appeared on the screen. Trystan opened it, and we began making our way through the photographs. After a while, I tuned out, tired of hearing Trystan go into such agonizing detail on what each expression meant. I'd had no idea that a twitch of arrogance could mean so many things and be interpreted in so many ways. I like reading people, like guessing what's behind the masks, continuously curious about what's inside their minds. I like it when I can determine what they might be thinking with a reasonable degree of accuracy.

This was like dissecting a frog for Biology class.

I watched the images move past with a detached eye, recalling the details of the evening — the perfect martinis, the delicious food, and the sub-optimal ending, made slightly better by the limo ride back to the city, sipping champagne, bathed in silence.

Jim sat with his arms folded across his chest, gripping his biceps. He watched the parade of pictures, a variety of micro expressions moving across his face as he listened to Trystan's analysis, or rather, Diana's analysis filtered and embellished by Trystan. He nodded occasionally, leaning forward after a while as if he was having trouble focusing.

About twenty minutes into it, he asked Trystan to pause. "I have a more general question."

Trystan settled back on the couch.

"If these expressions are driven by subconscious thoughts, how am I supposed to control them?"

"Not all of them are driven by the subconscious."

"But when they are?"

"For starters, we'll focus on the ones that aren't. For example, when you have the urge to dominate a conversation, we'll work on training your mind to pause for a moment and consider whether you might get a new, valuable piece of information if you quell your thoughts for even a few seconds. Your expression will change accordingly, and your potential clients will have a positive reaction."

Jim laughed. "I don't see how that's possible. I'd operate like an awkward kid. I can't be second-guessing myself at every turn. My success comes from great instincts. And acting on those instincts." He looked at me. I returned his stare, unblinking. He smiled and held my gaze with equal intensity.

So that's how it was. Neither of us would back down.

He turned his attention to Trystan and nodded his head toward me. "Has anyone studied her micro expressions?"

I spoke quickly before Trystan could insert his opinion of me, or try to smooth over Jim's obnoxious objectification. "We're not here to talk about me."

Trystan smiled. "The study of micro expressions is something everyone can benefit from."

I felt my jaw clench as I waited for him to take back control of the meeting. I wondered if he realized he'd lost it.

"I'd like to interpret some of the looks on *her* face," Jim said.

Trystan's expression remained neutral. "Do you have any other questions about how we're going to implement strategies to control the impression you're giving to potential clients?"

Jim settled back in his chair. He crossed his legs and laced his fingers behind his head, elbows extended, man-spreading with his arms. "Not right now."

Trystan returned to the photographs. The images began marching again, one after another — Jim facing forward, left profile, right profile, smiles that ranged from smirks to grins to open-mouthed laughter, and the occasional look of amused tolerance. There were a few where I thought I detected a look of lust. Diana described all three of those as hunger or desire to control. I wondered whether she'd seen what I was seeing now and was diplomatic in her assessment, or if she didn't see it. Or, was I seeing something that wasn't there?

I couldn't imagine she'd choose political correctness

over truth in her analysis — the point of everything we did was to be brutally honest. A person can't up their game if they don't know where the weak spots are.

So. That meant she didn't see it. Then the question remained, was I seeing something that wasn't there based on my experience of him, or even my view of the world in general? Or were there gaps in the micro expression theory? Both were plausible.

It shook me. I pride myself on my ability to read people. If I was projecting my own bias, then how many things had I misinterpreted over the years? My recent obsession with the cross around Stephanie's neck supported the idea that I was projecting. It was unsettling, and I didn't like the sensation.

Trystan continued tapping the key to advance the photographs. Jim glanced at his watch. "I think I've taken in what you wanted me to get from this exercise."

"Let's see it through to the end," Trystan said. "Only a few more."

As he spoke, he tapped the key. An image appeared on the screen.

Jim squinted. "Huh?"

Trystan said, "What the hell?"

I didn't move, staring.

There was Stephanie, larger than life, looking guilty as sin. She stood in front of Trystan's bookcase, her head turned as if someone had spoken to her. But did she look guilty? Or was I projecting that as well? I did not like this questioning of myself. I wished I could leave the room and go for a run. I needed to think.

"What's…how did this get into the file?" Trystan looked at me.

"I'm not sure." I gave him a perplexed smile.

He looked back at the screen. He was silent as he drank in the details of his office, obvious in the photograph. There was no need to decipher a micro expression on Stephanie's face.

Trystan advanced to the next photograph. Another picture of Stephanie, then a third.

Finally, Jim's photos reappeared. A picture of him taking a sip of his after-dinner drink. Trystan spoke quickly, pointing out how the look around Jim's eyes became more predatory when he consumed alcohol. He suggested Jim avoid drinking when he was pitching to new clients. Trystan rambled on in this way for several minutes, repeating himself, his mind clearly still circling the photographs of Stephanie.

I knew Diana hadn't included them deliberately. She hadn't even been sure she wanted to show them to Stephanie. She would never disrupt a client meeting so flamboyantly. She must have pulled them off her phone and mixed them up with the other images as she rushed to load them to the folder by her early-morning deadline.

I knew how she would respond to the news of her mistake — horror.

I did not know how Trystan would respond. It wasn't how I'd hoped to use the photos, but now that he'd seen them, things might work out quite well.

61

The minute Trystan and I were settled in the cab, I texted Diana. I'd expected Trystan to start talking about the misplaced photographs, but he said nothing. His head was turned to look out the window as we sped past buildings and lurched through intersections, the driver constantly pressing his advantage against the other vehicles.

Pic mishap.

Diana texted back two question marks.

5 pics I gave you showed up in Jim's profile.

She sent back an emoji with an alarmed face, no need for a micro expression interpretation. It was followed by a string of more alarmed yellow faces. Those hairless yellow icons that are nothing if not the emotion consuming their faces, have a way of saying what words can't.

As if to confirm my thought, she sent a string of three more faces — gritted teeth, bugged-out eyes in a state of disbelief, and finally, a face with a tear dripping from the eye.

I wrote back — *Fixable.*

Trystan and I rode the entire way in silence. It wasn't uncomfortable. I didn't have the sense Trystan was upset with how the meeting had gone. The photograph meant nothing to Jim, and I was sure he'd already forgotten it. There was no damage to our reputation.

But clearly, he was trying to figure out what was going on. I assumed he didn't think I was involved, although eventually, he would come around to wondering who had taken the guilty shots. Right now, he was most likely fixated on why Diana had it and what Stephanie was doing in his office.

It wasn't as if we locked our doors, as if there was never a reason for one of us to be in another's office, but I'd done too good a job with my camera. She looked caught in the act. She looked guilty — possibly because, in her mind, she was always guilty.

The cab stopped in front of our building. The silence between us continued as we crossed the lobby and waited for the elevator. Once the doors closed and we were alone in the iron box, Trystan spoke. "Did you take those photographs of Stephanie?"

I'd had the entire ride back to consider how I might respond, but I'd squandered the minutes. Now, I was left swallowing and trying to think fast. Keeping it simple was best. I might not have to admit to my doctoring. If he ended up speaking to Stephanie, she might not make the accusation, knowing that I had simply created evidence for what I'd caught her doing. I shouldn't rush to give too much information too soon. "I did."

"Why was she in my office?"

"I don't know."

"Does she know you took it?"

This was trickier. I spoke slowly. "Yes."

The elevator stopped, hesitated, and then opened its doors, bringing an end to our private conversation for the moment.

Inside the suite, Stephanie and Diana were in their offices, keyboards clacking. Trystan walked down the hall, entered his office, and closed the door. I dropped my bag in my office and went to Diana's. She looked at me, her face echoing the series of emojis she'd texted.

I'd half expected her to be angry with me, blaming me for creating the image, for putting her in a terrible situation. But the expressions that transitioned across her face didn't include anger.

"Should we get an early lunch?"

Without speaking, she grabbed her purse. I returned to my office for my bag, and we left quickly before Stephanie could join us.

Inside the elevator, she collapsed against the wall. "We screwed up."

Mostly *she* had, but I wasn't completely uninvolved. Still. She hadn't been careful. There had been no reason to move that photograph off her phone.

She closed her eyes for a moment. "What did he say?"

"Not much. He wanted to know if I took the picture."

"I should have told you I didn't want to do this."

"I thought you were concerned about her ratting you out for…for whatever."

"I was…I am." She sighed.

The doors slid open, and we entered the lobby.

"Where should we go?" she said.

"Dim sum?"

"Perfect."

We exited the building and walked almost ten blocks to an upscale Chinese restaurant in the Theater District. When we were seated at the table, a basket of steamed dumplings already nestled between our plates, two glasses of sparkling water in front of us, she clicked her plastic chopsticks against each other. "This is too much drama. I don't like it."

I didn't say anything. I'm rather fond of drama. I wanted to see what Stephanie would do when she saw the photograph. I was still curious what she'd been looking for. And I wanted to know what Diana had done to give Stephanie leverage over her. Now, maybe I would find out.

I put a dumpling on my plate. I filled the tiny side dish with soy sauce and a healthy dose of chili oil. I dipped the dumpling into the mixture and put the entire dumpling in my mouth. I chewed slowly, savoring the tang and the warmth of the noodle. I swallowed. "It's probably not a big deal. He might ask Stephanie about it. She can tell him whatever lie she wants. After that, I'm sure she'll say something to me, and I can tell her to retract the other lie. She probably doesn't even think you're involved."

"I don't want her to get fired."

"Trystan doesn't strike me as someone who fires people on a whim."

"No, I suppose not." She took a dumpling and used her fork to cut it into quarters. She picked up one of the tiny wedges and ate it without the benefit of savory sauce. "I love this job. And I already blew it once." She ate another wedge, chewing carefully.

"How did you blow it?"

She rearranged the napkin on her lap so the points fell over the sides of her legs.

"I won't tell him," I said.

"The more people know, the greater chance that I'll…"

"I think you can trust me more than Stephanie. And if I know, maybe I can help make sure she gets the message."

She didn't meet my eyes. What I'd said was a rather

flimsy premise for revealing a secret, but she didn't appear to be thinking about that. She seemed more disturbed by what she'd done, more upset that she'd risked her job, as she seemed to believe.

The dumpling cart came by, and we ordered three more items to share. I sipped my water and waited for her to make up her mind that she really did want to tell me. I could see it eating at her, I could see that she sort of hoped I would reassure her it wasn't that terrible. Unlike Stephanie who most likely had a lot of guilt she wanted to inflict on others.

"I guess I'm already in trouble, if she decides to betray me." She leaned forward. "I recommended a friend to Trystan. When the photographs came back, she hounded me to let her see them." She nudged her lime into the water and took a long swallow of bubbling liquid. "I knew I shouldn't, but she was a friend. And it didn't seem like it would hurt anything."

"That's not so terrible. What's unethical about it? I guess if that's not the process he wants to follow, but still…"

"She hated several of the pictures. A few that really had good data in terms of her micro expressions. She was embarrassed by what the photographer had captured, and upset that her face looked fat." She laughed. "I explained to her over and over that no one but her and Trystan, and me of course, would ever see them. She couldn't stand it. Couldn't bear the thought of Trystan seeing her in such an unflattering light. Couldn't bear the thought that they even existed. She asked me to delete them. We went around about it for almost a week. And finally, I did. I deleted them."

"It's still not a crime."

"I know, but I screwed him over. I left him with very

little value-add in terms of feedback on her expressions. At that time, we didn't take as many photographs as he has you do now. So there were only a handful left."

I nodded. I didn't see how it robbed the value-add, given that the whole thing was a rather elaborate game.

"At this point, it's not just that I undermined his ability to help a client. It's that I lied to him. He wants everything we do to be transparent."

I nodded. He had made a point of that.

"I wish I could just clear the air. Start over."

"Maybe you should tell him. That would defuse Stephanie."

"I can't. He trusts me. He thinks I've been completely transparent."

We ate our dim sum, ordered more, and ate that, letting our conversation wander around other things. She didn't mention it again. And we never talked about what might happen next, what she would do if Trystan asked her how the photograph found its way into Jim's collection.

62

An invitation to lunch with Trystan was something that happened rarely. When Stephanie saw the text message asking her to join him at a steakhouse — all dark corners and subdued, private conversations — she knew it probably wasn't going to be a good thing. He certainly wasn't offering her a job as the photographer. And she doubted there would be a raise, because what had she done to deserve one?

It briefly crossed her mind that Alexandra and Diana had conspired against her. That they'd confessed their sins to Trystan and made her look bad. He might be taking her out to reprimand her for what was essentially blackmail. For creating a toxic work environment. For undermining the camaraderie of their tiny venture.

She slid into the booth and smoothed her skirt over her legs. She tugged the fabric where it had pulled up on the left side, revealing part of her thigh — white and dimpled as it squashed on the firm vinyl bench.

He ordered for both of them — filet mignon, medium rare, with Caesar salad, served alongside the steak. He took a bite from a roll without adding butter and put it on his plate. "I'll get right to the point."

She swallowed. She wanted a roll, with a thick layer of butter, but couldn't be chewing bread and gnawing through crust while he delivered whatever terrible news he was so eager to hand her.

"It's come to my attention that you've been going through things in my office."

She swallowed. She took a sip of water. "Why do you think that?"

"I was direct with you, I'd appreciate the same."

She picked up a roll, tore it in half, and spread several scoops of butter across the inside surface. "I did. I'm sorry." She took a bite. Of course Alexandra had betrayed her. She took another bite, searching for comfort in the butter sliding across her tongue.

"Why did you do it?"

"I misplaced something. I wasn't sure if it ended up in your things."

"What did you misplace?"

He was right. There was no point in dodging the questions. "The one-pager Jim Kohn wrote. His information regarding the areas of his life for which he feels ashamed."

"I see." He pushed the bread plate to the side, making room for the meal being carried toward them.

He didn't speak while the plates were arranged in front of them and ground pepper was sprinkled across their salads. When they were alone again, he sighed. It was a deep, defeated sound as if he'd lost something or someone important. "Jim asked me not to include that in his profile," he said.

"Why didn't you tell me?"

"Your job is to input what you're given."

"I thought I'd lost it."

He narrowed his eyes, staring into hers until she was forced to look away. "Had you read it when you first received it?"

She shook her head. "I saw it in the envelope when I first went through it, the day it was dropped off. I always check that everything we ask for is included."

"And you didn't read it?"

She swallowed. "I thought I saw my name on it. But Diana came into my office, and I stuffed everything back. The next day, that page was gone. I thought I'd lost it when I pulled the papers out to check they were all there. That maybe it fell on the floor, that the cleaning service…"

He held up his hand. "Jim asked me to get rid of it. He regretted what he'd written."

She stabbed her fork into a piece of lettuce. She ate several forkfuls of lettuce and two croutons before responding. He should be regretting a lot more than what he'd written. She swallowed. "What did he say about me?"

"I wasn't aware that you knew him."

"I met him once. Before he was your client."

"Where was this?"

She paused. Was there a point in lying? Would anything happen if he knew? He still wouldn't *know*… "He was in a relationship with someone I'm…close to."

He leaned back and studied her face. She kept her head bent over her plate, shoveling in food as if she hadn't eaten in two days, feeling his eyes on her. Maybe he did know.

"You should have mentioned it."

"Our meeting was brief."

"Still. I like things…"

"…To be transparent, yes, I know." She bit into the second half of her roll and tore off a large piece, not caring if it looked gluttonous. He would realize she was unable to speak for a moment.

"You should have asked about it."

She nodded, chewing. *He* should have told her about it. If he wanted transparency, why was he going through her locked desk, taking a document she was responsible for tracking from its receipt, through inputting it, and archiving it in the secured file cabinets?

He ate several pieces of steak while she continued to chew the roll. It resisted her effort to transform it into a consistency she could swallow. It moved around inside her mouth like a large wad of putty, thick and dense, in danger of causing her to choke on her saliva.

Alexandra stood up to Trystan. Why shouldn't she? Maybe he liked that. Maybe she'd been too meek, despite the assurance that the meek would inherit the earth. So far, she hadn't inherited a single stone. She finally managed to swallow the bread. "You went through *my* desk."

"I did. And I suppose I should have asked you for the document instead of taking it. I apologize. But as I said, he was frantic and full of regret."

It didn't seem fair. That was it? He *supposed* he should have asked? He apologized as if that were it, and yet she was in some sort of trouble that he still hadn't defined. His apology wasn't a true apology, not with excuses tacked on the front and back of it.

"Please don't go into my office again," he said. "It makes me think I can't trust you. If you need something or have a question, ask. We don't have secrets here. You know that."

"And yet, there are secrets all over the place."

"Such as?"

"If I knew what they were, they wouldn't be secrets."

He laughed.

She cut a slice of steak and ate it, chewing slowly to absorb the flavor. She felt calmer, hearing him laugh, but she was still angry. His desk was off limits, but hers was not?

"What appears to be secretive?"

"Besides part of Jim's profile?"

He pressed his lips together and said nothing.

This was her only chance. If she didn't speak her mind when he'd opened the door, whatever frustration she felt from here on out was on her. She had to lay her cards on the table. If she didn't take this opportunity, there was no chance of things working out the way she'd hoped. The way she needed things to work out. "It's a bit of a mystery why you hired Alexandra."

"That's not a secret. She's very good at what she does. Do you have an issue with her work?"

Stephanie let her steak knife clatter onto the plate. "She's not *good* at it. She's just learning. She doesn't know anything about photography except what she learned in that class." She took a deep breath. "That should have been my job. It was my idea to bring the photography in-house, and I wanted it. I'm qualified, at least as much as she is."

"I see."

"I don't think you do."

"You and Alex have different skills."

"She is not skilled as a photographer."

"Actually, she's picked it up quickly. She has a perfect sense for what I'm looking for. She has strong people skills. She knows how to take control of a situation, and she's not afraid to do what's necessary to capture the images we need."

Stephanie pushed her plate away. The steak was half-eaten, but she didn't care. She was sick to her stomach with the heavy food and his condescending attitude.

"Don't take offense. I'm being transparent."

"Yes, you are." She no longer cared. She was utterly defeated. If she weren't paid so well, she would start looking for another job today. But for now, she'd have to put up with things as they were.

Alexandra had tattled on her. She'd stolen her job and made her look bad to Trystan.

Worst of all, without the photography job, she'd never have a chance to rip a hole in Jim's life — a small, pathetic payback for what he'd done to Eileen. Jim Kohn had no shame, so she couldn't imagine what he would have written. "What did he say about me? In his essay?"

"I don't think delving into that is helpful. I've ignored it and so should you."

She could imagine. Maybe she'd ask him herself.

63

I saw Trystan and Stephanie come back from lunch. They parted ways outside her office door without speaking. A moment later I heard the door to her office close, followed by the sound of Trystan's door latching shut.

Did this mean lunch had not gone well? I'd assumed he'd taken her out to discuss her intrusion into his office. Had she accused me of using Photoshop to make her look guilty, trying to argue she was not? Had she complained that I'd lied about why I wanted to photograph her? The minutes ticked past. If the answer to those questions was *yes*, I expected I'd hear almost immediately from Trystan. But my phone remained silent, and the two doors remained closed.

He waited until everyone was getting ready to leave for the day. It was dark outside. It felt as if we'd worked far into the evening, although it was only five-forty.

I looked up from my desk, and he was standing in the doorway.

He tapped his finger on the doorframe. "Do you have a minute before you head out?"

"Sure."

"In my office."

I followed him down the hallway. As I passed their offices, Diana and Stephanie both said good-night, their gazes lingering with curiosity.

I sat in one of the chairs facing his desk. I crossed my

legs, settled back, and folded my hands on my lap.

"How did the photograph of Stephanie get into the file with Jim's pictures?"

"It was something I showed Diana, and there was a mix-up."

"When did you take it?"

Any lie I offered could easily be taken apart by speaking to Stephanie. I wondered why I hadn't foreseen this when I first considered the idea. I suppose I thought it would all be out of his range of awareness. I thought I'd handle it between me and Stephanie. "I caught her looking through your office a few weeks ago. After I took some practice shots of her, I was fooling around with Photoshop. I decided to see if I could recreate what I'd seen." Sometimes, plain honesty is best. It ends up providing future credibility. Even though this wasn't technically plain honesty, it had the ring of truth.

"Why?"

"Practicing my new skills."

"You won't have a need for Photoshop in this job."

"I know."

"The images need to be unvarnished. That's the whole point."

"Yes, I know. But Leon mentioned it, and I wanted to learn how to use it. Just for my own satisfaction. And I did see her going through things in your office. I just didn't have my camera with me."

He nodded. He seemed to be concealing a smirk that wanted to force its way across his lips.

"I thought about showing the photo to her."

"Why?"

I looked down at my clasped hands. "I don't feel

comfortable working with someone I can't trust. What's to keep her from going through my office?"

"It's important to me that we maintain a harmonious environment here."

"I know."

"There seems to be friction between you and Stephanie."

"Is that what she said?"

"Is there?"

"I think we got off on the wrong foot."

"I need you to work on correcting that," he said.

"Sure. No problem. Is she working on it also?"

He studied me for several minutes. "Thanks for making sure you establish a good working relationship with her. As I said, it's important." He pushed his chair away from his desk.

"What was she looking for in your office?"

"It was nothing."

"Nothing?"

He sighed. I expected he was thinking about honesty. And transparency. "Just a document from Jim Kohn's initial input."

I thought back over the reams of information provided to me about our clients, a firehose of information in just a few days. "What document?"

"It's not important."

"Is something missing? Anything I need to know?"

"Nope." He walked around the desk. He shook my hand, which seemed out of place, but I gave him a firm grip in response. "She inserts herself where she doesn't belong," I said.

"Be kind to her." He leaned back over the desk and

clicked the mouse to lock the computer screen.

"I don't understand."

"Most of the time, only a fraction of what's going on in other people's lives is visible on the surface."

"I know that."

"Then consider that Stephanie made a bad judgment call. Sometimes, emotion takes over."

I gave him a tender smile. I placed my hand on his forearm. "Is she okay? It would help me to work better with her if I knew what was going on."

He sighed. "I suppose it's not really a secret. She has a daughter. Early twenties."

It was certainly a secret to me. She hadn't said a word. She looked young to have a daughter that age.

"You need to keep this to yourself. No exceptions."

"Of course. But if it helps me understand…"

"I think it will. Her daughter was in a relationship with Jim Kohn."

"Oh."

"As I understand it from what Jim wrote, Stephanie blames him for causing her daughter to abandon her religious upbringing. Jim wrote about it in his thoughts about shame. He doesn't accept the blame, of course. And he shouldn't. The girl is an adult. She made her choices."

"And they broke up, I'm guessing?"

He nodded. "Jim wrote some unflattering things about Stephanie's zealous views. She saw her name on the paper but says she didn't read it. When she saw it was missing from the package, she went looking for it."

A daughter. I pictured Stephanie's face. I guessed her age at thirty-seven or thirty-eight.

"I'm only telling you so you'll cut her some slack. She let her feelings for her daughter and what happened influence her behavior at work, but I'm confident this is the end of it."

We walked out together, and while he talked about various other clients, my mind raced in circles. Was the woman displayed in the twenty or thirty photographs in Jim's study, Stephanie's daughter? Did Stephanie know all those pictures were still decorating his study as if he expected her to return to him?

64

I knew I was going to kill Jim anyway. For me. Carrying out Stephanie's vendetta, whatever the details were, didn't enter into it, but she would be an unwitting beneficiary.

He was a man willing to pay thousands of dollars for Trystan's support in getting to the next level but was completely oblivious to why he didn't even deserve to be at the level he'd already achieved. There was no doubt I wasn't the first or the only woman he'd demeaned and pawed and tried to take possession of. The world would be better without him. The world didn't need his *improved* self that would make him successful with the political and sports and entertainment crowd, which he lusted after with even more enthusiasm than he lusted after me. I was a diversion on his way to something better — power.

Having his seed in the gene pool would not move the world in a positive direction.

It wasn't just his attitude toward women. It was his attitude toward me, toward a woman who was a de facto employee. He treated me as if I were his personal property. He acted as if taking his picture and attending his dinners and lunches meant he had some kind of claim on me. In his mind, I existed to serve him in whatever way he desired.

During business meetings, a woman is expected to sit there and take lewd comments in stride. She's expected to let condescending or degrading conversation wash off her back

— it's just casual, meaningless chit-chat. The men can laugh and chortle and talk about how women get so pissy or feisty when they're mocked, as if we're adorable monkeys, swinging by our tails from the bars across the tops of our cages, hooting and scratching ourselves, jumping down, eager for a bit of applause or a peanut.

Speaking up is rude. Speaking up means you're a bitch. Speaking up disrupts the meeting. Jokes are supposed to be accepted as jokes and comments making you out to be inadequate are not meant to offend, and if you take offense, it just proves that girls are too emotional.

I'm not driven by emotions, but it doesn't mean I don't take offense. I just don't engage in emotional rants. I wait. When it crosses a line, I'm not going to let it continue.

A man like Jim Kohn will never recognize that women are equal human beings. We aren't entertainment, and we aren't sex toys, and we aren't going to be weak and needy so he can feel important, stupid so he can feel smart. We aren't there to decorate his study with photographs of our perfectly poised selves.

It wasn't that I wanted to see him suffer. I don't like suffering. I just wanted him gone. It was possible his clients would be devastated, losing his obvious skill at making money multiply as if it were rabbits having sex. But they'd find someone else. Pete, for example.

All forty-seven floors of that building were occupied by men and women who were equally skilled at spinning straw into gold. Other people knew how to do what Jim did. Even Rafe and Victoria appeared to have a handle on it, although from a less sophisticated angle.

Possibly, Jim wasn't even all that skilled. It might simply

be luck. Exactly like Rafe and Victoria — gambling in a legal arena. The entire planet complicit in legalized, authorized speculation. We all want money, and if we don't have work we're passionate about, we want to acquire money by magic — slot machines or the lottery, the stock market or a windfall inheritance. People like Gavin, who are obsessed with the work itself, have money flow into their lives without thinking. Teachers not so much, I suppose. But it's true for athletes and actors, scientists and physicians, and anyone else who loves her work.

For me, photography had some potential for work that consumed me and brought in money. It seemed to fit who I was with what I like doing — watching people and studying their behavior. Still, it's not a career that's going to lead to the kind of money a woman needs to live out her life with all her desires satisfied, answering to no one.

Right out of the gate, Jim came close to spoiling my interest in taking photographs, making me an object for his enjoyment instead of yielding to the few skills I'd acquired in my class and the natural ability that came from always noticing how people were behaving.

For a while, I considered whether I was two-faced. I'm more than happy to use my appearance to get what I want, to manipulate men, and the occasional woman. But I don't like it when my appearance is used to classify me and put me into a box and turn me into a toy. But then I use it to escape that box. Trying to pluck apart the threads of what I think about female beauty and female objectification is a laborious task. My head ached from turning it around, looking at every facet. All I knew was that Jim tried to take possession of me and I didn't like it.

Killing a client was risky. But only risky if I revealed my thoughts about him to anyone I worked with. As far as Trystan knew, I tolerated and appeared to respect Jim. That's what he saw when I shook Jim's hand, when I offered appropriate smiles and kept my mouth shut as offensive words spewed out of the man's mouth. As far as Stephanie knew, he wasn't a problem.

Although Stephanie didn't enter into my decision to kill him, I did think about her daughter. To think that she'd abandoned what she believed, that a man had that power over her, and then casually removed her from his life was disturbing. Maybe she allowed him that power, but knowing what I knew of him, it was more likely he'd simply taken it.

65

Portland

Mrs. B and I were assigned to make an evangelism call on a woman who had visited the church only once. This woman had marked on the visitor card that she'd learned of the church through an online ad. In the space provided, she wrote with sharp, jerky words that she wanted prayers for her marriage. Her husband had abandoned her for another woman. She wanted him back.

It was a large request. I wondered whether Mrs. B believed that god was up to it.

It surprised me that they allowed a teenager to participate in a conversation that could easily turn to sordid details. Normally we were vigilantly protected from anything even remotely related to divorce or affairs or any subject that carried an undertone of sex that hadn't been sanctioned by marriage to one man or one woman, virgins in the marriage bed until death parted you.

I suppose they had to visit this woman one way or another, and the teenagers at Pure Truth Tabernacle were the first to be trained in this *highly effective* program for bringing salvation to the ignorant and unrepentant.

Before making our visits, we met at the church for a pep talk and prayer. Then we went out, two teenagers to one adult leader. In my case, there was only me and Mrs. B.

She led the way to her white Toyota Camry and opened the passenger door for me.

She drove casually, hardly seeming to notice the other vehicles on the road as if she thought she had a path carved along a heavenly, gold-paved boulevard. Miraculously, we arrived at Kate Pervain's house without anyone honking at us, or worse, running into us. I thought about offering to drive us back to the church after our visit, but it was unlikely Mrs. B would let me have the wheel of her car when her husband had instructed her to watch over me.

The house was set back from the street and surrounded by a low brick wall. Behind that wall was a second wall of trees that prevented anyone from seeing through the enormous picture windows that looked out from the living room, dining room, and breakfast area.

A feeling of desolation filled the house — five bedrooms and four bathrooms, a family room and a dining room and a three-car garage. A large swimming pool and patio and lawn in the backyard. All of it for Mrs. Pervain. Mr. Pervain, she told us, was living with her younger sister in a studio apartment. All he needed was space in which to *betray their marriage vows, several times a day.* She gave me a sideways glance, checking to see whether I understood her euphemism.

I smiled naïvely.

We were seated in Mrs. Pervain's lavish living room. On the table in front of us, seated on square stone coasters, was a mug of coffee for Mrs. B and a glass of cola with ice for me. I'd become a coffee drinker over the past year or so, but it wasn't offered. I decided not to make an issue of it. Something cold, with an ice cube to chew on if I got tired of listening and not talking, was a good thing. And I'd been instructed by Mr. B not to say a word beyond the niceties. Of course, he wasn't there to enforce that, and I wasn't certain his wife was as firm in the belief that I should keep my mouth shut.

For nearly an hour, we listened to Mrs. Pervain describe her love for her husband and her devotion to her sister, and the shocking betrayal by the two people she treasured most.

During this time, Mrs. B sipped coffee, nodded and smiled. She said absolutely nothing about how Mrs. Pervain would respond if she died that night, arrived at the gates of heaven, and was asked why she should be admitted.

"I feel that if I stay on my side of the bed," Mrs. Pervain said, "I'm making space for him to come home. I would never speak to my sister again, of course. She betrayed me with such cruelty. Vicious cruelty." She hissed slightly. "I can hardly breathe when I think of it." She took deep, gulping breaths as if she needed to prove to us that she was speaking the truth.

"It's such a shame," Mrs. B said.

"I don't understand why she would steal my husband. I was so good to her."

I took a long swallow of coke. "Did she steal him, or did he steal her?" I said.

Both women stared at me.

I think they'd forgotten I was there. Neither one answered. After a few minutes of silence, Mrs. B asked Mrs. Pervain which song she'd liked the best when she attended Pure Truth Tabernacle's morning service.

"I don't remember the songs. Not really. All I remember is that they made me cry. Most things do." Her eyes filled with liquid. She grabbed her coffee mug, holding it with both hands. She moved it close to her mouth, her hands shaking. She took a tentative sip, then continued to hold it close. "I also set a place for him for dinner every night."

"Is that healthy?" Mrs. B said.

"What do you mean?"

"Perhaps you need to let go."

"You don't let go of love. If I continue loving him, and making room for him in our home, he'll return. I'm sure of it. He'll see that she can't satisfy him, not really. Not the way I can. I know him."

Mrs. B's head jerked toward me. She smiled, stretching her lips into a wide grin. "Alexandra, maybe you should go watch TV." She looked back at Mrs. Pervain. "Is that okay with you?"

"I'm fine," I said. "I'd rather not watch TV."

Mrs. B turned back to Mrs. Pervain. She smiled, then gave Mrs. Pervain a hard stare, clenching her jaw. I could feel the electricity coming out of her, trying to send telepathic messages that sex or anything hinting at sex should not be mentioned.

To ease her mind. I put down my glass and folded my hands, pressing my icy fingertips on my knuckles. "If you were to die tonight, Mrs. Pervain, and god asked why you should be allowed into his heaven, what would you say?"

"Oh, Alexandra. I don't think that's necessary." Mrs. B scooted closer. She put her hand on my leg. "Let's just have a friendly conversation. There's no need to bring death into it."

Mrs. Pervain looked thoughtful but said nothing.

"I thought we were supposed to…"

Mrs. B's fingers tightened on my leg. "We don't know what it's like to suffer the kind of betrayal Kate has had to endure. Let's be patient."

I moved my leg. After a moment, she released her death grip. I picked up my glass and shook a piece of half-melted ice into my mouth. I sucked on it and let them continue talking about all the things Mrs. Pervain was doing to *make space* in her home for Mr. Pervain's return.

In the car, Mrs. B said nothing about the conversation. When we were a few blocks from the church, she eased her foot off the gas and let the car glide slowly through the residential streets. "I think we can tell Mr. B that our visit was successful, but that Mrs. Pervain needs more time."

"Time for what?"

"Well, time to consider her life. Don't you think?"

"Maybe."

"And we can tell him we had a nice visit. I'll tell him your behavior was admirable."

"If you say so."

She didn't turn. She smiled absently, staring through the windshield. There were tears on her cheek. I guessed that in some way, she felt betrayed.

Mrs. B and I made all of our visits as a team until the program came to its end a few weeks later. Never once did she ask anyone what they would do if they died that night and were accosted at the gates of heaven.

66

New York City

Jim was not going to be as easily led as some of the other men I've killed. Maybe my thinking was influenced by my stereotype of New Yorkers — sharp and smart and wary. The other thing was that I didn't know him as well as some of the others, which would mean he'd have more alarms going off if sex with me seemed too easy. I didn't think he would buy a sudden change in my behavior, a sudden melting toward him, a complete change in who he perceived me to be.

I needed to take my time. First on the list was a fake ID. In Australia, I'd managed to persuade a hotel clerk in a small coastal town to accept cash payment for a room without providing any ID. That was not going to happen in New York City. I could persuade Jim to arrange for a room, but the more action he had to take, the more it might come across as one of those things that he'd view as too good to be true.

A drink in a hotel bar and a room I already possessed would be smoother, less for him to think about. Of course, once I used the ID and a dead body was found in that room, the ID would be useless. Still, for a hundred bucks, it was worth it.

I dyed my hair platinum blonde, put on a bright blue turtleneck shirt, inserted my new lovely green contact lenses, and applied makeup that included blue eyeliner and eyebrow color lighter than my own. I set my camera on the tripod, pointing at a blank wall, and took ten shots of my face. I selected the one with the blandest expression and filled out the online form for the ID, uploading the photograph along with payment.

While I waited for the driver's license to arrive in the mail, I made my usual purchases — plastic bags, duct tape, and rope, scissors and cleaning supplies, a wig of long brown, wavy hair, and a black all-weather coat that covered me to my knees. I also bought a pair of fashion eyeglasses with large red frames. I bought a new gym bag, one that was less bulky than my usual bag, so it would be easy to glide through a hotel lobby without looking like I was lugging all my worldly possessions.

I purchased handcuffs and scarves, roofies and ecstasy. Because of his wariness, it would be tricky to get a roofie slipped into Jim's drink. Instead, I would invite him to be a willing participant in taking ecstasy. The drug would disable him, make him easier to manipulate. Not as thoroughly as a roofie, but enough.

Five days later, I had my new ID — Carrie Lancer, age twenty-eight, from San Diego, California. There's nothing like a total cliché to help people remember you the way you want to be remembered.

When they saw my blonde hair, my co-workers had stared with open mouths, afraid to speak. I'd whispered to Diana that I already regretted it, and she nodded in agreement.

The clerk at the front desk hardly glanced at my photo, not commenting on the red glasses, concerned only with scanning the license. I didn't like that the record of it would be left behind, later confiscated by the police, but I'd been assured that the website where I ordered it was operated by people who were pros at keeping their skills and their customer list private.

Reserving the room for three nights was a knife in my gut. Manhattan hotel prices already knocked the breath out of me, but I needed flexibility. Jim was a busy guy. Even choosing the three dates I had was taking a chance. He might not be available for any of them. I was counting on him at least squeezing me in for a drink, eager to see where things might go. I also hoped I was buying an extra day before he was discovered by putting out the *do not disturb* sign.

I sent him a text message, asking whether he wanted to meet for a drink.

He responded immediately with a simple, straightforward, *Yes.*

I suggested Thursday evening, and he agreed.

He asked whether we'd be reviewing photographs. I said, *no.* He asked whether Trystan was joining us. I said, *no.* He asked whether it was business or pleasure.

I texted back — *Which do you prefer?*

It was fifteen minutes before I received an answer.

Pleasure.

Maybe I'd overestimated his wariness.

At work on Thursday, my nerves were jumpy. I was anxious to move forward. I couldn't focus on the photographs of Pete that I was reviewing with Diana. I couldn't stop checking the time, couldn't stop fiddling with my platinum hair, couldn't stop getting out of my chair to stretch my arms over my head and behind my back. I'd gone for a three-mile run that morning, and every morning that week, but I felt like I'd been stuck in a chair in a tiny office, staring at a computer for a week.

If Jim said anything to Trystan about meeting for a drink, I would have to cancel my plans.

"Why can't you sit still?" Diana said. "You're making me nervous."

"I'm feeling cooped up. These offices are so small. Being inside my apartment now that it's cold…"

She shrugged. "Welcome to New York. Unless you're rich, you're confined."

"I suppose that's true anywhere, to some degree."

"Probably. But sit still, or we'll never finish this." She slid the scroll bar to move the next set of photographs into our viewing range.

"You took an awful lot of pictures. I'm not sure we need all of these, but each one has a slight difference, and I don't want to toss the most telling ones."

"It's probably faster just to make notes on all of them than to spend time debating which ones to keep," I said.

"True."

Nevertheless, she continued studying the screen, and I continued squirming and checking the time.

My bag was stashed in the room at the hotel. I'd checked in early the evening before. I was already dressed for our date.

I'd settled on a camisole top with navy blue pants, navy high heels, and a jacket that buttoned just below my collarbone so no one in the office would see the sexy top underneath.

It had added to my squirminess, being all buttoned up like that, but I couldn't bring a change of clothes to work without inviting questions. And I didn't want another armload of things to carry out of the hotel when I was finished with Jim.

Now, I just had to wait. And try to settle down.

67

Jim kept me waiting in the bar for twenty minutes. After ten minutes, I'd expected a text to let me know he was running late. After fifteen, I was irritated. I began to wonder whether he'd changed his mind.

When I looked up and saw him weaving among the tables toward the end of the bar where I sat with an empty stool beside me, I took a long, slow breath. I eased all the irritation out with my exhale. I couldn't let petty complaints interfere with my plan.

I smiled.

"I didn't expect so much traffic. Thought I'd never get here." He eyed my platinum blonde hair but said nothing. He slid onto the empty stool. "How do you want your martini?"

"I'll have a glass of Chardonnay."

"I thought you were a martini-aficionado."

"Chardonnay is fine, for now."

He lifted his left eyebrow slightly and turned to look for the bartender. He ordered two glasses of wine. When they arrived, I raised my glass toward his. "To knowing how to treat a girl right."

He grinned. "You got it."

I took a sip. "I need to thank you again for the flowers. They always open the door."

He nodded. There wasn't a trace of discomfort anywhere in his jaw or eyes or the tilt of his head. He was happy to continue taking credit for flowers he hadn't sent, letting the goodwill carry him wherever it would. "I'm glad you're not one of those women who holds grudges. Gets all riled up at an innocent pass."

"I can't imagine a woman who doesn't like a man to express interest. It's all about timing."

"I completely agree. My timing is rarely off."

"This time it was."

"And now the timing is favorable?"

I smiled and moved so my hair fell across my brow.

"Is that why we're having drinks?"

I leaned closer. I let my breath wash across his face as I spoke. "Is that all we're having?"

"Dinner?"

I unbuttoned my jacket and let it fall open in the front.

He took several quick sips of wine. "This is not what I expected."

"What did you expect?"

"A drink. You giving me a lecture about respecting you."

"I did say pleasure, didn't I?"

"You did. But women never say what they mean, so I expected it was to put me off my game."

"What game is that?"

"You know."

I didn't, but I let it go.

I took a sip of wine. I placed my glass close to his, letting my baby finger slide away from the others, touching the side of his hand. He relaxed his hand on the bar, and I moved mine closer. He ran his finger along my index finger, down to the webbing, pressing gently, then dragging it up to the tip of my middle finger. He mapped the shape of my entire hand this way.

"I did something kind of crazy," I said.

"What's that?"

I moved my hand out of reach.

He picked up his wine and swallowed some. He glanced at my glass. "Do you want another?"

"Don't you want to hear what I did?"

"Sure."

"I booked a room here."

"In the hotel?"

"Yes."

"You don't waste any time."

"Life moves fast. What would be the point of wasting time?"

"I don't disagree," he said.

"What do you think?"

"What I'm thinking is — does Trystan know we're meeting?"

"Of course not."

"This is not the vibe I've been getting from you. I'm a little surprised."

"Then why did you kiss me?"

"Because I wanted to. But now…" He picked up his glass and swallowed the last of the wine. "So, another?"

"Or we could head upstairs."

"The vibe I'm getting is, this is too…It seems as if you want something."

I smiled and touched his hand with my pinky again. "You're misreading it. I've finished photographing you, so we no longer have a working relationship. Don't you realize that?"

He nodded. "I'd just like another glass of wine."

"There's a bottle in the room."

He pulled his phone out of his pocket. He scrolled through email for a few seconds, tilting the phone so I couldn't see the details of what he was looking at.

It wasn't clear whether he distrusted me, or he wanted to get back in the power position. Maybe a woman had never taken the lead with such a definitive plan before. He looked anxious, and I wanted to believe it was the latter reason. I needed him to quit stalling and let his lust consume the logical areas of his brain that were telling him this was too easy or suggesting that a woman is never this aggressive about wanting sex, so there was something else going on. A woman is never going to arrange a room and invite a man to join her without demanding he buy dinner first, or at the very least, milking him for that second drink.

He dragged his finger across the screen.

The bartender paused in front of us. "Two more?"

I shook my head. Without looking up, Jim did the same. And yet, the methodical movement of his finger across the surface of his phone didn't change. Was there an email from Trystan he wanted to show me? Was something else going on? The jitter below the surface of my skin returned.

I crossed my legs in the opposite direction. I pulled the sides of the jacket toward the center of my body. Instead of buttoning them, I held onto them, keeping them close to each other.

Jim placed his phone face down on the bar. The bartender moved toward him and handed him a glass with the receipt curled inside. Jim took out his credit card, and the glass disappeared. A few minutes later, it was returned. He scribbled his signature and stood.

I slid off my stool.

"Lead the way," he said.

Once again, desire suffocates logic and caution. Or maybe it's entitlement.

68

Inside the room, Jim was even more uncertain than he'd been in the bar. He settled into one of the two armchairs in the corner and stretched out his legs. He grabbed the bottle of Cabernet I'd left waiting and read the label. He placed the bottle on the table again, ignoring the opener and the glasses beside it. He unknotted his tie but left it looped around his neck.

I had an urge to wrap it around his throat and pull it tight, foregoing the dance, but what would be the fun in that?

During the course of our time together, less than an hour so far, he'd become completely passive. I wondered if he was testing me. I began to worry that he was performing his own dance and whatever I had planned would get derailed by something he'd mapped out with equal care.

I walked to the table and picked up the bottle and opener. I sliced off the foil and turned the corkscrew into the cork, pressing firmly and rotating it quickly.

"Did you used to be a waitress?" he said.

"No."

"You certainly know how to open a bottle of wine."

I poured some in each glass and put the bottle behind the glasses. "You don't have to be a server to enjoy learning how to manage a bottle of wine."

"Most women don't know how."

"Is that right?" I picked up a glass and handed the other

to him. I took a sip. It needed some breathing room, like me.

He didn't drink any of the wine. "What are we doing?"

"You don't seem all that thrilled to be here." I put down my glass, took off my jacket, and tossed it on the bed.

"I'm not sure what's going on."

"Really? You really don't know what's going on?" I walked toward him. I leaned forward and placed my hands on his knees, offering him a nice view of my breasts as they spilled over the edge of the camisole.

"This is just… You were so cold every time we met for the photography sessions. At my party…you…and now you're acting like a woman who needs a guy to fertilize her egg right this instant because her clock is ticking."

I laughed. I straightened and picked up my wine glass. "You need to relax." I took a sip. "How about some ecstasy?"

"I'm not into that kind of thing."

"You don't like it?"

"Never tried it."

"Then how can you know you're not into it?"

He shrugged. "I like to face reality."

"Is that why you were salivating for a second glass of wine? Because, reality?"

"Alcohol is different."

"How do you *know*, if you've never tried it?"

"I just know."

I went to the closet and opened the door. I reached into my gym bag and pulled out a tiny plastic bag with two tablets inside. One was a small breath mint. There was a tiny nick in the side that showed me which was the tablet I needed to consume.

Discussing it any further would result in more

resistance. If we debated drug use, his passive mood might shift. I felt the start of an argument. I sensed him digging into his position that he wasn't interested in getting high. I returned to where he was sitting. I took the wine glass out of his hand and settled myself on his lap. I unsealed the tiny bag and dropped the tablets onto my palm. I picked up the one with the nick and put it in my mouth. I pinched the other and touched it to his lips. He remained motionless.

I put my mouth on his, easing it open. At the same time, I settled myself more deeply into his lap. His lips parted, and I slipped the tablet into his mouth. Fortunately, he left it there.

I picked up our glasses. I handed his back to him and took a sip from mine. I put my hand on his leg and began massaging it while he drank some of his wine. After a few minutes, I took the glasses again and set them on the table. I kissed him and felt his body begin to yield to mine.

It took about twenty minutes before I was aware the ecstasy was kicking in. The benefit of this drug was that he was more interested in prolonging our kissing. His movements slowed, and I could see him living in an alternate reality to mine, one where we were filled with giddy affection for each other, one where we had endless time for expressing that affection with our bodies.

After a while, I pulled him to his feet and tugged him gently toward the bed. I removed his clothes, trying to keep my head turned away from the sappy smile on his face, the loose form of his lips, the tiny giggles that escaped every few minutes. Yes, giggles. It was unsettling and kind of creepy.

I helped him lie down. I dragged the scarves across his body until he closed his eyes and sighed. I whispered about the fun we were about to have while I tied his wrists with two scarves, knotting them multiple times. I bound his ankles with another scarf. He talked nonsense the entire time and seemed to be mostly unaware of what I was doing. He was aroused and ready, but didn't push to move forward, seeming to be content with his own sensations.

Once he was restrained, to be extra certain I had complete control, I wrapped the rope under the bed and over his body, also tying that with several bulky knots. I turned on the TV, increasing the volume on an action movie to just below the level where a neighboring room might complain to the front desk.

The last thing I did was cut a piece of duct tape and place it over his mouth. He moaned and twisted his head, but didn't fight violently. The thick tape would leave marks on his skin, which would make it less likely the death would be considered an accidental over-indulgence in sex games, but I felt secure with my fake ID and my red eyeglasses and neon blonde hair.

I placed a garbage bag over his head and taped it in place. There was enough air that he took several shallow breaths before instinct took over and he began to thrash as much as the scarves and rope allowed. I went into the bathroom. He was groaning, but it wasn't terribly loud. I turned on the water for additional white noise so I didn't have to listen. I really do abhor suffering. But we all experience it, so I try to face it with equanimity.

When I returned to the bedroom ten minutes later, he was no longer moving.

I cleaned with my usual diligence, packing up the wine and glasses. I stuffed my suit and high heels into the gym bag and put on black leggings, a white long-sleeved T-shirt, a white hoodie, socks, and running shoes. I scrubbed my face, scouring the sink and counter with cleanser when I was done. I put on the wig and swept a microfiber cloth across the counter and floor, grabbing my own and the wig's fallen hairs.

I removed the plastic bag from his head. I pulled the tape off his mouth. There wasn't a red mark after all, so maybe I'd gotten lucky, unless a technician found traces of adhesive in his stubble. I untied the rope and smoothed the bedding where it had been crunched by the pressure of the rope.

Standing near the door, I gave the room one last look. It was spotless, no doubt cleaner than it had been when I'd checked in.

I put on slim leather gloves, opened the door, and stepped boldly into the hallway. Skulking out of the room would attract attention. No one would remember a nondescript woman with a gym bag, as long as she didn't behave oddly.

The hallway was empty.

In the lobby, no one even looked at me. I left the hotel and walked home, enjoying the bite of the cold night air. Finally, my nerves had settled, and I felt at ease in my skin again.

69

Pete could not focus on relaxing for my camera. All he seemed capable of was contorting his face in confusion and a hint of grief over the ugly death of Jim Kohn. He was fixated on the ugliness. He didn't like that a man's sex life was exposed to the world as Jim's had been in all the online news outlets, and even in the New York Times. He didn't like that Jim was found naked, that he was tied up as if that somehow symbolized the powerlessness of all men when their desire overtakes them.

He was flabbergasted by Jim's stupidity in getting into whatever situation he'd gotten himself into. He felt compelled to relate each publicized detail as if I hadn't read any of the same news reports. "Not that I was always an admirer of the guy," he said. "But it makes you feel vulnerable."

I took several shots in quick succession when he said that, the vulnerability obvious in every crease of his face.

He dragged his hand across his eyes. "I'm not in the mood for this today. I should have rescheduled."

We were standing in Central Park, shivering, which is why I wanted to keep moving about, snapping photos. He'd written in his profile that he felt grounded in Central Park, for a reason he couldn't define. His only guess was that it made him aware of his connectedness to a city where he'd grown up, a city he rarely traveled out of much farther than upstate

New York or across the river to New Jersey.

Trystan had suggested it would be useful to capture that environment to see if there were insights Pete could gain regarding his true self and whether his extreme caution was an inherent part of him, or something others had placed on him.

The ridiculous nature of this idea was lost on Pete.

Honestly, I was on the fence. I knew it was absurd, manufactured by Trystan, and yet, it felt true in some way that I couldn't define. "Not being in the mood might be a good thing," I said.

He sighed.

"Let's walk to the natural history museum." I put my camera strap around my neck and replaced the lens cap. We walked quickly, silently agreeing that warmth was our top priority. The park was almost empty, even more than on a typical mid-morning Monday. There were a few runners puffing out steam into the frigid air, and dog walkers that are never deterred by cold weather. But the usual stream of older people taking leisurely strolls and parents pushing babies and toddlers was missing. The benches were unoccupied.

"It's such a shock," he said. "I had to read the article four times to really believe it was him. He seemed like a guy that no one would ever bring down."

"I'm sure."

"His clients must be devastated."

"Won't his firm carry on without him?"

"I suppose they'll follow his model, but I expect the wind is taken out of their sails."

"You never know."

"I can't stop thinking about it."

"Maybe we should talk about something else." I'd wanted Jim out of the world, I didn't want to spend an entire morning talking about him as if he were someone to be mourned.

"He didn't have any kids. I wonder where his estate is going."

"Maybe his ex-wife?"

"His first wife died in a plane crash."

"And his second?"

"There wasn't a second."

"Since you specified first, I thought…"

"Yeah. Not sure why I said that. I guess I thought he might end up with that woman he was seeing, but I guess it fell apart."

"Is that the woman in all the photographs?"

"Not sure what you mean."

"At his house. There's at least twenty-five of them."

"I've never been to his home."

"It's the same woman whose photograph is in his office."

"Yes, that's the one."

"What was the story with her?"

"He was pushing every contact he had to get her into a modeling career."

"She's very good looking. Beautiful, actually."

"Yeah. Not sure she had the personality, but he wouldn't let up. He was convinced she would be a supermodel. An internationally recognized face. A woman created by him, more or less."

"Why would he care about that?"

"He needed someone famous on his arm, and in his bed."

"It's weird that he has her photographs all over if they aren't together."

He laughed. "Women read that so differently."

"What do you mean?"

"Women read the presence of a photograph as an inability to let go, pining for someone you've lost. It's not that at all. It's a cloak. It says, *you can trust me. I'm not after you, I'm already attached.*"

"I'm sure all women don't view it that way. It could put some women off. I don't think most women want a man who's already attached."

"You'd be surprised," he said.

I said nothing.

"Anyway, he dumped her because she didn't have that fire — success at all costs. I thought if he worked with Trystan, he would sort out what he's looking for."

I nodded and gave him a thoughtful smile.

"It wasn't originally my idea. One of the other women who works for Trystan suggested I refer him. The one who does scheduling."

I stopped walking. "Stephanie?"

"I think so, yes. Stephanie."

He kept moving, and I hurried to catch up. "Why did she suggest that?"

"She said he wasn't living up to his potential."

"So she knew him fairly well?"

"I don't know...she must have. I never thought about it. Never asked her. Everyone wants to improve their potential, right? Jim certainly did. And I thought...Anyway, he rushed into it and jumped the queue ahead of me."

"Right."

We stopped outside the American Museum of Natural History. I took a bunch of photographs while he continued verbalizing his shock. He went on for so long about how upsetting it was to have your personal life exposed like that, I started to wonder whether there was something he feared exposing.

Most people harbor that fear, even if it's far from the center of their thoughts. So maybe it was merely the shock of seeing that exposure. No one thinks they're going to die forty years before their *time*.

When I pointed out that if you're dead, it probably isn't that upsetting, Pete demanded to know how I could possibly know that. I wanted to laugh, but he wasn't in a laughing mood. His distress was all over his face, still.

70

Listening to Pete made me want to spend time at the gym, clearing my head of a conversation I hadn't wanted to have, but I needed to go back to the office and download the photographs to Diana's computer. It was a few minutes after twelve when I arrived. The offices were silent. All the doors except the one to the conference room were closed. I wasn't sure whether they'd gone to lunch or were all behind their doors, thinking about Jim. Possibly, Trystan was calculating the loss of revenue.

I did feel bad about that. If I'd had more patience, I could have delayed until after Jim paid his final invoice, but I couldn't wait. I wanted it taken care of. Now, I could relax. Trystan would make it up with other clients. Maybe the death would bring us to the attention of Jim's colleagues. Maybe Pete would talk more about us when he emoted his feelings about Jim's unseemly death.

The moment I settled in my chair, Stephanie appeared in the doorway. "Did you hear?"

"Hear what?"

"Jim Kohn died."

"Yes, I heard."

"They think he was murdered!"

I lowered my voice to a near-whisper. "It's tragic."

She folded her arms and stepped into my office. She uncrossed her arms and tapped the door lightly until it swung closed. "You don't seem very upset."

"I said it was tragic."

"But how do you feel?"

"I feel it was tragic."

"It's terrible to say this, but he wasn't a very nice person. You're better off without him. I can see you're trying to hide your feelings, but really, it's true."

"I'm not hiding any feelings. And I wasn't with him."

"I had the impression you were."

"Your impression was wrong. Maybe it was affected by your own feelings, so you saw something that wasn't there."

She sighed. A guilty look flashed across her face. She wrapped her arms around her upper body, more tightly this time. Her voice trembled. "I feel terrible." She unclasped her arms and took a deep breath. Her voice grew stronger. "You know, you'll probably understand this…I'm almost glad he's dead. It's like karma, although I don't believe in karma. Not really, at least not that word. But maybe justice." She stroked her cross and turned her gaze toward the window as if she was seeking some sort of confirmation.

"Why was it karma?"

"He wasn't a nice man. He was…I just feel like maybe things can improve now."

"What happened? Why don't you sit down? It sounds like you're upset."

"I'm fine." She moved toward the door.

"I think we started out on the wrong foot," I said.

"No we didn't. I took you to breakfast. If anything's wrong, it's not my fault."

"Don't you think we can have a better working relationship?"

"I haven't done anything wrong," she said. "Not really."

"I shouldn't have taken that picture of you."

She went to the chair and pulled it closer to my desk. She heaved herself into it as if she'd been waiting weeks for words that sounded halfway apologetic. "Thank you for saying that. Trystan was pissed."

"I don't think he gets particularly pissed."

"Well, he wasn't happy. But I think things will be better now. With Jim gone."

"It doesn't sound very Christian to wish someone dead."

"I didn't wish he was dead. I didn't want him dead. I'm just...relieved."

"Pete Torkenson mentioned you knew Jim before he became a client?"

"Not really. I met him, that's all. I just wanted to reassure you that you'd be fine without him."

"Even though I wasn't *with* him, what makes you say that?"

"I guess it doesn't matter if you know. Not now." She took a deep breath. "He was engaged to my daughter."

"Your daughter?"

"I don't talk about her much. It's too painful. She... he..." Her eyes filled with tears. She grabbed at her cross, pinching it between her thumb and forefinger. "I feel like an angel came and took care of this for me." Tears spilled over her lashes and ran down her cheeks. "Not that I want anyone to die. But he brought it on himself. My daughter was a beautiful girl, but he took that and turned it into vanity. He filled her head with terrible things. He told her she should become a model, sell her body like a piece of meat. Go chasing after money and fame. He twisted her and took advantage of her and made her someone she's not."

"I don't think modeling is selling your body."

"In a way, yes it is. It makes it all about your shape and your face. Beauty should come from inside. He told her she'd be famous. He hired men to photograph her and kept introducing her to agencies, pushing, pushing. He wouldn't stop pushing."

"She didn't want that?"

"Of course not. I raised her to be pure in spirit. But she changed. He pushed so hard, it's all he talked about, and after a while, that's all *she* talked about. She stopped eating like a healthy girl." Stephanie put her hand to her mouth. She coughed and choked back a sob. "Once he got his hands on her, she started spending hours in front of the mirror. She wore ridiculous clothes, terrible clothes. Ugly and evil, sometimes showing far too much of her body. Fashions that are popular, and makeup that gives women evil-looking faces. She lost her soul. She wasn't happy unless people were looking at her, telling her how gorgeous she was."

"It sounds rough. What's she doing now?"

"Still chasing that. She's done okay, but it was never good enough for him. He wanted her face recognized all over the world. He wanted her to put herself *out there*. Whatever that means. No one needs that."

I nodded.

She stood suddenly. "I don't know why I'm telling you this. I guess I'm so relieved. She can be free of him. I feel so…I guess I'm happy."

"That's good." I smiled. "But there's nothing wrong with being a model. Maybe she likes it."

"It doesn't last. In a few years, she'll be too old, and no one will want her. I just hope it isn't too late." She wiped at her cheeks. "Please forgive me for telling Trystan you were flirting with him."

"You need to tell Trystan. Your lie damaged his business as much as it affected me."

She sighed. "I know."

I smiled. "I'm glad things are settled."

She looked toward the window, but there was nothing to see from where she stood.

71

Telling Alexandra that an angel had rescued her was not a fantasy. Of course, Alexandra had smirked. Even if it hadn't shown on her lips, Stephanie felt the condescension, the patient tolerance of *ignorance*.

People disbelieved in angels to their detriment. They were there to help the human race, and if Alexandra wanted to look down her nose, then she could just try making it through life without any assistance. It was her loss. Eventually, she would run up against her limitations. Everyone did. Eventually, she would suffer, not that Stephanie wished that upon her, but it was inevitable. And when that day arrived, there would be an open door for Stephanie to introduce Alex to the peace that came from trusting your Creator, and the angels.

Angelic assistance had definitely intervened for her and Eileen. That man's death would set Eileen free. She would wake up and see what kind of creep he truly was. Dying tied up like that, wanting perverse sex. It should have been obvious all along that he craved degradation. That's what he'd done to Eileen, and now it had come back on him. He wanted to turn Eileen into an object that people leered at. She'd seen those women in magazines — modeling clothes no one could afford. Their eyes were soul-less.

Stephanie prayed to God that her daughter wasn't engaged in that sort of depravity. When images of Eileen disrespecting her body flashed through Stephanie's mind, it was like oil splashed in her eyes. Her vision blurred and she lost all sense of where she was.

Eileen cried when she heard the news of Jim's death, of course. But it hadn't stopped her, just a day later, from spending an hour and a half in the bathroom, painting her face, turning herself into a plastic doll that would pose in all sorts of ungodly positions to sell unflattering and dehumanizing clothing.

Still, now that he was dead, Eileen would no longer lie in her room at night, wanting something that would destroy her soul. She would no longer slide that gaudy ring onto her finger and sit in her room, gazing at it with longing.

Eventually, maybe, it would seep into the deepest parts of her that she'd only done it for him, to get his love, if the affection of a man like that could even be called love.

Gradually, over time, Eileen's heart would soften. Time would dim her experiences with him, time would edge her further away from the delusion she was chasing. Already, at twenty-seven, she was too old for reaching the heights of modeling success. It was absurd, thinking of twenty-seven as *old*. A girl of that age was barely past puberty. But that's what the world wanted. Teenagers. Girls who weren't yet allowed to vote or drink a glass of wine. Often, girls who weren't old enough for a driver's license.

Stephanie didn't know why she'd told Alexandra about her daughter. She'd known she needed to ask forgiveness, and the rest had bubbled out of her with a force of its own. Alexandra had been mildly interested, at best. She listened, said a few words, and left Stephanie feeling unsatisfied. You told people stories so they would feel some of what you felt.

Alexandra seemed to feel almost nothing. Her response to the request for forgiveness proved that there was something dark inside of her. And just because she'd asked forgiveness didn't mean she wasn't still keeping an eye on Alexandra. Over time, the truth, whatever it was, would become clear.

Time took care of most problems. Stephanie wondered why it had taken her so long to learn that lesson. Time had removed Jim from their lives and time would make Eileen forget the lies he'd told her. Sadly, time would fade Eileen's skin and the shimmer in her eyes, and eventually, her chances at a modeling career. That was a good thing.

Picturing him dead brought Stephanie pleasure every minute of the day. She liked knowing he'd been humiliated in public, even if he wasn't conscious to experience it.

She'd been so consumed with her own plan — becoming Trystan's photographer, taking awkward pictures of Jim, posting them on Instagram, shaming him with all sorts of hashtags about his disgusting character. It was a weak plan, but it was the only one she'd had. She even had a username that hid her identity — Evil_Jim_Kohn.

This was so much better. She felt she'd won.

The day her precious baby came into the world was as fresh in her mind as her daughter's skin had been when Stephanie cradled the newborn infant. Breathing in her baby's sweet scent, she was reminded of the aroma from an open box of chocolates. Her baby's eyes were clear and full of utter and all-consuming love for her mother. Everything about her, the tiny soft fingernails, the fingers themselves with their delicate, perfectly-formed knuckles, her round toes and the curl of her feet when she stretched — every cell stunningly perfect. The texture of brand new skin and untarnished breath were an endless source of pleasure. And then, that smile.

Watching the world damage that precious child, relentlessly scarring her skin with falls from swings and climbing equipment, greasy foods marring her teenaged face with oil and blemishes, and the odor of sweat and unwashed hair. It was heart-breaking to see what the world inflicted, what the animal nature of human beings was subject to.

Worse, were the wounds to her spirit. The cruel little girls who made Eileen cringe and hide her beautiful soul, the boys who made her ashamed of her lovely body, and the media that made her hate everything about herself that didn't fit their air-brushed standards.

Then, like a swan, Eileen had emerged into a stunning woman, only to have that man batter her confidence, prod her faith, persuading her she was nothing without male attention and female envy, without more money than she could ever spend in a lifetime. She was nothing without a life legitimized by a camera and fame.

Every time she thought about it, Stephanie tasted vomit in the back of her throat.

The rage boiled inside. She'd gone to Jim Kohn's office and screamed at him. His staff thought she was a woman who had dragged herself out of a rat-infested alley. They called the police to remove her from their opulent offices.

She had assured Jim he was carving out a place for himself in the sulfurous torment of hell, and that's where he was now. She was confident.

72

Trystan stepped into my office and closed the door. He gave me a hard stare. "Did Jim confide in you? Did he mention anything that suggested his life was in danger?"

I laughed. "No."

Trystan acted as if I was harboring other documents from Jim, keeping back photographs — something that revealed a darker side of his life. Trystan had come to the conclusion that the humiliating state of Jim's corpse was a set-up. It was very insightful of him. The man had excellent instincts. But he spoke as if he believed I was curating our clients' backgrounds, an exercise that would be self-defeating to our purpose. Sometimes I wondered whether I fully understood our purpose.

I thought about the hidden document outlining Jim's shame. The man didn't possess any shame. From what I'd gathered, the shame he'd expressed was simply a tirade at being called on his shameful behavior. How he categorized that as shame was beyond me. I might not experience shame myself, but I know what it is. He seemed oblivious.

Trystan glared at me. "You're sure? Think."

"We didn't talk that much."

"What about at the dinner party? Did you see anything? Anyone who might…I don't know…any women who seemed bitter? Or angry? Anyone who wanted to punish him? Did you see any tense conversations?"

"No."

"I just can't...I feel like this is connected to us, somehow."

"Why would you think that?"

"We were intimately involved in his life. We should have seen something," he said.

"Did *you* see anything?"

"No. I keep trying to reconstruct all of our meetings, the things he said."

"Nothing about sex was ever discussed, so how would we have known?"

"I have an uneasy feeling. The police will be talking to us."

"But they'll talk to everyone he knew. They aren't singling us out."

"Yes, but I want to provide useful information."

"We don't have any useful information."

He studied my face, staring into my eyes, waiting for me to say more, although I wasn't sure what he expected. "Why would he be in a hotel room reserved by some woman from San Diego when he has an apartment in the city? It doesn't make sense."

"Maybe it wasn't a woman," I said.

"A woman reserved the room."

"Maybe she was an admin."

"Okay, but that's not really the issue. The issue is *why?*"

"It's not our job to figure it out," I said.

"We should feel some responsibility."

"Because...?"

"He was our client."

"I didn't know we were supposed to feel responsible for

their private lives."

"We're dealing with all facets of their lives." He went to the window. He opened the blinds wider and looked out. He pulled the cord and raised the blinds, looking into the distance. "I've never known anyone who was murdered."

I remained silent.

After a few minutes, he turned. "It's deeply disturbing. You feel as if there must be something you could have done to prevent it."

"What would that be?"

He shrugged. "The feeling won't leave me."

Given the mental changes he aimed to make in our clients' lives, he was collapsing too easily into uncontrolled thoughts. Letting his mind run amok.

I stood and put my hands in my pockets. I was tired of sitting at my desk while he explored the interior of his mind, looking for something that wasn't there.

73

The following day, a detective came by to speak with all of us. He spent less than five minutes with Diana and Stephanie. I understood later that Stephanie got away with a tiny white lie, telling the man, with her eyes opened wide to evoke naiveté, clinging to his gaze, that she'd never met Jim Kohn.

Trystan spoke to the detective for the longest amount of time, but the questions were routine — How did they meet? What did Trystan know about Jim's personal life? His sex life? His financial situation? Had Jim ever expressed fear of anyone seeking to hurt him?

They asked me the same questions. They wanted to know what I'd observed at his party. They asked to see the photographs. Diana moved them all to a thumb drive which he dropped into a plastic envelope.

I told him there were no women at the dinner who appeared to be antagonistic toward him. No men either. I did not have an alibi, but they accepted my explanation that I'd stayed home, eaten leftover takeout Chinese food, gone up to the roof for a cigarette. No one had seen me coming or going. Not everyone is going to have an alibi in life. Lots of people spend many evenings home alone, unprepared to be questioned in a murder investigation. But of course, I had no reason to kill him. None of us did, and so they were reasonably satisfied.

They didn't seem to expect any of us would have useful

information. I think they were more interested in Jim's clients, in anyone who had lost a lot of money under his management.

Later, Stephanie told me the detective came to her apartment to speak with her daughter. Stephanie had made sure to be out that evening. The interview only lasted two minutes because the night of the murder, Eileen had been out to dinner with a few girlfriends. The timing was quite fortunate for her.

Of course, the detective would continue to investigate, but in his mind, the provocateur and his staff had been relegated to the status of a personal trainer. He didn't think we had anything valuable to offer. He didn't seem to realize the extent of the information we collect on our clients. He might have had a field day with all of those details, but as they say, you don't know what you don't know. It's a fact that directs the course of many lives.

Trystan continued to feel irrationally responsible for Jim's murder. It surprised me. I'd thought he was more like me — easily moving past disturbances that tripped up other people for weeks, sometimes years. Maybe it was a male thing. Maybe, like Pete, he was suddenly aware of his own vulnerability. Women are used to that feeling. Men, not so much.

74

That evening, Victoria and Rafe were standing outside my door when I arrived home. Victoria held a large brown paper bag with twine handles. It emitted the savory aroma of Indian food. Rafe was carrying three boxes of cigarettes.

He held them out to me. "For the ones we bummed."

"It's not necessary."

"Oh, but it is." He smiled.

Victoria lifted the bag. "We brought dinner."

"I'm not..."

"Just being neighborly. We haven't seen you around." She laughed. "We figured you were working too hard."

"Much too hard," Rafe said. "Dinner. Conversation. A bottle of vino..." He raised his other hand which held a bottle bag with a dark blue background covered in silvery snowflakes. "Then a smoke on the roof. Just what the doctor ordered after a rough day at work."

"I didn't have a rough day at work."

Victoria laughed. "Every day at work is rough."

"Come on, be a good sport. Let's chill," Rafe said.

I shrugged. I was starving. The food smelled amazing, and the longer I stood there, the more it settled into the air around me, wafting its way into my stomach with the promise of satiation. "Okay. Sure."

I unlocked the door, and they followed me inside. I pointed to the cabinets where the plates were kept and went into the bedroom to change. I closed the French doors. They offered minimal privacy, but the bedroom was dark, and if they wanted to make the effort to look, that was their issue.

I put on jeans, Ugg boots, and a soft black sweater.

We sat at my table and Rafe filled three glasses with Zinfandel. Victoria chattered about her desire to travel to India while we scooped out jasmine rice and Butter Chicken, Alu Gobi and Alu Matar, Chana Masala, and Tandoori Chicken. After Victoria's toast to the Hindu god of the night, we dug in.

The food tasted as amazing as it smelled. The wine was pretty good too.

Our stomachs full, we bundled up in thick jackets and hats and scarves. We went up to the roof with one of the new packs of cigarettes and a second bottle of wine that Rafe had grabbed from their apartment.

"We still need to have you over to show you our business set-up," Rafe said. "Vic told me you were curious."

Was I? I would have described it as casual interest. I rested my head on the back of the couch and looked up at the sky we'd toasted earlier. There were no stars. I'd hardly noticed the weather that day, too caught up in the detective's visit. I tried to consider scenarios in which he might ask more probing questions. I wondered how long they would pursue a case that had no physical evidence and no witnesses.

"What's on your mind?" Victoria placed her hand on my leg.

My muscle tensed. I shifted my position so that leaving her hand there became awkward. She let it slide away. "Nothing," I said.

"Your ash is about to fall off."

I looked at my cigarette. I leaned forward, and as I moved it over the ashtray, the column of ash fell away. I put the cigarette to my lips and sucked in smoke.

"So what is it?" she said. "What has your brow crunched up like that?"

I thought for a moment. There was nothing I wanted to say. Even a lie seemed more trouble than it was worth. I blew out a thin stream of smoke.

"We realized, we know nothing about you," Victoria said. "We've hung out and taken a class together, and we know hardly anything about your job, except that it's stressful and doesn't seem to pay what you need to live well in Manhattan."

"And we don't know shit about the men in your life," Rafe said.

Victoria echoed him in a shrill voice. "We don't know *shit*!" She laughed, softening her tone.

"We want to be friends. But you're a bit standoffish," Rafe said.

"Am I?" Movement caught my eye. I looked toward the door that led from the stairwell onto the roof garden. Kent stood there, watching. I waved him over to join us and then the conversation shifted to normal things, if there was any concept of normal anywhere in the vicinity of Victoria and Rafe.

I was on my third cigarette, most of my wine still in the glass.

Silence settled over the group for several minutes, then Rafe spoke. "If you died tonight, would you be happy with how you'd lived your life?"

Victoria gave him an adamant and victorious-sounding, *yes!*

Kent shrugged and grunted a non-answer.

I smiled, but I wasn't sure if they could see in the darkness. "That's a very personal question," I said.

I looked out at the skyscrapers surrounding us, the glowing lights from windows and along roof lines, and felt that it was a decent substitute for the stars, for now.

75

New York City has a mythology that's hard to define.

It views itself as the queen of cities, and that's certainly true for the United States, but the entire world? Maybe it's got more than its fair share of American vanity in its blood.

The mythology is warranted because of all those towering buildings on a tiny island, the distinct districts, like small towns of their own. It's the financial center of the nation, the heart of theater, and all the arts, really…and its lore — *If I can make it there, I'll make it anywhere.*

The mythology had captivated me. I felt the excitement of the city course through my veins when I walked the numbered streets and avenues, when I rode the subway, when I sat in the roof garden, and even inside my apartment with its French doors that transformed the three and a half rooms from a cramped, down-at-the-heels shoebox into something charming.

Rafe and Victoria made my building an entertaining place to live. Sooner or later, I'd figure them out, and find out what they wanted from me. Before that, I'd find a way to get Kent talking about the guy who lived in my apartment and left so abruptly. There was a lot to do, but for now, I just wanted to enjoy living in the Big Apple. Corny, but true.

The next day, after lunch by myself at Sardi's, a place I absolutely had to try, I stopped at a tourist shop and bought a key ring. The fob was Lucite formed into a tiny black T-shirt with red letters — I *heart* New York.

It was a total tchotchke, but I loved it. Anyone who saw my key ring would peg me as a tourist. But who ever really saw my key ring? It had only three keys — one to my apartment, one to the main door of the office, and a beautiful antique key.

The iron key was about two-and-a-half inches long, with a single thick tooth at one end and an intricate opening shaped like a three-leaf clover at the top.

I'd removed it from Jim Kohn's key ring.

I had no idea what it opened, but it was so unusual, I was compelled to find out.

Letter From Cathryn

Thank you so much for choosing to read *The Woman In the Photograph*. Your support is greatly appreciated, and I hope you enjoyed the book as much as I enjoyed writing it. I especially hope you enjoyed Alexandra and her unique take on the world. If you enjoyed the book, I would be extremely grateful if you could take a few moments to leave a quick review. It's always great to hear what readers think and it can also help others discover my books. Any recommendations to friends and family are also very welcome! I love hearing from readers so please feel free to let me know what you thought via my Facebook page or Twitter. You can even contact me directly through my website. To make sure you don't miss out on my upcoming releases and more, you can sign up to my mailing list at my website: CathrynGrant.com

Thank you again for all your support – it is greatly appreciated.
Cathryn.

Book Ten:
Look for *The Woman In the Storm* in 2019.